Contents

Acknowledgments	vii
Preface	ix
The Letter	1
The Clarke's Tale	6
Wedding Bliss	12
The Violinist	16
New Ventures	23
Jacobite Rebellion	31
Proud Preston	58
Flight from Preston	70
Battle of Preston ~ Day One	84
Battle of Preston ~ Day Two	107
Battle of Preston ~ Day Three	124
Executions	135
Home and Away	150
Trials and Tribulations	166
The King's Bedchamber	175
Sunday Escapades	178
Tower Hill	188
Exodus from London	194
The Bubble Bursts	212
Chesterfield	221
Drawing on Trust	227
Elopement	237
Epilogue	241
Appendix	243

Also by Malcolm Brocklehurst

The Secret History of Christianity
ISBN 978-1-84529-763-3

The House of Cavendish ~ Out Roads
ISBN 978-1-60860-307-7

I would like to dedicate this book to my Grandfather; the late Arthur Storey without whose legacy of research into our family history back to 1734, this novel would not have been written.

Arthur Storey my grandfather spent many years trying to trace a will but to no avail but the family story of the lost fortune has haunted me all my life and so with Chamade which is a military term to describing a drum beat or trumpet sound to herald a truce, I present THE HOUSE OF CAVENDISH ~ PRESTON CHAMADE, which is the second novel in the trilogy of the Cavendish saga.

Acknowledgments

I wish to thank my family and friends who supported and encouraged me, especially my wife who suffered through the difficult long hours of solitude during my research for this book. She has been a part of the haunting quest left in the legacy from the moment I received it.

Grateful thanks go to Mrs Elaine Brown in the Reference Services, National Library of Scotland for her detailed research into the regimental officers who served under General Wills at the Battle of Preston.

Grateful thanks are given to the Chetham Society and to Chris Hunwick for granting permission to reproduce the map titled 'The Taking of the Town of Preston from the Rebels by King Georges Forces' as printed in the 'Lancashire Memorials of the Rebellion' by Samuel Hibbert. The book is V in the Old Series printed in MDCCCXLV for the Chetham Society.

Thanks go to Allan Emmerson; a retired graphic illustrator for reproducing the pen and ink sketch of the map 'The Taking of the Town of Preston from the Rebels' as prepared in the field at Preston by cartographers to King George I.

I wish to thank the Blaby Mill Stables Leicester for information regarding horse travel and care.

A sincere thank you to Ros Westwood the Derbyshire Museums Manager for all the information on early eighteenth century travel conditions in the Peak district which was most valuable and also grateful thanks goes to Lisa Langley-Fogg the local studies Librarian at Derby county council for her full and efficient response in sourcing other information relative to Buxton Spa circa seventeen fifteen period and to Chris Latimer City Archivist Stoke on Trent City Archives for advice on transport through Staffordshire and the coaching inns located in the Newcastle-under-Lyme area.

Thanks to Catherine Brighty of the Islington Archaeology and History Society for information on Islington and the area in the early eighteenth century.

Grateful thanks to Pat Rogers for her research into the Jacobite occupation of Lancaster in seventeen fifteen. Pat is an author and poet and fellow member of Cleveleys Writer's.

And finally thanks to Middleton & Jones Solicitors of Chesterfield, Derbyshire; for help and research into their archive department.

Preface

The *House Of Cavendish ~ Outroads* was the first in a trilogy of historical novels. *Outroads* was set against the backdrop of Elizabethan and Stuart politics and spanned a period of English history (1560-1710). The Cavendish saga began with Henry Cavendish; the eldest son of Bess of Hardwick, who according to historical records fathered several illegitimate sons around the shires and his procreations were particularly active in Derbyshire. He seduces a clergyman's daughter; the young lady, Sylvia became his life long mistress with Henry providing a small manor house for her and their son Robert Cavendish.

On his maturity and after the monarchy was restored, Robert sets forth to seek his fortune in London where he makes the acquaintance of Samuel Pepys who becomes his benefactor and a life long friend of the family. On Samuel's advice Robert invests in the import of tobacco from Virginia and soon becomes a wealthy man. He marries and starts to raise a family at Cavendish House in Newington Green in London but the plaque strikes London and the grim reaper enters Islington; a village near to Robert's home. The Cavendish family flee back to their ancestral home in Derbyshire but inadvertently carry a damp parcel of tailor's cloth on their coach for delivery to the village of Eyam. The village becomes decimated with the plaque but the self sacrifice of self-imposed quarantine by the villagers saves the spread throughout the county. The London outbreak of the plaque is finally eliminated by the Great Fire and Robert and his family return to Cavendish House to rebuild their lives. The family fortunes ebb and flow through the Dutch wars with family members tragically killed in naval actions.

In the near arctic conditions of a London winter Robert dies and his son James inherits and takes over the family investments in the Virginian tobacco trade. The horrors of the slave trade become apparent when James receives a letter from a doctor in Bristol about events witnessed on a slave ship. The Cavendish family sell their tobacco investments and become anti-slave traders and re-invest their wealth in the Hudson Bay fur trade coupled with the birth of Canada as a nation, but their past involvement in the horrors of the slave trade still haunts their consciences . . .

The House of Cavendish – Preston Chamade is its sequel and is set within the framework of historical events encompassing the Jacobite rebellion of 1715 and the events through until 1734. The novel touches upon the lives of real people when the author's ancestor; Elizabeth Cavendish, inherits a fortune and elopes with her groomsman and lover William Clarke.

So who was Elizabeth Cavendish? Was she a descendent of Bess of Hardwick of Chatsworth House and Hardwick Hall? We will never know but a possible ancestral link was given in *Outroads.*

The story handed down through generations of our family is that in 1734 Elizabeth Cavendish fell in love with her groomsman and he being below her station in life, and knowing he would lose his job and that there was no chance to marry, the couple eloped. Before they eloped Elizabeth made plans; she had an inheritance of ninety five thousand pounds, which by today's standard is approximately ten million pounds. The facts recorded by Arthur Storey my grandfather are that after the couple eloped they had a son and Elizabeth bequeathed her inheritance in trust to that son. Subsequently the son married and had a daughter who was the author's maternal great, great grandmother.

The House of Cavendish ~ Inroads will be the final book in the trilogy and will be a factual account of the family history after seventeen thirty-four Events that involve the loss of the fortune bequeathed by Elizabeth Cavendish and culminates in the family's involvement in the Russian Revolution of 1917.

Descendants of William Cavendish

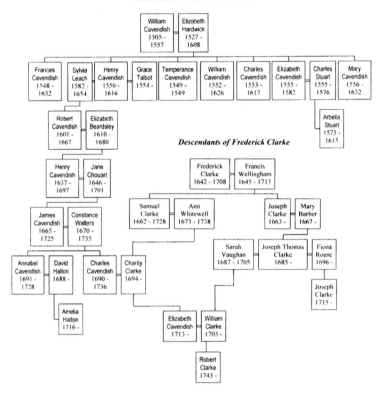

Descendants of Frederick Clarke

The Letter

James and Constance Cavendish were sitting in the library at Cavendish House. The winter had been long and cold and that February night in seventeen hundred and ten, a log fire was glowing in the grate. Occasionally a spark from the embers cracked as the flames leapt to cast warm shadows around the room.

Annabel their daughter was playing the harpsichord and had just completed a difficult rendition of a simple melody. Charles her brother had sat and listened in a veiled attempt at brotherly interest accompanied by bored silence. James rose, poured a glass of claret for each of them then he motioned for Annabel to join them.

"That was very nice, my dear, but Mother and I have something we wish to discuss with you both." James coughed, sat down and said, "Your mother and I made a decision a few years ago that when the time was right we would acquaint you both with what we feel was the ill treatment of slaves on slave ships. The evidence I have and which proved a life changing factor came in a letter from a Doctor Roberts who served on a slave ship that the Cavendish family owned. I received the letter about ten years ago."

James now handed a folded and creased document to Charles and a silence descended on the room as Charles then Annabel read the letter.

To James Cavendish

Dear Sir.

I hope that this correspondence finds you in good health.

As you are aware I fulfilled my obligations to serve you on one voyage as a doctor to care for your investment of your human cargo on the good ship Bristol bound for Africa and the Virginian tobacco plantation in the New World. I fulfilled my duties and was paid off earlier this year by your agent at the Llandoger Trow Inn in Bristol in May 1700.

But such were the barbaric actions of the crew as condoned by your Captain Speers that my conscience is heavy and I must relate the facts to you for you to take any action you feel appropriate.

After we sailed from Bristol we made a good passage to the coast of Africa. For three days, the male slaves were taken on board and forced below decks into the larger holds on the lower decks, then for a further day canoes transported female slaves with their children. Females were segregated from the male slaves and it was heartbreaking to listen to the women trying to comfort their children as they too were packed between decks. Finally, with two hundred humans stowed as living cargo aboard the ship and my signature on the trading manifest that the slaves were healthy, we set sail on the twenty-fifth of March for the New World.

I must state, Sir, that at that time all was normal aboard the ship for the treatment and transportation of the slaves. The crew said that the conditions were the same that exist in hundreds of other slave ships. However, we were only three weeks into the middle crossing, and being early spring our ship encountered heavy seas.

Captain Speers ordered the ship's portholes to be covered during the storm to stop the ingress of seawater and due to the work of sailing the ship, the crew did not have time or the opportunity to clean the slave decks. Soon the smell became unbearable. After fourteen days of bad weather it was so bad below decks that — and I am sorry to admit it - I had to refuse to go below to tend to the sick. Slop buckets were no longer available and the slaves were forced to void their bladders and bowels and to lie in their own excrement and urine. The captain then battened down the hatch covers to keep the stench from pervading the rest of the ship.

Over the next few days the conditions in the holds got very bad. There was very little fresh air to breathe and the crew had to tie rags over their noses to make very quick visits to hand out the meager food rations of one bowl of gruel and one bowl of water to each slave before beating a hasty retreat back into the fresh air above decks.

Praise be to God that four weeks into the voyage the bad weather finally cleared, the heavy seas abated and the crew formed bucket brigades to try and swill out the holds.

As you must be aware from Captain Speer's report, during those four weeks, twenty slaves died and as is normal practice on slave ships, their bodies were thrown overboard.

I now come to the event that has so troubled me. Captain Speers used the period of fair weather to give the slaves an airing and gave the order for the women and children to be brought onto deck for a time. At the end of their time on deck, the Captain allowed three of the females who were unencumbered with children or babies to remain on deck.

We were sailing in the mid-Atlantic in May and with the dark seas and low horizon, dusk fell early. It was a long night but by lantern light, the crew abused and raped the three women. From the confines of my cabin I heard the cries of these poor women for hours until gradually all fell silent. As dawn broke, I ventured on deck, where I discovered one of the females was dead, and one was so badly abused she died within the hour despite my efforts to save her. The third poor girl was forced below decks in a state of shock into the confines of the stinking fouled hold. The two dead females were thrown overboard, their deaths recorded in the ship's logs as due to sickness.

That morning it was as if the events of the night were nothing to Captain Speers who gave the order for the male slaves to be brought on deck in batches of twenty and given an airing whilst the fair weather continued.

Much to my shame, I remained silent during the long months till I was safe ashore in our blessed England. I fear that accidents could so easily happen and I was alone and in fear of my life had I voiced disapproval or protested whilst at sea.

I know, Sir, that you will do what your conscience directs and therefore,

I am, Sir,

with great respect

Your most obedient and Humble Servant

Henry Roberts Doctor

In silence Charles folded the letter and handed it back to James; Annabel had tears in her eyes.

"So now you know why our family sold our investments in the Virginian tobacco trade and re-invested in the Hudson Bay. You also remember our dear friend Samuel Pepys?"

James paused as Charles and Annabel nodded. "While he was alive we felt duty bound to stay by him in London but when he died seven years ago, I promised your mother we would stay in London until you both reached an age where you were on the social scene and we could then make a decision. Those years are now passed and this year we will decide if our family is to move back to Ufton Manor in Derbyshire. Charles my boy, you have an insight into our financial world and know how I do my business, how do you feel about moving and travelling back to London twice a year to protect our interests?"

Charles remained in thought for a moment, then looking at Annabel for some support but finding nothing in her demeanour, he replied in a totally unexpected manner. "Sir, I have on several occasions visited the home of Samuel Clarke and his wife Ann; he is one of your fellow merchants, and I have met Charity, his very agreeable daughter. I have been meaning to speak to you, Father, about my future with this young woman and I would ask if you will speak to her father on my behalf. If it is agreeable and I marry Charity, then it would be most suitable if she moved with us to Ufton Manor. It would also be beneficial to our business if her father would act as our agent here in London and what better connections could your agent have than to be my father-in-law?"

Constance nodded her approval and smiled. "I think your father will speak favourably for both of us."

"That settles that problem," said James. "I shall arrange to meet with the Clarke family. Introductions between the families will not be deemed necessary as Samuel and I are business associates and we often meet at Lloyds Coffee House to discuss shipping news.

The Clarke's Tale

At the first opportunity, James called on Samuel Clarke and his wife Ann. They discussed the proposed marriage but before agreeing to the betrothal, James explained in detail his plans to move his family back to their ancestral home in Derbyshire and Samuel agreed that if a betrothal was arranged, neither he nor Ann would object to Charity living at Ufton Manor in Derbyshire after the wedding. Samuel also agreed that he would help protect the Cavendish business and shipping interests and act as their agent on the proviso that Charles visited London at least twice a year to advise on the Cavendish wishes.

In the spring of seventeen hundred and eleven, with the winter furs from Hudson Bay safe in the London warehouses, Charles and Charity were joined in wedlock at the church of St Mary Aldermary in Bow Lane.

The spring sun had very little warmth in it as friends and relatives from both families gathered in the church before the ceremony and sat listening to the strains of the choir singing a selection of cantatas.

Charles waited nervously before the altar for his bride to arrive and James was engaging him in conversation to help calm him. "You know, some notable personages have been married within this church. I think John Milton, the poet, married his third wife here in 'sixty-three and of course this is the church were your mother and I married back in 'sixty-nine. I hope you have as many happy years with Charity as I have had with your mother. She was pure when we married, I trust Charity is also."

"Father, how could she be any other? We are always chaperoned and tonight we will enjoy our union for the first time."

At that moment the mood of the music changed. Charity, a radiant seventeen year-old bride on the arm of her proud father, entered the church wearing a wedding dress of pure white silk. The gown emitted a sound like a rustling restless wind as the material slithered across the stone floor, while the bride, carrying a spray of orange blossom to signify her purity, walked sedately down the aisle followed by a very young boy carrying an ornamental cushion on which Charity could kneel in prayer. Above her head the unique plaster vaulting of the church ceiling glistened white and ornate.

The couple made their vows and then with Charity on his arm, Charles proudly escorted his bride down the aisle to the porch followed by the young pageboy. Friends and family followed and gathered outside to applaud the happy couple. To one side Constance stood in conversation with Samuel's wife. "Your daughter looks beautiful, and that dress, the silk material is fit for a queen."

Ann beamed with pride. "It is beautiful, and Samuel obtained the material at a bargain price through a merchant trader of the East India Company, but you must not say I told you so."

The two mothers; Constance and Ann smiled at the secret shared as Samuel and James joined them. "I will lead the way," Samuel said. "We are all retiring to Ye Olde Watling Tavern for refreshments and to drink good health to the newlyweds, though I think that Charles would rather be away with his new wife."

"Hush, Sam, you will make Charity blush and suffer the vapours," said Ann. Charity simply smiled demurely as Charles took her arm to guide her over the cobbled stone road as the group strolled over to the tavern.

When the group was inside, Samuel guided his party to a private room at the rear that he had previously booked.

"Now please," he said, "those that wish, be seated – and landlord, eight bottles of your finest Portuguese wine." Then addressing James he said, "We have ceased drinking the French wines, the tax on them has become prohibitive and I find these Portuguese wines superb and much cheaper."

At that, an elderly gentleman who was next to Samuel and Ann coughed loudly to clear his throat then spoke loudly so all could hear. "We are all here today to celebrate the coming together of two families. My name is Frederick Clarke and as the senior member of the Clarke family, I bid you welcome. Let us hope our families and our business ventures both prosper with this union, and may I add that as Samuel's father, I see he has inherited some of my habits for being thrifty, economical and frugal."

Laughter echoed round the room as the group relaxed and began to converse with each other. James nudged Samuel in the ribs with his elbow. "Your father has you there, but I must admit the quality of this wine is very good and as you say, it saves on the tax."

Constance and Ann just smiled, for they shared the secret of the source of Samuel's cheap silk material for the wedding dress.

"So, Charles, you will be carrying my cousin off to Derbyshire?"

Charity interrupted the gentleman that had spoken. "Charles dear, this is my cousin Thomas." Charles shook his hand. "And this is his young son William who was my pageboy and carried that cushion most properly. Didn't you, William?" Constance added.

The child nodded and smiled.

"You did very well, William," Thomas said, then turning to Charles he added in a low voice,

"William's mother, Sarah, died in childbirth, but it is six years since and time for me to marry again." Thomas turned to the young lady at his side. "And may I introduce you both to Miss Fiona Rouse; she and I are also to be wed this year."

Charity and Fiona's hands touched in a gentle handshake.

"We shall hope to be invited to your wedding," commented Charles, "and may you both be as happy as we hope to be."

It was into the early evening before Charles and Charity managed to persuade James to send for the family coach to take them back to Cavendish House.

James's coachman, old Ben McQuire, drew rein and feeling his age, he climbed hesitantly down from his driving seat. He was approaching his sixtieth year and his employer had been good to him since the time ten years previously when Ben was attacked and left half dead on a Bristol quayside. Only the prompt actions of a doctor aided by the thickness of Ben's skull had saved him from brain damage and possible death.

James noticed that Ben's agility had decreased; his legs were not as nimble as they were and he wondered how much longer he could carry on driving the coach in the inclement weathers and how much longer he could employ him. And there was Ben's wife Vivien who still worked in the house as a serving maid and cleaner; she too had to be considered in the planned move make to Derbyshire.

"Now, Ben, take Charles and Charity back home, then you can retire for the night. Mrs Cavendish and I shall be staying with the Clarke household tonight to let the newlyweds have the privacy of their first night in Cavendish House alone. Come at noon tomorrow to the Clarke residence in Bunhill Row to drive us home."

"Yes, sir."

"Oh, and Ben, be very careful, be aware the lanes to Islington and Newington Green seem to have become infested by highwaymen and footpads these days. Have you a pistol?" James enquired.

"I have, sir, and don't you worry, I will get Master Charles and his new wife home safely."

James helped his daughter-in-law to board the coach and Charles mounted the step behind her. Ben closed the coach door and climbed up onto his seat then taking the reins and with a flick of the whip, the coach trundled off into the evening twilight.

Inside the coach Charles took Charity in his arms. The cool silk of her white dress enhanced the soft warmth of her bare shoulders and arms. The couple kissed and Charity's lips parted as her tongue sought his.

The coach lurched on over the ruts in the road but it didn't distract the lovers. Charity seemingly never noticed as the coach drove down Bunhill Row past her old family home; she was too distracted as Charles untied the cord that held the bodice of her dress and cupped her breast in his hand. He felt her quiver as he nibbled her nipple and with his other hand he searched beneath the layers of the silk dress as she parted her legs for Charles to caress her for the first time.

"My dearest Charity," he whispered into her ear, "I love you so much."

His hands caressed her and she gasped as her heart began to beat faster. "And I love you, my darling, but let us wait until we are home. But don't stop what you are doing to me now, I feel such joy."

Charles was surprised; he hadn't known that ladies had such feelings. Gently he continued to caress Charity until she began to tremble and her legs stiffened, her back arched and she was gasping for breath. Slowly Charity regained her composure smoothed her dress and gave Charles a demure glance.

"My dearest, I felt like I was taken to heaven and back again; I hope you to do that to me every time when we make love properly."

Charles sat with his breeches damp, not daring to complain that he had been frustrated while Charity clung to his arm and whispered confirmations of her undying love . . .

* * *

It was totally dark when Ben pulled rein outside the family home in Newington Green. He climbed down from his seat; placing the mounting steps at the door of the coach, he opened the door and helped Charles climb down safely. Charles turned and offered his arm to Charity, and Ben noticed as he stood back to allow Charles to help Charity descend gracefully that his mistress's eyes seemed to be sparkling in the moonlight. Ben smiled, noticing that Charity's dress seemed slightly disarranged.

"Thank you, Ben. You may take the coach over to Miller's Farm. After you have taken care of the horses, you and Mrs McQuire may retire for the night."

"Goodnight, sir." Ben turned to lead the coach and horses the short distance to the farm.

The front door of the Cavendish house had already swung open and on the threshold stood Mrs McQuire who had witnessed her husband's departure.

"Welcome, Mr Cavendish, and can I offer my own and my husband's good wishes for a long and happy life together," Vivien said as she made a half curtsy.

"Thank you, Mrs McQuire," Charles said. "And now please stand back while I carry my bride over the threshold of her new home." With a sweep of his arms he lifted Charity off her feet and while she held on firmly with her arms around his neck he carried her into Cavendish House.

Wedding Bliss

Vivien had ensured that there was clean linen and new covers on Charles's bed. Now she stood waiting to be dismissed.

"Good night, Mrs McQuire," Charles said as he took Charity's hand and guided her towards the stairs. "I have already informed Ben we shall not require either of you again tonight."

"Goodnight, sir," Vivien replied. You won't be having much sleep tonight, she thought as she remembered her young days with Ben.

Vivien walked to her quarters to await her husband. Tonight he was in for a surprise; she too felt feelings she had not had for some time. Romance was in the air as she hurried to her room, with dreams of her own youth.

* * *

Charles pushed the bedroom door open and stood behind Charity. Putting his hands around her waist, he pulled her back into his arms and gently kissed her neck, kicking the door shut with his left foot. The couple were alone at last.

Charity looked hesitantly at the large four-poster bed as she untied her bodice while Charles still held her in his arms; then the couple slowly began to remove each other's clothing. At seventeen, Charity had the body of a mature young woman. Her breasts were well formed with large nipples, each encircled in a brown halo. Charles's eyes wandered to the light brown curly hair that covered her intimate parts.

He stepped away, pulled back the covers and slipped into bed. "Do not be too long joining me," he whispered, "I fear it is chilly and I need you to warm me."

Charity climbed into the bed and Charles pulled the covers over them as she curled into his arms.

"Touch me like you did in the coach," Charity whispered, but Charles could wait no longer and she felt him trembling in anticipation as he moved his body to cover her. Charity gave a small cry as he entered, then he was thrusting deeper as if to touch her heart. Charles moved faster and faster. Charity began to breathe heavily and then, all too soon it was over. As he regained his breath, he lay by her side with a contented look on his face and whispered, "That was beautiful, but I think I was too quick for you, my love. Did you feel anything?"

"That nice feeling began to start within me, my love, but then it disappeared just as you finished. Next time you must first caress me longer and it will be better for me, but for now I am happy just to be here with you."

Charles glowed with happiness then fell asleep. When he awoke, he moved his hand so his fingers sought her and she gave a small tremble. "That's nice, touch me just there; kiss me, Charles, and keep touching me for it makes me tingle with love for you."

Dawn was breaking when they finally both fell asleep in each other's arms.

* * *

The spring flowers bloomed and died, summer fruits ripened and were picked in the orchards as Charles and Charity continued to enjoy their honeymoon with passionate nights of love.

In the autumn of seventeen hundred and eleven, the Cavendish family were invited to attend the wedding of Thomas Clarke and Fiona Rouse, and once more young William was pageboy.

In the Cavendish home, Annabel was showing little interest as a London socialite; her interests seemed to be more in reading and art. Consequently, James and Constance began planning the sale of Cavendish House, which was in a rural and still very fashionable area of London.

"I think we are moving at the right time," James commented to Constance one evening as they sat at table. "These rural surroundings will not survive another decade; the city expansion is already beginning to absorb the outer villages and I am afraid our village will disappear into a part of the city. I have spoken to Ben and Vivien about their future when we move and he says since they have no family in London, they will remain in our service and come to Derbyshire with us."

But the plans to sell were delayed when in seventeen hundred and twelve Charity announced she was pregnant and it was decided to await her safe delivery before submitting her to the trauma and upheaval of a family move.

In the spring of seventeen thirteen, Charity gave birth to a daughter whom they named Elizabeth and the move could now be put into operation. Over the following weeks, the better pieces of the family furniture and the heirlooms were packed into wooden boxes. The larger items such as beds and tables were left behind for the new occupants of the house. Finally, on a bright sunny day in early June, the boxes were loaded onto four horse-drawn carts ready for transporting to Derbyshire.

Seven days later, James closed the door of Cavendish House for a final time, stepped out onto the lane and looked up at their old home whilst Ben helped Constance, Annabel. Charles, Charity and baby Elizabeth into the coach. Eventually James climbed aboard.

Ben removed the mounting steps, he helped his wife Vivien up onto the seat next to him; gripped the whip, and with a flick of his wrist the horses took the strain as the coach made out-roads from Cavendish House, the London home that Henry Cavendish had purchased almost fifty years previously, to begin their new life in their ancestral home at Ufton Manor.

Elizabeth Cavendish was going home . . .

The Violinist

The festive season in their new home was a cheerful one. Snow decked the countryside and the family enjoyed the warmth of log fires in contrast to the coal fires that had been the fashion in London. The winter was milder and seemed shorter that year and all too soon spring was upon them once more.

"I think we made the right move away from the city smells, it is so lovely here in the country," commented James as the family sat for breakfast.

"I agree, even Annabel seems settled, she shows little interest in reading and art since you introduced us to the Halton's at Wingfield Hall. She can't seem to stop talking about young David Halton. If she doesn't lose interest, we may have to start making arrangements for a formal betrothal." said Constance.

"Well that will get sister out of my way," said Charles, "incidentally where is she this morning?"

"Oh, she just has a touch of the vapours" said Constance, "she said she wanted to stay in her room, but I think she may be writing a poem for David."

"So it's serious then," said Charles, "anyway, to change the subject, I shall have to go up to London in the next week or two to see how Samuel is handling our affairs and to arrange for the arrival of the new season furs. Hopefully all our ships will make the safe passage home from Hudson Bay this year."

"So when will you be leaving? Will Ben be taking you in the coach?" enquired Charity.

Before Charles could answer James interrupted, "I think you would be better going by horse, so long as you are well armed."

"I think so too," replied Charles. "If I ride only by day, with three stops at inns and allowing for a week of business matters in the city, I should be back within two weeks."

Charity's anxiety at being parted from her husband for the first time since the wedding peaked two nights later when she realized that he was departing in the morning. As they lay in their four-poster bed, Charles did his utmost to calm her, but her tears kept flowing and it was only with Charles showing great tenderness, and after they had made love, that Charity calmed down and fell into a euphoric sleep. As she lay asleep, cradled in his arms he realized how much he was going to regret being parted for two weeks.

Early next morning, in the courtyard and cradling baby Elizabeth in her arms, she was again tearful as Charles kissed them both farewell. Elizabeth watched as he mounted the horse that Ben had brought over from the stables. Noticing the pair of flintlock pistols in the saddle holsters and knowing they would be primed, her hand went to her mouth in a gesture of anguish. Then she saw the rapier hanging at his side and although not an accomplished swordsman, she knew he was prepared to give a good account of himself if he was attacked, but she prayed he would not have to do so and would return home safely. With a farewell wave to his family, Charles turned the mare towards the lane and rode off in the direction of Derby. Three hours later he entered the outlying hamlets of the city and having ridden the first twenty miles from Ufton Manor, Charles decided both the horse and he should rest for an hour. Crossing St Mary's Bridge, he found himself in a maze of streets. Heading his horse onto the widest of the lanes, he rounded a final bend into Iron Gate Lane and reined in at the Dolphin Inn. Dismounting, he led her into the cobbled courtyard.

An ostler ran out and took the reins. "Make sure my horse is watered," Charles told him, "I will continue my journey in about an hour." He removed the pistols from the holsters and put them in his travel bag then made his way inside.

An hour later, after a hurried meal of cheese and bread and a half a flagon of ale, Charles was out in the cobbled yard. Placing his pistols back in their holsters; he gave a cheery thanks to the lad and placing one foot in the stirrup he was up in the saddle and cantering out of Derby; into the age-old lanes that led towards Royston, to join the Roman road known as the Ermine Way down to London.

A couple of miles along the way, he slowed the mare to a trot and then to a gentle walk. Alternating the pace of their travel with pauses for a short rest, he occasionally leaned forward and touched the mare's ears; speaking words of encouragement to her for they were two solitary companions travelling alone along long lanes and rutted roads.

Charles halted by a stream to let the mare drink and from his bag he took a piece of cheese and some bread that he had purchased from the innkeeper. Then after a short rest he remounted the horse and gave her an affectionate slap on the neck. "Come on, girl, another seventeen miles and we can have a good night's sleep in Wadesmill." The mare turned her head as if to look at him and walked on . . .

Charles finally reined in under a swinging sign proclaiming that the thatched-roof hostelry before him was The Feathers Inn. The mare snorted and shook her head . . .

* * *

Charles strode into the step parlour, "Travelled far, sir?" the paunchy innkeeper said.

"From Derby, and tomorrow I hope to travel the remainder of my journey to London. Have you a room for the night?"

"You be lucky, sir, and that's a fact; the London-bound coach has not arrived; when it does I have no doubt I will be sleeping 'em in the barns." The innkeeper laughed at his own joke. "'ave you stabled your horse, sir?"

"Aye," said Charles. "Your ostler took him round into the yard when I dismounted."

"Well, if yer go through into the lion parlour on the right, I will bring you our cook's special meat pudding and a flagon of ale."

Charles thanked him. "It's a large coaching inn you have, I expect you meet all types of travellers."

"Aye, we do, sir. We can stable up to a hundred horses and sometimes we get two or three coaches a day going to London, which makes the stable yard a dangerous place. In fact a couple of years ago we had a tragic accident involving a young girl who was earning the odd penny or two from travellers by playing her violin as the coaches pulled into the cobbled yard. The driver said he never saw her as she stepped too near the iron-rimmed wheels. She was run down before she could even play a note on her 'g' string and there she lay dead, her crushed young body lying in a pool of blood next to her broken violin."

"How sad," said Charles.

"Aye, sir, but there is more; some travellers have told me that they have been woken in the middle of the night to the strains of a violin being played. One traveller even said to me that when he awoke to use his slop bucket, he glanced out of his window and thought he saw in the moonlight, a young fair-haired girl playing a violin in the courtyard."

"Your ale must be very strong," Charles joked, "to have such effects."

Charles ate ravenously of the hot crusted meat pie and vegetables and drank a second flagon of ale before retiring to his room for the night.

He awoke at something like four in the morning and swore he could hear the faint strains of a violin playing a haunting refrain . . .

Gradually, though, he found himself drifting off into deep slumber.

* * *

His head was aching when Charles came to; he doused it in cold water and immediately his mind cleared, 'Did I imagine that violin music' he asked himself? He gathered his personal items, packing them into his travelling bag along with his pistols. It was later than he intended as he stepped out onto the corridor and made his way downstairs to the parlour to partake of breakfast before resuming his journey.

"Your ale certainly gave me a head," Charles said to the innkeeper as he was departing. "I awoke and thought I heard that violinist playing in the night, but it must have been my imagination."

The man smiled. "Take care, young man. That girl died a tragic death and folks around here say she only appears and plays to warn of possible danger. But then it's just a country tale and I bid you have a safe journey, sir."

The journey from Wadesmill to London through Epping Forest was about thirty miles and that day Charles had planned to set off at dawn and arrive late afternoon. But as he collected the mare from the stables his departure was already a few hours' late. Climbing into the saddle he headed south. All was at peace with the world, the spring sun shone as the mare trotted towards a wooded dell. A chorus from the birds in the woodlands and from the occasional upland pastures was ringing in Charles' ears when two men leapt out from the shrubbery into the path of the mare. The man to Charles' right grabbed the horse's bit while the man to the left pointed a pistol.

"Get off yer horse," the robber holding the bridle shouted.

Keeping the mare's body between him and the man holding the pistol, Charles flung his leg over the saddle. As he dropped to the ground his right hand instinctively grasped the butt of one of his pistols in the saddle holster. He rolled to one side and with his free hand he cocked the mechanism, aimed and fired; the highwayman took a step back, a look of surprise on his face as a gaping wound appeared in his chest. Blood erupted and soaked the torn remnants of the mans tunic; he stood swaying for a second then fell to the ground dead. The mare, its reins now released, reared, snorted and galloped off down the lane. Charles, already on his knees, dropped his pistol and drew his rapier. Turning on his heel to face the other assailant, he saw him standing frozen in an attitude of disbelief.

It was that second of ineptitude that saved Charles, who lunged at his second attacker. The man gave a sudden cry as the tip of the rapier pierced his forearm. Keeping hold of his pistol the man turned and running, he disappeared into the shrubbery leaving Charles panting with adrenalin coursing through his veins. The whole episode was over in less than a minute. With his arms at his side and the tip of the rapier touching the ground, he had one attacker lying dead at his feet. But he had another worry: the other assailant was still at large and armed and although wounded was probably lurking nearby. Charles had no horse, his other pistol was in the saddlebag and all he had with which to defend himself was his rapier. Then he noticed that the dead man also had a pistol, foolishly he had placed it in his belt to have two hands free to catch hold of the horse during the attack. Charles took it and picked up his own discharged weapon and and put it in his waistband; then with the rapier in one hand and the dead man's pistol in the other, he now felt that he could face any obstacle as he set off in pursuit of his horse. Charles didn't follow the lane; instead he entered the woods, keeping parallel with the lane, using the trees to give him cover in case the other assailant decided to lay in wait for him. After an hour of careful coursing through the forest glades, Charles entered a low-lying meadow; crossing it, he rejoined the lane. On the horizon at a distance of about a mile, he saw his mare grazing from the short lush grass. He quickened his pace and as he approached the horse, she lifted her head, stared at him, and then with recognition she slowly walked over and nuzzled his shoulder. With a tear in his eye, Charles patted the mare then gripping the reins and with one foot in the stirrup he mounted and the pair set off once more at a slow trot.

Two hours later, Charles finally rode out of the lane in Epping Forest and into a tiny settlement called Fiddlers Hamlet that had a small inn. What a coincidence, he thought, last night I dreamt of a ghostly girl violinist who supposedly heralds danger, this morning I am waylaid in Epping Forest by villains, and now I arrive in Fiddlers Hamlet just twenty miles to our old home in Newington Green and discover an inn named the Merry Fiddler.

Climbing from the saddle, Charles left the mare to graze on the green. As he walked away to rest and partake of a tankard of ale at the hostelry, the mare lifted her head and shook it, snorted, and then with her brown eyes she gazed soulfully at her fellow traveller . . .

New Ventures

Charles had ridden through several outlying villages encircling London before he halted the mare on Newington Green and took a nostalgic look around, remembering his youth, recalling playing games on the lush green grass. He gazed at Gloucester House built at the south-west corner of the Green, where Sir Thomas Halton lived with his wife Elizabeth. Charles used to play bat and ball with their son William. Charles sighed; he hadn't seen his childhood friend since the wedding when William married a young woman named Frances. Charles wondered if he had made a career for himself in the army. The mare snorted, bringing Charles back from his reminiscent mood, and he regained his composure as his thoughts returned to his present surroundings and his eyes took him to the portal stone that old Henry Cavendish had inscribed above the front door of their old home; it read 'Cavendish House'. Charles was pleased the new owners had not renamed their abode and with a kick of the stirrups, the mare trotted off the green towards Bunhill Row and the home of Samuel and Ann Clarke.

* * *

Charles paid and dismissed the hackney driver that had driven him from the Castle and Falcon in Aldersgate Street where he had arranged to stable the mare and grasping his saddlebag firmly in his hand, he rapped on Samuel's front door.

"It's good to see you, Charles, come in," Samuel said as he took Charles' cloak and saddlebag, "Where have you stabled your mount?"

"At the Castle and Falcon, it's not too distant and the mare will be well groomed."

"She will indeed, now come in and rest. How is our daughter Charity and baby Elizabeth?"

"Fine," he replied but at that moment Ann came into the entrance hall and embraced Charles, curtailing any further conversation until the three were sitting comfortably in the drawing room exchanging family news.

After some time they retired to the dining room for an early supper before Charles, exhausted from his long ride and hazardous encounter with the highwaymen, begged an early night.

"In the morning I will tell you of my encounter with two robbers and also the visitation by the ghost of a female violinist that I experienced at an inn."

"Oh, Charles, you cannot leave us now without telling us more," said Ann. "I shall not sleep a wink till I hear these accounts from you." But Charles was already half asleep at the table.

"His story will keep till morning," said Samuel as they escorted Charles to Charity's old bedroom.

The bedroom had a tallboy in the corner for the storing of linens. A delicately carved four-poster bed hung with drapes and a bed cover was placed along the back wall. Facing the foot of the bed was a dressing table with compartments and a mirror. In the other corner of the room was a washstand with a ceramic bowl and jug, and concealed underneath was a chamber pot. Charles was grateful to see that Ann had filled the jug with cold water; he quickly undressed, washed his face and hands, then walking over to the bed, pulled back the covers and fell onto the bed, asleep within moments; there were no ghosts or thoughts of Charity to invade his dreams that night . . .

* * *

"Did you sleep well?" Ann enquired as Charles presented himself for breakfast.

"Excellent, thank you, Mrs Clarke," he replied to his mother-in-law as he took a seat at the table.

"Now, Charles," said Samuel, "my wife has kept waking me during the night with concerns about these stories you have to relate to us; so please don't delay any longer, tell us what befell you."

Charles then recounted how the landlord at The Feathers Inn had told him about the fair-haired girl playing the violin and how she had been killed by a stagecoach. "The weird thing is," said Charles, "I heard the strains of the violin playing in the night and next morning the landlord said I should take care as the 'violinist' only played to warn of danger. Then a few hours later I was attacked by two armed highwaymen."

Charles next gave Ann and Samuel a full account of the attack and how he had defended himself, leaving one villain dead in the forest.

It was almost noon before they had extracted all the details from him. "We shall dine out for a season on your escapades," Samuel joked. "But now shall we discuss your family trading account?"

Ann got up from the table and suggested that her two men folk would be more relaxed discussing business in the drawing room.

"All your ships returned safely from Hudson Bay," said Samuel as the pair settled themselves into two comfortable chairs. "The furs this season were of exceptional quality and I managed to sell them at a very good price and I used some of my money to invest in the South Sea Company."

"What on earth is that?" said Charles

"It's a new company and seems a very good investment with the government," replied Samuel. "After the recent war with the Spanish, part of the Treaty of Utrecht gave us the right to send one ship a year, to engage in the slave trade with the Spanish colonies. Well good old King George saw an opportunity and has granted a trading monopoly to form the South Sea Company to have the exclusive right to trade slaves in Spanish South America and I have invested in the company."

"And what will the company do with the profits?" Charles asked.

"Apparently after the first voyage; Mr Walpole the Prime Minister has the idea to sell more shares in the company and use the money to pay off debts from the war."

"Excellent, but not for me" said Charles. "as you well know, the Cavendish's ceased slave trading some years ago, however I do think that it is time for me to consider new markets and ways to expand the Cavendish business."

Samuel produced a couple of leather-bound ledgers in which a bookkeeper had entered the trading figures for the previous season. Charles studied them for some time before closing them and sitting back.

"If I could make a proposal, Charles," Samuel said. "I believe that the county of Lancashire is not too distant from where you live in Derbyshire, and it has come to my attention from listening to other traders and shipping agents at Lloyd's coffee house that there is a small town in the north that may soon become a new port in competition with Liverpool. The town is called Preston. I have already spoken to some traders here in London and at the moment they say that the river into Preston, although hard to navigate, can be dredged. Reports say there is a single quay on the river and small ships are beginning to trade with the Baltic ports for the importing of iron, timber and hemp."

Charles listened in silence as Samuel continued, "My thoughts are that you could look at the possibility of trading furs direct from Hudson Bay into the Baltic ports and then import the timber and hemp back into Preston. It's just an idea, but you may be able to get an interest in developing this port with a little investment."

Charles said he would discuss the possibility with James when he got back to Ufton Manor.

That evening Samuel suggested that Charles join him and Ann for dinner at the Albion on Aldersgate Street.

"Prepare yourself for a feast, Charles. The Albion is one of the best eating houses in London and I have the table bill of fayre for this evening; it consists of eleven plates all served with wines." Charles took the bill from Samuel and read

Thick Spring Soup
Dorees a l'Italienne
Salmon
Whitebait
Escallopes de Ris de Veau aux Petit Pois
Poulet a l'Eclarte
Chines of Mutton
Ham and Salad
Ducklings, Goslings, Asparagus
Fruit Jellies, Pastry
Ratafia Creams, Compotes of Oranges

"You will have me returning home to Charity with a London paunch, but for one night I suppose it will not be noticed."

* * *

Samuel had requested a hackney coach to drive the three to the Albion.

"I think you will be pleasantly surprised by the company that attends the Albion," he said as they set off, "I seem to remember your father saying that a lot of your business contacts were maintained through the parliamentary introductions made by your old friend Samuel Pepys. When I last saw your father, he said that in the eleven years since Pepys died several of those contacts have also passed away, but tonight; you may find one or two old friends frequent the Albion. It's a fashionable place where gentlemen can take their ladies; much different from the usual bawdy inns."

As Charles entered the establishment he looked about and saw that there were individual tables each covered with linen table covers, and although it was still early evening, each table was illuminated with twin candelabras. A buzz of conversation filled the room.

A waiter escorted Samuel, Ann and Charles to a corner table; Charles had just taken his seat when a young man who was seated at the next table stood up and said, "Good evening, Charles."

The young man held out his hand. "It's good to see you after, oh, let me see, it must be at least four years; you came to our wedding, remember?"

Charles stood up and now took the hand of William Halton. Then excusing himself for a moment from Samuel and Ann, he stepped over to the adjoining table and briefly let his fingers touch the offered hand of William's wife.

"Good evening, Frances, I hope you are keeping well. I haven't seen you since your wedding."

Frances smiled, but before she could answer, William interrupted, "Will you and your companions join us at our table? We have so much to talk about."

Charles took William to where Samuel and Ann were seated. "Samuel, may I introduce William Halton, he requests that we join him at his table." With the introductions dutifully made, William summoned a waiter and requested that he make the new seating arrangements.

The wine flowed freely as they relaxed with the warmth of good food and pleasant company, but towards the end of the evening, the conversation grew more serious as Charles questioned William. "What is the latest news regarding Queen

Anne's health? We are so out of date up in Derbyshire; our news is possibly three weeks old."

"We all fear that we shall see a new monarch this year," William responded. "The queen is in failing health with severe gout; she never has been a healthy person and I think that is proven by her not being able to produce a living heir to the throne notwithstanding about seventeen pregnancies."

"I always felt so sad for the Queen," Frances said. "As a woman, I know how she must have felt having miscarried so many times."

"So do you think there will be a return to a Stuart monarchy," said Samuel, "or will the Act of Union that united England and Scotland seven years ago make it impossible for the Stuarts to reclaim the throne?"

A young man at the next table ceased conversation with his guest and leaned closer to try and overhear William's conversation.

"Oh, I have no doubt we may see some rebellion by the Jacobites led by James Stuart, but my fellow peers suggest that George, the great-grandson of James the First who is the Elector of Hanover, has a legitimate claim to the throne." William leaned forward to keep his voice low as he continued, "I have it from one good authority that he will be invited to England to end the reign of the House of Stuart forever and we may soon have the House of Hanover on our throne."

Their conversation had not gone unheard by the young gentleman seated at the adjoining table in the company of a young lady. The man was Charles Radclyffe; the brother of James Radclyffe, the Earl of Derwentwater. Both were related to James Stuart.

It was late into the evening as the conversation drew to a close when Ann said, "I regret but I must be excused for I am feeling very tired."

"Of course," William said. "It has been a pleasure to meet you and Samuel." Then turning to address Charles he added,

"Next time you are in the city do call on me and we can arrange for another dinner party. Frances and I still reside at the old family house in Woodford Green although we are having some alterations done to make the house more fashionable. Father is possibly commissioning a young architect recommended to him by the Earl of Mar so you may not recognize the interior when you see it."

Charles Cavendish left London a week later, unaware of the events that would befall him due to the comments overheard by the ardent Jacobite sympathiser Charles Radclyffe.

The comments regarding parliament's plans to forever exclude the House of Stuart from the throne were verified by Radclyffe a few days later, when he had a secret meeting with the Earl of Mar, who, since the union of Scotland and England in seventeen hundred and seven, had been Queen Anne's Scottish and British Secretary of State.

Jacobite Rebellion

A copy of the *London Gazette* reached Chatsworth House in August seventeen fourteen announcing with sadness that Queen Anne had died on the first day of that month and George Prince Elector of Hanover was to be crowned king of Great Britain. Within days the news had spread through the county and when it arrived at Ufton Manor it immediately caused consternation.

"What is happening, are we to have a foreign king now?" Constance asked at the breakfast table.

"I really have no idea," said James. "What is your opinion, Charles? When you were in London a few weeks ago, was their any speculation in the coffee houses of who might be a successor? I mean, was this Prince George of Hanover ever mentioned?"

"He was, but it's all very complicated and to do with the fact that Queen Anne's father, James the Second, was a Catholic but parliament deposed him," Charles said. "Incidentally do you realize that it is twenty-seven years since the government invited William of Orange, or we should say William the Third, and Queen Mary to accept the Protestant throne?" Charles sipped from his coffee. "And that is what may now cause a problem, because with both of them long dead and now Queen Mary's sister, Queen Anne, also dead, parliament fear that the Jacobites may try to start a rebellion and proclaim James Stuart as the lawful king to maintain the House of Stuart. To be honest it is a legitimate claim to the throne but he is a Catholic and I heard that if he gave up his faith, parliament would accept him, but he refuses."

"So," James said, "this Prince George is the favourite because he is a Protestant and being the great-grandson of

James the First, he has a legitimate claim and will bring a Hanoverian family dynasty to the English throne."

"That's about right Father, but whatever happens, I am sure our country is going to witness some troublesome times," Charles commented as he rose from the table.

"Praise the Lord, we are far enough away from it all here in Derbyshire," Constance added as she went with Charity to attend to baby Elizabeth. How little she knew . . .

* * *

Parliament announced their appointment of George Prince Elector of Hanover as the crowned king of Great Britain and sent the news post-haste to the Hanoverian Court, but the prince, with stolid Teutonic character and regard for conformity and preparation, did not rush to his new kingdom. His cortege was ponderously slow as it meandered its way through the European towns of Minden, Hengelo and Utrecht with civic receptions, toasts and speeches at almost every settlement through which his party travelled. A special reception took place in Utrecht to celebrate the first anniversary of the signing of the Treaty. A treaty that finally brought an end to the War of Spanish Succession that had embraced most of Europe and the West Indian colonies for a decade; a decade in which half a million soldiers had been killed.

Eventually a copy of the *London Gazette* reached Chatsworth House informing the nation that after delays due to adverse winds and bad weather in the North Sea, Prince George had finally landed at London Greenwich on twenty-ninth of September. The *Gazette* went on to announce that the coronation of King George I would take place on the twentieth of October seventeen fourteen.

When the news reached Ufton Manor, Charles's response was immediate. "Father, this is too important an event for our family to miss, The nation is about to witness a new royal house on the throne and I need to be in London to talk to my contacts to see if any political changes will affect our business investments in the Hudson Bay which had Prince Rupert as its founder. Ben can drive Charity and me in the coach. We can stay at the Clarkes' residence on Bunhill Row. I also have some business I wish to discuss with Samuel, so it will be a wonderful opportunity to conclude our business for this year."

The journey to London passed without incident and this time the violinist failed to play, even for Ben . . .

But after the coronation a wind of change began to sweep through Whitehall. King George shunned the Tories in favour of the Whigs and as a consequence the Earl of Mar lost his position as Secretary of State for Scotland, just one of the factors for the failure of the coming rebellion.

In the spring 'Bobbin John' as the Earl was nicknamed, because of his ability to switch political sides to his advantage, travelled in secret to hold meetings at the Jacobite court of James Stuart in the Netherlands. At the meetings it was arranged for the Earl to raise the Stuart standard in the highlands of Scotland.

At the penultimate meeting, the papal legate advised the Earl, "Plans are in place, and when you raise the Stuart standard in the Highlands, this court will support the rising with an invasion of French Jacobites. We suggest a suitable place for the landing would be at the Holy Island of Lindisfarne, off the Northumberland coast. Our intelligence sources report that Mr Forster, a prominent man in the area, can raise local Jacobite militia to support the invasion, so you must inform him by secret dispatches of the plans.

A week later, after a final meeting at the court, Bobbin John, the Earl of Mar, returned to England with plans already forming in his head for rebellion but forgetful of informing Mr Forster of the landings . . .

* * *

The servants at Ufton Manor had decked its rooms with holy and mistletoe. It was the first festive season for the Cavendish family in their ancestral home. Large fires warmed the rooms as the family watched the snow falling onto a white landscape. All was calm and warm, then came the thaw and all too soon it was spring, followed by a flaming June that heralded prospects of a good harvest for the villagers.

Towards the end of August, James and Charles were deep in conversation as they took an evening stroll down the lane towards the Peacock Inn. "Father, when I was discussing our business affairs with Samuel in the spring, he advised me that the Lancashire town of Preston could be a developing port to compete some day with Liverpool. Samuel told me that, although the river is hard to navigate, small ships are already trading with ports on the Baltic for the import of hemp, timber and iron. I thought I would travel north to Preston to investigate the possibilities of our family investing in the new port."

Father and son walked across the cobbled yard at the front of the inn and climbed the three steps up to the font door. "Enough talk of Preston for a moment, Charles. Do you want to drink a tyg of wine or share a flagon of ale?"

"Ale for me, Father." The pair sat down at a long bench.

Peter Kendal the inn keeper left the table in the corner where he was in conversation with David Halton from Wingfield Hall.

"Good evening, Mr Cavendish, what can I serve you?"

"Good evening, Peter," said James, "a flagon of ale and two tankards, please."

Charles looked across the room to the corner table and addressed young David, "Good evening young man, how are your parents? I haven't seen them for some time but I am sure we shall see more of you all now that Annabel and you are friends."

David stammered an embarrassing, "they are in fine health, sir." At the moment Peter the innkeeper returned and placed a pewter flagon and two tankards on the table in front of James.

"Grand weather, sir, should be in for a good harvest this year."

"Let's hope so," replied James.

James filled the two tankards and as Charles faced him again, he said, "You know I am not young, in fact I shall be forty-eight this year, and although I ride every day, I have never ventured north of Buxton. I think I will ride with you for company and for your safety. Together we can assess the possibilities of this business venture before committing to any financial undertaking. When are you thinking of travelling?"

"I know you mean well, Father, but are you sure you want to face three or four days in the saddle, stopping overnight sometimes in flea-ridden inns?

"My mind's made up, Charles; the exercise will do me good. We are only into October so it will still be a pleasant time to be travelling."

"Well, if your mind is made up, we had better break the news to Constance and Charity and I think we should make a start as soon as possible. I don't fancy going over the hills to Buxton for I have heard that you need a guide and there are tales of some unscrupulous guides leaving you abandoned to the wild men who live in the caves up on the hills. I suggest we go the longer but safer route into Derby and then we take the well-used road though Newcastle-under-Lyme, which I understand is the road the London travellers take to Warrington then to Preston. From there, the road goes on to Lancaster."

* * *

Two apprehensive wives stood in the cobbled courtyard of Ufton Manor to wave farewell to James and Charles, the same courtyard where fifty-five years previously, James' grandparents, Robert and Elizabeth Cavendish, had waved farewell to their son when he left to seek his fortune in London. A journey that with the assistance of Samuel Pepys paved the way to laying the foundations for the wealth of Cavendish House.

Now it was the turn of Constance and Charity to wave farewell to their loved ones . . .

* * *

Dusk was falling as James and Charles crested the ridge and saw the small town of Newcastle-under-Lyme nestling in the valley below them. As they rode down the main street into the town centre James saw what seemed to be a new two-storey rectangular brick structure standing on an island site in the middle of the High Street. The building had a hipped roof and an external support of stone pilasters surmounted by a cornice and a balustraded parapet.

James and Charles drew rein and Charles leaned forward in the saddle to speak to a man passing by. "Good day, fine sir. Can you tell us were we might stable our horses for the night and find clean beds?"

"Good evening, sir. Yer can try the Star Inn on Timber Market. It's not too bad a place, just ride past another two streets on yer left and you'll find it."

"Thank you kindly. We are just admiring that large new brick building in the centre of this road. What is its purpose in a small town like this?"

"Ah, sirs, that's the new Guildhall. It was only built last year and we are very proud of it. It's a public building. As you can see, the upper floor level is built on those open round brick arches, four on the long and two on the short sides, and underneath it's supported by three pillars. The townsfolk use the ground floor on market days."

"You are well versed in the building. How come you know so much about it?" said James.

"Ah, you see, sir, I am a carpenter and I worked on some of its construction. Now I will bid you farewell and a safe journey." And with a brisk step the carpenter walked off into the dusk.

"Come on, my boy, let us find that inn." James and Charles kicked the stirrups and both horses walked on. The street was deserted but there on the left was a swinging sign over a timber-framed building proclaiming it to be the Star Inn.

Charles and James rode the horses under an arch bracing tie beam into a small stable yard. Dismounting, Charles held the horses while James entered the inn to enquire for accommodation. He soon returned. "We are in luck. Hand the horses to the stable boy; they have a room for the night."

As dawn broke on the second day of their ride Charles and James awoke, washed and quickly dressed and were in the saddle by five in the morning for the forty-mile ride to Warrington.

James was very quiet as they rode. "You're deep in thought this morning," Charles said after the pair had ridden in silence for about thirty minutes.

"Oh, I was just contemplating; thoughts keep filling my head. Your grandfather Henry Cavendish was a great man for storing historical details and I suppose it came from his father's associations with Chatsworth House. Your grandfather always seemed to have information that wasn't known outside of military or government circles. Well, he used to relate those tales to me as a boy." James grew silent for a few moments then he said, "Lancashire, into which we are travelling, was the scene of several massacres during the civil war. One terrible event took place at the town of Bolton. From what your grandfather told me, Lancashire was mainly for the royalists and traditionally Catholic. It was only in some towns that parliament had a majority of supporters, Bolton being one of them. Well, apparently the Bolton townsfolk, led by a Colonel Shuttleworth, built earthwork defences around the town and waited for the royalists to attack. I think the first one came in the February of 'forty-three but it was beaten off. Then at the start of 'forty-four, Cromwell sent about three thousand men to garrison the town but a few months previously James Stanley the Earl of Derby was in charge of a contingent of the royalist forces at nearby Warrington when the king transferred a large proportion of the Earl's best troops to the king's main army at Oxford. The king was already losing the war and the Earl and his depleted army were hemmed in around Warrington by parliamentarian forces. The Earl then received bad news that his wife, the Countess of Derby, was besieged at Lathom House by parliamentary forces led by a Colonel Alexander Rigby." James paused as the pair entered a dip in the lane; high banks on each side made it a perfect place for an attack, so, kicking his stirrups, James called to Charles to ride. Within minutes the pair where out of the cutting and the horses reined in to a walking pace.

"I had the most uncomfortable feeling that we could have been attacked back there," said James.

"If you had experienced an attack like I did, Father, you would realize they happen without warning. But now you have regained your composure, you were telling me of the predicament the Earl had with a small royalist army at his command and his family home under siege a few miles away. What a predicament; your wife is defying the enemy to protect your home and the family honour. The Earl must have questioned, 'Do I march to save her?' Did he attempt to lift the siege?" Charles asked

"Apparently not," said James. "He held fast to his king but Lady Charlotte must have been a very remarkable woman to resist the parliament forces in such a manner. I don't know much about her but I do know Lady Charlotte lived at Lathom House; the Stanley family home. Father told me that she had assembled a militia of seasoned sharpshooters to defend it, as it was the last royalist stronghold in Lancashire.

"During the siege, those sharpshooters inflicted significant losses by sniping at the parliamentary officers. I believe the siege lasted for four months. At the beginning, Lady Charlotte had a garrison of three hundred against two thousand parliamentary soldiers," James went on. "The Earl was unable to defend his home or family because he had to wait for Prince Rupert who was on a march from York to attack Bolton. James Stanley then felt obliged to join him by breaking out from Warrington and on the way he had news; a rider delivered word that Lathom House had finally surrendered to the forces of Colonel Rigby; the siege was lifted and the Countess was safe."

Charles was deep in thought listening to James recount the history of the county through which they were riding. "I don't know how you can store all this knowledge in your head, Father."

"Ah, the secret, my boy, is to be interested in the subject. I have always had a desire to learn about our ancestors and our heritage. Your grandfather just kept feeding me with information. Anyway, to continue: when Colonel Rigby took Lathom House, he and his men joined Colonel Shuttleworth and the garrison at Bolton, which meant there were about four thousand soldiers now stationed behind Bolton's earthen defences. I expect Prince Rupert and the Earl of Derby had not expected to find the town so strongly defended but irrespective of the foul weather and in heavy rain, Rupert ordered four infantry regiments to attack immediately."

"How do they get men to fight and kill under such bad conditions?" Charles questioned.

"I suppose it's the discipline," said James. "Anyway, the attack was aggressive but they were beaten back with severe royalist casualties including Colonel Russell, the commander of Rupert's own regiment of foot. Apparently what happened next triggered the final atrocity but it was left to a contingent of Colonel Shuttleworth's defenders to commit the first act. All the soldiers in the attack were English although two of the regiments had just been released from service in Ireland. The defenders took some prisoners and believing one of them to be an Irish Catholic, they hanged him. When word reached the royalists of the hanging, the regiment of Sir Thomas Tyldesley that was recruited mainly from Catholics in Lancashire regarded the hanging as an affront to their religion and consequently when Prince Rupert ordered a second attack, which was led by the Earl of Derby; the attack was fuelled by sectarian anger against the puritans of Bolton. The royalists stormed the walls, carrying the fighting through into the town with savage hand-to-hand street fighting. Apparently the royalists massacred over a thousand townsmen and soldiers and it is said the Earl of Derby took a leading part in the slaughter on that terrible day in the May of 'forty-four."

"It's no wonder that Cromwell had King Charles beheaded for crimes against his people," said Charles. "Civil war always seems to bring out the worst in us when brother fights brother. Thank the Lord the days of war on English soil are over."

It was a poor prophecy that Charles uttered as he and James rode down the road and saw a coaching signpost that told them it was eight miles to Holmes Chapel. "We are approaching a hamlet; I think we will rest here for an hour," said Charles. "It's almost mid-day and then we can ride on to Warrington before dusk."

True to his forecast, dusk was just falling as the weary pair rode into Warrington. In the distance they saw a stagecoach departing through an archway from a courtyard; Charles and James rode on. Over the archway a sign proclaimed "Ye Olde Lion 1690". On a smaller sign, James read that the inn was a halt for the Liverpool and London stagecoach and that horses could be changed for a small payment. Father and son rode into the yard and dismounted; almost immediately an ostler took the reins of both horses and led them away.

"Evening, sirs," a ruddy-faced innkeeper greeted them. "Wilt thou be wantin' room for the neet?" he enquired.

"Yes, for two persons just for the night."

"Reet, sirs, one room it is. Would yer be wantin' suppa? We 'ave some Lancashire black pudding or some potage and reet fine ale."

"The pudding sounds fine for me," said Charles. James dissented and chose the potage.

The pair walked over and took two high-backed chairs at a long oak-planked table. A well-dressed man of Charles' age sat quietly studying some papers but otherwise the hostelry was devoid of clients except for a couple of young men sitting at a corner table.

Possibly getting drunk before going to their squalid homes, thought James.

"Good evening, sir I hope we won't disturb you?," said Charles as he sat down, "only you look so deeply engrossed in your papers,"

The man looked up and smiled. "No matter, I can do with a wee bit of company," he said, putting the documents into a well-worn carpet-bag with handles.

"That's a very convenient method to carry documents and papers," replied Charles without commenting on the man's Scottish accent.

"Aye, very useful, I saw them being used when I was travelling in Europe. As we are fellow travellers and there is no one to introduce us, my name is James Gibbs." The man offered his hand to Charles and James.

"This is Charles my son," replied James, "and my name is James Cavendish."

Their conversation was interrupted by the innkeeper, who brought flagons of ale and said their request for their supper meals would be ready soon.

"To continue now that your victuals are taken care of," said the man, "Do you by chance have a house out at Woodford Green; Cavendish House, I believe it's named?"

"We did live in London at that house but we sold it last year and moved back to our family home in Derbyshire," said James.

"The reason I recall the name," said Gibbs, "Is that I am an architect and I had cause to visit a gentleman named Sir Thomas Halton who owns Gloucester House on the green. I have been approached with the offer of a commission to make design changes to his fine house."

"How coincidental," said Charles, "It is only a few months since I was in London and happened to meet William Halton and his wife Frances at a supper party. He mentioned in conversation that his father Sir Thomas was commissioning an architect to redesign the interior. So did you train in Edinburgh? From your accent you're a Scot, are you not?"

"That's correct, I was born in Aberdeen and had a good education but when my parents died fourteen years ago I was only eighteen so I went to live with relatives in the Netherlands. Not knowing what to do with my life, I contemplated becoming a priest and I travelled to Rome where I enrolled in the Scots College founded incidentally a century ago by Pope Clement Eighth for the training of priests for the home mission. But the life was not for me so I left the college and was tutored at the Baroque architectural school of Carlo Fontana. It was then that I happened to meet the Earl of Mar, who became my patron, and last year he obtained my first important commission for me in London. I am to design the church of St Mary-le-Strand, in the City of Westminster and that is how I happened to be in London and how Sir Thomas Halton heard of me. But I do not think I shall be able to work on his house so I have recommended the work to another. For the moment I am just travelling up to Scotland on business and have stopped in Warrington as it may be the town for a future commission for me."

The innkeeper returned carrying their suppers; a plate of black puddings and a bowl of potage. "Thank you, landlord," said Charles. "You have very few travellers tonight. Is it normally this quiet?"

The innkeeper looked at the three, then said, "Haven't you heard the news? I got a London Flyer through here two days ago; he was on his way to Liverpool with news that some gentry, the Earl of Mar, was suspected of being a Jacobite sympathiser, whatever one of them is. An' because yon new King Georgie didn't re-appoint him as Secretary o' State or summat, the Flyer said the Earl who is Scottish took the sulks and disappeared for a short time. Rumour 'as it 'e went off to meet with the Stuarts in Holland then he went home to Scotland to support the cause of James Stuart and raise his standard and a rebellion. Anyway, there's been hardly any travellers from London since that all 'appened on't twenty-seventh o' August."

James Gibbs looked apprehensively at Charles and James. "I know what you laddies are a-thinking of me an' me talking about my patron being the Earl of Mar, but I had no knowledge of any of this. Tonight I shall stay here, in the morrow I shall go post-haste back to London."

"I think a very wise decision," said James. "What shall we do, Charles? Go on to Preston and finish our business or go home?"

"Oh, I cannot see any trouble befalling us in Preston and we are so near, we may as well complete our journey."

Dawn was breaking as Charles and James stood in the stable yard bidding farewell and a safe journey to James Gibbs. Their farewells were interrupted by a horseman galloping into the cobbled yard; the rider dismounted and shouting for the ostler to have a change of horse ready in fifteen minutes, the rider hurried into the inn.

A stable boy who was holding the reins of Charles and James' horses said, "Summat up and that's a fact, sir. That is't London Flyer wit'news."

Charles, James and Gibbs hurried back into the inn to listen to the man; what they saw and heard was most disconcerting.

The rider was slouched at a table with the froth from the tankard of ale around his lips. After swilling the ale around his mouth to wash the dust away after the hard ride, he spat the ale onto the floor, took another long draught from the tankard and still panting from exertion he leaned back and closed his eyes.

Unable to contain himself, James Gibbs shouted, "News, man; what news d'yer bear?"

The rider opened his eyes, wiped his lips with a sleeve, stretched his legs and for a moment remained silent. Then, gathering his breath he said, "its grave news, I fear. On the sixth of September the Earl of Mar proclaimed to the Scottish clans that James Stuart was the lawful sovereign and although the Pretender to the throne is still in the Netherlands, the Earl raised the old Scottish standard in his name. The lowland and highland clans formed an alliance and now the Jacobites have marched south. Last week they captured Perth without opposition and the news is that the Jacobite army has now grown to eight thousand fighting men. There is some good news: the Duke of Argyle with two thousand loyal clansmen held Stirling and saved Edinburgh and the Earl with his superior forces has yet to make a move south into England. At the moment, my news is, the rebellion is contained north of the border. Now, sirs, I am rested for a brief time and must be in the saddle for my news to go to Liverpool."

The London Flyer rose to his feet, threw sixpence on the table for the ale and made his way to the door.

"Farewell, ride well and we hope the next Flyer bears better news," shouted the innkeeper. The door closed behind the man and a silence pervaded the room.

Moments later the silence was broken as Charles and James made a hasty withdrawal, bidding farewell again to Mr Gibbs and wishing him a safe journey in view of the news they had just received. "Come on, Charles, the sooner we finish our business in Preston and get home the better."

In the yard an ostler still stood with the reins of their horses gathered in his hands. As Charles climbed into the saddle, James took hold of the reins, giving the boy an additional sixpence, then James also climbed into the saddle and the pair rode north.

* * *

A week before James and Charles left Ufton Manor to ride north into Lancashire, and unknown to them; parliament had ordered the arrest of the Northumbrian Squire and member of parliament; Sir Thomas Forster, who was a suspected Jacobite sympathiser. But Forster had fled north and at Greenrig in Northumberland he had proclaimed the Old Pretender, James Stuart, as James III, lawful king of England, and in support he raised a cavalry force of three hundred men. Fired up with enthusiasm for the cause, he led his cavalry north and attempted to take Newcastle but failed. But the standard had been raised and rebellion was in the air . . .

* * *

In Scotland the time had come for 'Bobbin John', the Earl of Mar to make his move; and a bold move it was as he called the Lords and Lairds of the clans to gather in the Forest of Mar at Braemar for the autumn hunt; an annual event that usually lasted for a week. As usual the strongest and fleetest of hunters accompanied by hundreds of beaters with hounds ran on foot to hunt for the deer that were fat after a summer of grazing and as evening fell on the first day the hunters returned to camp. Storytellers vied with each other for attention amidst the joviality. Pipers mingled with the crowds displaying their skills with the bagpipes, and the skirl of the pipes lingered on the evening air. Fires were lit and soon the smell of roasting meat cooking on spits filled the nostrils.

The Earl of Mar sat at ease with the Lords and Lairds, watching and listening from the comfort of a rustic bower that was decorated with heather, fir boughs and rowan berries. The Earl had set the scene and slowly he rose to his feet and raised his arms. In one hand he held high the Stuart standard. A hush slowly descended on the assembly. The earl lowered his arms and firmly planted the standard into the ground before him, then in a commanding voice he began, "Fellow clansmen, I welcome you to this gathering. I beg you enjoy the food and hospitality of friendship and the brotherhood of the clans but more importantly I want you to know that I hereby assert the undoubted right of our lawful sovereign, James the Eighth, to the crown, and the relieving of the kingdom from the oppressions and grievances, arising particularly from the union of the two kingdoms and the heavy taxes levied, and the large debts imposed for the maintenance of foreign troops."

The gathered clansmen cheered and the shouts rang out of "No union", while some shouted, "No malt tax". Then the cry was taken up and "No salt-tax" gradually transformed, accompanied by the rhythmic stamping of feet, into the general chanting of "No taxes, no taxes, no taxes . . ."

The mood of the gathering was at fever pitch; it was time for the Earl to again raise the Stuart standard high, this time proclaiming, "Men, you must fight for the relief of our native country from the oppression and from the foreign yoke that is too heavy for us or our posterity to bear."

The pipes began playing in unison and for once there was unity as the gentry on the bower sat down and began planning the order of battle.

"As the Mackintosh clan will form the largest battalion in our invasion of England, I hereby appoint the Laird of Mackintosh, my good and trusty friend Lord Lachlan, as commander in chief."

Lord Lachan stood and received the applause of gentry on the bower. "I'll be a-thanking of yea," he said addressing the Earl, "an' me and my fine ladies will not be letting yer down. If I am yer commander in chief, sir, then I mus' be 'avin a good fighting brigadier to lead my battalions in the days to come and I can think of none better than my nephew, Old Borlum, William Mackintosh the Laird of Macintosh."

The pipes continued to play as the Earl of Mar nodded his agreement, and then in a low voice he began to address his staff officers. "I have a communication from a Mr Forster in Northumberland who intends raising the Stuart standard in Newcastle and he writes that he will ride to meet us with three hundred cavalry. So, Brigadier, how many men do you need for this undertaking and how will you get them across the Firth of Forth?"

Old Borlum, as Brigadier Mackintosh was familiarly called, sat quietly for a few moments. The Earl of Strathmore, Lord Nairn and Lord Charles Murray waited in expectation. Finally Old Borlum addressed them. "This is going to be a hazardous undertaking and I must have the best and fittest body of soldiers. I think two and a half thousand men should be sufficient to rouse our Jacobite supporters in England to arms. I know I can rely on the Mackintosh clansmen but will you and your regiments ride with us?"

"You have our support," the three Lords voiced as one.

"Very well, gentlemen. I now have a large commitment of men and I will take the greater part, which will be the best of your own regiments, but," Old Borlum now turned and spoke directly to the Earl of Mar, "I only have one problem now. How do I get two and a half thousand men and supplies across the Firth of Forth?"

* * *

Old Borlum Mackintosh searched for days for a solution to his problem, then it came to him in a flash of inspiration: he would utilize the local fishermen to ferry his reinforcements across the estuary in readiness for an attack on Edinburgh.

All the plans were in place; fishermen had been contacted and on the evening of the ninth of October under the cover of a thin drizzle of cold rain, Brigadier Mackintosh made a successful crossing. Immediately he instructed his commanders to form the two and a half thousand Jacobites into groups of forty men in preparation for their march on Edinburgh.

The rebel clansmen had marched barely five miles and had just entered a short shallow valley; the sides of which was scattered with rocks and boulders, when a couple of sheepherder's cottages set in a small clearing that was free of rocks and boulders came into sight. The walls of each home were formed of loose stones under a roof covered with clods of turf supported on fir tree branches. To the marching clansmen the homes were part of the normal landscape but from a distance and to any Englishman coming north they looked like gigantic molehills. From one '*molehill*' a wisp of smoke plumed upwards from a peat fire through a stone chimney. Of the inhabitants there was no sign or evidence that the rebel army had even been seen or heard.

"Possibly the families are loyalist," Mackintosh said to an officer who was sucking on an empty pipe.

The rebel clansmen, who a moment before had been marching with their flags flying, their drums beating and the skirl of the pipes echoing around them, grew silent as a rider galloped into their columns. Reining his horse to a halt in front of old Borlum Mackintosh the rider gasped, "Sir, there are enemy forces approaching and you are in danger of attack from a regiment of cavalry."

"Take cover and prepare to repel horse," shouted Mackintosh. The drummers began to beat out the order and the highlanders hastily took shelter behind the large boulders that where scattered around the hillsides.

"'Tis nay a place for cavalry," commented a pipe-sucking Jacobite officer.

At the head of the valley the Duke of Argyle sat astride his tough highland horse. The duke had rapid marched a small force of four hundred cavalry and two hundred foot soldiers from Stirling Castle, but now he halted his government troops.

The duke raised his arm and shouted to the cavalry commander, "Yer'l not be a-going in there amongst those rocks tonight, my bonny lads. Especially as we're outnumbered and it's nigh on dusk. We shall make camp here for the night." With his action he knew Edinburgh was saved and the rebels could not retreat back into the highlands. Giving orders to his officers to post guards, the duke settled down for a long night's vigil and silence descended on the valley.

But all was not still in the rebel encampment. The Jacobite rebels gradually slipped away under cover of darkness and by early dawn had reformed where the hillsides flattened out onto a coastal plain. Under the still dawn air and across the damp heath, the Jacobites set off at a rapid march towards Leith, the seaport for Edinburgh. This time it was a silent approach, no drums beating, no pipes playing.

Colonel Mackintosh, the nephew of Brigadier Mackintosh, gave orders for a detachment of his men to open the tollbooth and jail and release the prisoners then he addressed his aide; Lieutenant Colonel Farquharson, "We need food, drink and any fighting equipment you can muster. I think you should organise a raid on the custom house and seize its merchandise plus any ships in the harbour. Take what provisions are available and any arms and powder and report back to me."

Farquharson saluted and said, "Aye, an' we'll nay be forgettin' wee drams for the lads, eh, sir? I shall tell them laddies o'mine to bring brandy back to camp."

Lieutenant Colonel John Farquharson of Invercauld had four officers and one hundred and forty men of the Clan Chattan in his regiment, which he now deployed as a raiding party. It was almost midday when the raiders returned and the two thousand rebels barricaded themselves in the old fort at Leif.

* * *

The Duke of Argyll rose an hour after dawn but too late; he had lost the initiative and the rebels had slipped away and taken the fort at Leif. Realizing his cavalry was now useless and with only two hundred foot he could not take the fort, he retired to Edinburgh to review the situation. The answer lay at the castle. The Duke of Argyle requisitioned artillery pieces and using horses from his cavalry he ordered the guns to be dragged to the seaport.

"We canna' hold the fort against artillery," Brigadier Mackintosh said to his nephew and to Farquharson, "and I despair of the locals supporting our cause so I think we should make a tactical withdrawal across the estuary."

Taking advantage of the low ebb of the tide, the Jacobites slipped out of the fort and onto the sands. The tidal waters of the Esk rose to the calves of the rebels and as the column reached the middle of the river, the low ebb tide reached the knees of most, and a few of the height disadvantaged found themselves in waist-deep water. Disregarding the cold water, the Jacobites crossed in silence; a column of freedom fighters intent on a mission for their lawful monarch.

"You've done it, sir," Farquharson said as he rode alongside his colonel through Musselburgh. "I wager as of yet Argyle doesn't even know we've' gone. I will get a quick count to see how many men we've lost in the crossing."

Five minutes later Farquharson reported that they had lost forty men to the rising waters.

"We're not safe yet," said Colonel Mackintosh. "His artillery may be of little use now, and his cavalry can't catch us till the next low tide, so it's a rapid march to Seaton House where I guarantee some safety for us all."

The Jacobites repelled several attacks from Argyle's government troops, then on the third day news reached the rebels that lifted their spirits. Brigadier Mackintosh called his officers to a meeting and informed them that an express rider from Northumberland had brought news that Mr Forster had raised the Stuart standard in England and with three hundred cavalry was riding from Newcastle to meet the highlanders at Kelso.

As Old Borlum William Mackintosh led his slightly depleted rebel force away from the safety of Seaton House, Argyle's marauding force continued to launch a series of harassing attacks against the escaping Jacobites but after several days the attacks gradually grew less frequent as the Jacobites distanced themselves from Edinburgh.

* * *

The Scottish townsfolk of Kelso awoke on the twenty-second of October seventeen fifteen to witness an historical day; in the market place Brigadier Mackintosh called for the Lords and Lairds to stand in the centre of the square and a circle of gentlemen volunteers to form around them. In the churchyard the highland regiments led by Colonel Mackintosh and the Northumbrian cavalry led by Thomas Forster were drawn up in marching order. At the fore was the south-western Jacobites led by Lord Kenmuir. At a signal from Brigadier Mackintosh and with full colours flying, drums beating and bagpipes playing, the rank and file marched into the market square and formed a huge circle that filled the market place, around the Lords and Lairds

"Silence," bellowed a barrel-chested highland officer. A trumpet sounded and George Seton, the Earl of Wintoun, unrolled a proclamation and speaking in a loud commanding voice declared to a hushed crowd that King James was the lawful king over the realms of Scotland, Ireland and England.

As night fell, Old Borlum and his staff officers worked with frantic pace to concentrate the planning to merge the Jacobites into a single fighting force; the task was not made any easier by Thomas Forster's insistence that the rebels march south into England to meet up with English Jacobites.

"We have twenty thousand waiting to support us in Liverpool," Forster said.

"And do yer no understand, laddie," replied Mackintosh, my highlanders want to take and hold Scotland for King Jamie when he comes from Holland. And there is good news: two ships manned by French supporters are waiting for a signal to invade at Holy Island off the Northumberland coast to support our cause."

Forster hung his head and remained silent for a few moments. "So that's what it was all about," he finally muttered.

"What yer muttering, yer wee 'scuse for a man?" said Mackintosh.

Forster raised his head. "After we were repelled from Newcastle, we marched north to attack Berwick-on-Tweed and on the road we heard the news that two Jacobite sympathisers had been warned to expect a Jacobite invasion at Holy Island and had successfully taken control of the castle on the island. Apparently the master gunner at the castle was also the surgeon and barber. Well, it seems one of the local men, Lancelot Errington, had visited the barber to ask for a shave and during conversation he discovered that most of the garrison was absent in the town. After his shave, Lancelot hurried home and spoke to his nephew, Mark, the pair then returned to the castle, claiming that Lancelot had lost the key to his watch. They were allowed in and overpowered the three people in the castle." Forster paused and held his head in his hands in despair. "That castle was one of the key points to the rebellion. I see it all now and I never went to reinforce the Erringtons. Next day a detachment of one hundred men was sent from Berwick to retake the castle. When the government soldiers approached, the Erringtons fled, but were soon captured and imprisoned in the tollbooth at Berwick. We heard that security was so lax that they tunnelled out and escaped. Oh, if only . . ." wailed Forster. "I gave up waiting for the French reinforcements because 'Bobbin John' never informed me they were landing at Holy Island, so we marched north into Scotland on the same day that two French ships signalled the island castle, but when they received no reply, they withdrew and sailed back to France."

"Aye, well, laddie, mistakes are made in war," said Mackintosh.

"Aye, an' the side that makes the most usually loses," said a sarcastic but philosophical Farquharson.

The discussions raged on for three days until the Highlanders finally agreed that the Jacobite army would march south into England to rendezvous with Lord Kenmure who on the twelfth of October seventeen fifteen had set off from his home with the intention of joining the Earl of Wintoun at Moffat.

On that October morning, in the stable yard of his ancestral home, William Gordon Earl of Kenmure and his clansmen had gathered. He had already said his fond farewells to Lady Kenmure and was now sitting astride his horse, ready to sally forth. In the yard Lady Kenmure gave a rallying cry: "Ride, my champions of the king, ride for Scotland; there can be no turning back. It is into glory that you all ride." William Gordon took heart as looked at the body of a hundred and fifty horsemen, including William Maxell the Earl of Nithsdale plus a number of the Roman Catholic gentry from the western borders of Scotland, together with their servants. Kenmure kicked the flanks of his horse with his spurs but the horse remained steadfast. Three times he urged the horse forward and three times it refused. Lady Kenmure stepped forward and taking off her apron, she threw it over the horse's eyes. "Now ride, never look back," she whispered as the animal was led forward . . .

She was never to see her man again.

* * *

At Moffat Lord Kenmure was joined by his brother-in-law, the Earl of Carnwath, and Earl Wintoun. They all now rode onward as a unit with three hundred men under the command of Lord Kenmure. Two weeks later, on the eve of the fourth of November, the Jacobite army led by General Forster, Colonel Mackintosh and Lord Kenmure reached Lancashire and were grateful when two days later they took Lancaster without opposition.

In traditional mode, the Jacobite army marched into Lancaster with swords drawn, bagpipes playing, drums beating and colours flying. The city was occupied without loss of blood and with fervour the proclamation was again read out at the market place declaring, "James III is our lawful king."

Celebrations in Lancaster began as the Jacobite officers and gentlemen soldiers dressed themselves in their finery and went calling on the ladies of the city; who, thrilled at the excitement that had descended into their dull lives, put on their finest clothes and invited their suitors to tea.

With zeal, five local gentry of Catholic persuasion joined the rebels. One of the gentry was John Dalton who now offered his ancestral home, Thurnham Hall as accommodation for the Jacobite peers.

The wine was flowing freely that night as Lords Kenmure and Murray and the Earls of Nithsdale, Derwentwater, Wintoun and Carnwath all dined on roasted lamb taken from the nearby Bowland fells. John Dalton was holding court at the supper table. "Our family name hasn't always been Dalton," he said. "All of us at this table belong to the Church of Rome and support the Stuart cause, consequently when an ancestor of mine, Thomas Dalton, fought on the side of the Charles the First in the Civil War, he lost the estates to Cromwell and parliament but Charles the Second restored the lands and the Hall back to our family. Thomas, incidentally, had ten pious daughters, all renowned for their adherence to the Faith. The ladies all lived in Aldcliffe Hall and were known locally as the 'Catholic virgins'."

"Not for long, I'd wager, if Charles had got amongst them," bellowed Charles Radclyffe, Earl of Derwentwater. The rest of the supper party joined in the merriment.

Laughing, John continued, "The Daltons continued to live at Thurnham Hall until Robert Dalton, my grandfather and the grandson of the original purchaser of the estate, died leaving only an heiress, Elizabeth Dalton, who is my mother. Now this is where our family is split because Mother married into another staunch Roman Catholic family and Father's name was William Houghton, one of the Houghton's of Houghton Tower and a family supporting George the First. Father decided to adopt Mother's name of Dalton."

"This should get interesting, John," Charles Murray said. "I hear from our spies that Sir Henry Houghton has positioned local militia at Preston."

"That is one of the circumstances of civil war, it sets father against son and splits families," replied John Dalton.

"Our family was split by religious differences," said the Earl of Wintoun, "one day I had a quarrel with my father and that same day I saw a band of gypsies on our estate. They frequently came onto the Sefton land, so I just walked out of the family manor and took off with them on their wanderings over Scotland, England, and onto the Continent. I never saw my father again."

Everyone at the table was now paying full attention to George Sefton as he recalled his adventures.

"I spent several years in France as a bellows blower and servant to a blacksmith. It was a wonderful carefree time; I was young and well educated so I had the pick of the local French girls who seemed to flock to the forge and workshop. When I began working on very small items of adornment for their ears, the girls couldn't do enough." He paused in thought. "Needless to say, I kept them happy. While working on those minute items, I also learnt how to mend clocks and watches and make springs for them. Then, after seven years of pleasure, I heard father had died so I went home and claimed my inheritance and here I am George Sefton, Earl Wintoun a trained blacksmith."

"Well, I don't think anyone will tell a better tale than that tonight, and if we need a new watch spring we know who to call upon." Amid raucous laughter from the assembled gentry, Charles Radclyffe rose from the table and said, "so I will bid you all a fair night's sleep, for tomorrow we must organize foraging parties to implement our weapons and food supplies."

* * *

While the gentry wined and dined; Old Borlum Mackintosh was not idle, he sent out scouting parties to requisition any powder and guns that where held in the city. The captain of one ship that was moored in Lancaster docks was forced to relinquish his barrels of powder and six small cannon, and a Catholic sailor from the ship volunteered to join the rebels as artillery captain. Finally, after two days of carousing, the army re-assembled and began its march south.

"It is nay going well," commented John Farquharson as he ate supper with his colonel. "We are getting no support, and remember the English don't support Catholic government. It was one hundred and ten years ago when Guy Fawkes found that out to his cost."

"Nay to worry, only two days' march and we shall all be in Preston and hopefully the Liverpool and Preston Jacobites will turn out in force," said an optimistic Mackintosh . . .

The Jacobite cavalry arrived in Preston on the Wednesday evening of the ninth of November but it wasn't until the following day that four thousand Jacobites foot soldiers were welcomed into 'Proud Preston' by the prominent Catholic town populace.

* * *

Unknown to the Jacobite leaders, a Reverend Robert Paul was on a collision course with them. The clergyman from Leicester with Catholic beliefs and Jacobite sympathies, had progressed into the Protestant church as cover for his genuine beliefs. When he heard that revolution had broken out in Scotland he collected letters of support from Catholic gentry in Leicestershire, and set out on the fourth of November to ride north to meet the Jacobite leaders on their invasion into England.

Proud Preston

It was late afternoon as Charles and James picked their way down the ravine, so narrow in some places they could scarcely ride abreast before the road widened to a small hamlet. A few whitewashed cottages and an inn was all that stood between them and a stone bridge spanning the River Ribble.

"I think we will stop for a brief rest before venturing up the hill into Preston," said James.

Father and son dismounted and hitched the bridles of their horses to a post outside the Unicorn Inn in Walton-le-Dale. Charles opened the door to the inn and was greeted by a cheerful innkeeper who had seen them ride down the ravine.

"Good day, sirs, you're not from these 'ere parts then?"

"No," said James, "just travelling; and we will have a flagon of ale to refresh us after a long ride."

"Travelled far?" the innkeeper asked.

"About twenty miles from Warrington."

"A dangerous road, there be footpads and the like, an' how lonely," said the innkeeper in a whisper. "But I hear there be government forces a'cumin this way,"

Charles and James sat down whilst the innkeeper continued to chatter. "There you be, sirs, two flagons mi'best ale and all furt'sum of sixpence. Best ale in t'area though I say it myself. Folk come fur miles to sup Thomas Cowpe's ale at the Unicorn. Blessin' be to God for givin' me the skill to brew such an ale." Thomas Cowpe bowed his head and made the sign of the cross.

Charles looked askance at James who now urged him to drink up and for them to leave.

"A fine ale," said James," as the pair left the inn.

"Travel safely," the innkeeper said, "and watch out for the Jacobites if you go north, for they are coming south." He shut the door behind them.

"I suspect he is a rebel sympathiser, and he seems very confident in flaunting his loyalties," said James. "I think that we need to conclude our business in Preston as quickly as possible and then leave.

The road out of the hamlet crossed the Ribble Bridge before ascending a steep lane that was the southern gateway into Preston. As Charles crossed the bridge he glanced over the parapet and noticed the spiky marshland grass growing through the sand that led down to the water's edge.

He nudged James' elbow. "Obvious signs of quicksand; I wouldn't want to venture down there to the water's edge."

"Good heavens," replied James, "you have just jogged something in my memory about the civil war and Oliver Cromwell. I seem to recall that in a report he was leading a squadron of roundhead cavalry through a ravine on the approach to Preston. That must have been the narrow lane we have just traversed. And royalists who were on the ridges above the ravine hurled down large fragments of rock. One rock nearly killed Cromwell and he only escaped by forcing his horse into the quicksand at the side of the bridge. You mentioning that marsh grass sparked off that distant memory. James, we are living history as we ride." How prophetic his words were to be . . .

Charles and James rode up the long steep lane that was lined with hedges. At the summit the road branched left into the town and right towards Clitheroe and the Pendle hills. A large house with a flat roof stood at the junction. Looking left James saw in the distance the spire of the parish church, a spire that in the coming days would provide commanding views of the surrounding fields and meadows and observations of troop movements in the lane that was aptly named London Road as it descended the steep hill to the Ribble

Bridge and beyond. Observations that would be crucial in the battle to come, but for now the spire seemed to be beckoning them towards the centre of the town and as they rode down Church Street on that November evening, the town was alive with the hustle and bustle of traders and townsfolk and farmers all going about their business. The majority of which were making their way to the market square for the Wednesday cheese market.

Charles looked about and saw the street was lined with wooden structured buildings mingled with the occasional brick building. One very large brick house on the north side of the street caught his attention; it had small lawns to the front and these were protected by iron railings and gates. "Obviously the abode of some wealthy person," Charles commented as they rode on. In the days to come they were to discover that it was Patten House, the family home of Sir Thomas Stanley, the Earl of Derby.

"Rein in here," James said as the pair rode through one of the two archways that gave an entrance to a courtyard of the Dog Inn. "We've travelled far enough and this inn next to the church will serve our purpose for a few nights."

* * *

At his command headquarters in Manchester, General Wills, the northern commander of the government troops was pacing the floor in expectation of news of reinforcements. The general had in his company his aides Colonel Cotton and Lieutenant-Colonel Richard Cobham, plus Staff Officer Major David Ward.

Two days previously, on the seventh of November, an express rider had delivered despatches assuring the general of reinforcements but until they arrived, Manchester and Liverpool were very much under threat from the Jacobite rebels in Scotland, who had now marched south into England.

A drumming of horse's hooves heralded the arrival of a rider and Staff Officer Major David Ward hurried outside to collect the orders.

"It seems that the promised reinforcements of two additional regiments of foot and one regiment of dragoons are still a few days' march away," said Wills to Colonels Cotton and Cobham. "Major Ward, immediately call a meeting of all my staff officers to discuss the situation."

With his officers assembled General Wills outlined the seriousness of the situation, "Gentlemen, we have to hold Warrington Bridge to stop the rebels. I shall take Stanhope's four regiments of dragoons and two regiments of foot, and hold the bridgehead. We will defend Manchester from that side of the river."

The general paused then issued an order to his aide Colonel Cotton. "Draft orders to the colonels commanding the reinforcing divisions requesting them to take up positions to the north of Manchester and defend the city if we fail to hold the rebels at Warrington."

In full battle order at dawn on the ninth of November, Stanhope's six divisions crossed the Warrington Bridge, circled to the north of the town and made camp in the meadows, preparing earthworks for the defence of the bridgehead.

A few hours later, General Wills and his staff officers, satisfied with the arrangements, rode back into Warrington and with his aides and second in command riding ahead, they were escorted under the arched entrance and into the cobbled yard to the rear of Ye Olde Lion. The same inn in which a few days earlier James and Charles Cavendish had met the Scottish architect James Gibbs, an innocent who was a patron of the Earl of Mar, the Jacobite Rebel . . .

The colonels dismounted and handing the reins of their horses to their aides who in turn gave instructions for the feeding and watering of the horses, and expressed to the ostlers the need to have spare horses available, day and night for instant saddling.

"Now let us go inside," said General Wills. His aide-de-camp Colonel Cotton opened the door and the military entourage consisting of Colonels Philip Honeywood, Richard Munden, Lieutenant Colonel Richard Cavan and Major Ward stepped into the primitive traveller's inn. The General's aide followed them and closed the door. Looking around he saw before him a long room with several oak tables and chairs. Along the edge of the whitewashed walls were a few benches. His observations were interrupted by the entrance of a ruddy-faced innkeeper from a rear room who now greeted them. "Mornin', sirs. Wilt thou be wantin' rooms for the neet?"

Colonel Cotton drew himself up to his full height and in a commanding voice said, "Sir, in His Majesty's name, we are requisitioning this inn for immediate use for our headquarters for the defence of Warrington. There will be General Wills plus myself and five senior officers and our aides; a total of fourteen, all guests of His Majesty for you to feed and bed."

The innkeeper attempted to remain calm but his heart was racing in fear of any conflict that might befall his inn and the town. With a tremble in his voice he said, "Reet, sirs, rooms it is. Would yer be wantin' suppa? We 'ave some hot meat pie or Lancashire black pudding or some potage and our ale is reet fine though I say it myself."

"We are all taken to red wine, if you can find any in this backwater of England," said Cotton.

"Bottles of the best you have and the meat pie will be sufficient," added Wills. "Mustn't upset the locals, Cotton, that's the first rule of engagement if you want a flea-free bed, though I'll wager a king's shilling he has none of those, eh, lads?" The rest of the officers laughed as the innkeeper hurried away to return shortly with six bottles of wine and fourteen pewter tygs.

"Yer food will be served shortly, sirs," he said, then relieved to be away from the militia he retreated to a back room.

The officers rearranged the heavy tables into a square formation in the centre of the room and kicking off their riding boots they sat down to relax.

It was late when the innkeeper, who had kept out of sight as much as possible for most of the evening, stepped into the room and spoke to Major Ward, "I 'ave some information that may be of use to his Lordship."

"He's not a Lord; he's a general," said the major and grasping the innkeeper's arms took him aside. "Now what have you to say?"

"Well, about two weeks ago two men arrived on horseback and met a third man at this 'ere inn. They pretended to be strangers but I think they planned to meet, cos, as I saw it, they were reet friendly. I heard the man who was a Scotsman say in conversation to the other two that he was a friend of that Earl of Mar chap, as what yer all hunting; the one who is the Jacobite rebel. Next morning, after I 'ad served 'em breakfast, the London Flyer arrived and the news he brought so alarmed the three of them that the two men left in a hurry to go on to Preston and the Scotsman said he was returning to London."

"And do you remember the names of these three fellows?"

"I seem to remember the Scots fellow calling 'em sumat like Cavendish and I think he called one of 'em James."

"Thank you, innkeeper. The general will be informed that you have been most helpful, and now I think another three bottles will be most welcome."

The man smiled and hurried away, while the major made a mental note to inform the general at the first opportunity.

* * *

It was first light at the government army headquarters; General Wills had spent a restless night, the responsibilities of his command weighing heavily on his shoulders. He had just completed his ablutions when a knock at the door heralded a rider with despatches. The man who entered the room, saluted and offered the general a waterproof wallet. Wills wiped his wet hands, sat down at a table, broke the seal and read his orders.

To General Wills, Commander in Chief Northern Division.

The government of His Majesty King George I under the Act of Union of 1707 do command you to proceed with great exertion and march with the forces at your disposal to the defence of the Realm at Preston in the County of Lancashire against the attack by the insurgent Jacobite army. When apprehended the leaders of the Jacobites, namely, The Earl of Mar, George Seton 5th Earl of Wintoun, William Maxwell 5th Earl of Nithsdale and James Radclyffe 3rd Earl of Derwentwater, are to be held at His Majesty's pleasure and charged with treason.

God Save the king.'

The government despatch dated a day previously on the eighth of November was drafted and signed by the head of state. He dismissed the rider telling him to rest and get some warm food; then he gestured to Colonel Cobham to join him. "Draft orders to General Carpenter at Durham and request that he march south west into Lancashire with the prime objective of preventing a further Jacobite advance towards Manchester and Liverpool and with the secondary objective of cutting off any Jacobite retreat back into Scotland. I want that drafted for my signature within the hour. Have a rider ready to deliver the orders the hundred and thirty miles to Durham." Colonel Cobham rose, saluted and withdrew to complete his duties.

Charles Wills sighed and rose from the table and turning to Major Ward he confided, "I fear in my heart that

Carpenter will arrive too late to save Preston. It may well be up to us after all. Major, call all the officers immediately, inform them we are riding within the hour"

* * *

In the encampment north of Warrington, Stanhope's six divisions were being called to order as trumpets sounded, sergeant majors barked orders, colour sergeants ordered their squadrons into line and the chosen men led by example. In two hours the six divisions were riding north on the Wigan road in the direction of Preston. The words of General Wills were very prophetic; before lunch another rider brought the bad news that Preston had been taken by the Jacobites.

* * *

The previous Wednesday Charles and James had taken a room at the Dog Inn, and after supper the pair strolled down to the market place. To their surprise they discovered a large open square, in which the weekly cheese market was a hive of activity. Booths had been erected by the village traders and farmers all offered samples of local produce before making a sale.

"It's a very good market town and the quality of theses northern cheeses far exceeds the quality we got when we lived in London," said James. "Let us pray that the docks and the rest of the town live up to the same high standards."

Preston was a cameo of the streets of London before the Great Fire; the only difference as far as James could see was the houses on the Preston streets had forged iron supports attached to the front frames from which oil lamps hung to provide partial street lighting that cast dark shadows into alleys that seemed to hold warnings of danger from footpads.

Charles and James wandered the town for two days talking to the local traders and civil dignitaries. As the pair strolled up Church Street on the Saturday evening, they were adjacent with Patten Manor House with its small grassed area to the front protected by iron railings and gates when James paused in thought.

Charles said, "I can see you are contemplating about something but I cannot see much profit from setting up trading links in this town. The town traders seem to be more interested in agricultural products; the docks are too primitive, even the river is un-navigable without a pilot to guide the shipping from the estuary. No, Father, I don't think this is for us."

"I tend to agree, Charles," said James, "but let us delay a decision until after Monday evening. Remember: we are dining here at Patten House as guests of Sir Thomas Stanley and he has graciously arranged for us to meet Sir Henry Houghton and Sir Francis Anderton plus some prominent guildsmen, so let us delay any decisions until after the event."

Father and son turned and strolled back towards the Dog Inn.

At the hour of seven on Monday evening the seventh of November, Charles and James opened the iron gates, walked up the short pathway, and ascended the two steps to the front door. Charles, drawing himself up to his full height, lifted the ornamental knocker and rapped twice. The door was opened almost immediately by a footman who stood aside as Charles and James entered. Charles placed his calling card on the silver tray that the footman presented in one hand and as James looked about him at the lavish furnishings of the entrance hall, the footman retired into a reception room. Moments later a young man stepped forth from the room to welcome them. "Good evening, gentlemen," he said as he offered his hand, "Sir Thomas Stanley." He turned to a middle-aged lady at his side and said, "May I introduce my mother Lady Elizabeth Stanley. My father Sir Edward is no longer with us to greet you. Sadly he passed away in May of last year."

Henry and Charles expressed their condolences and the four moved into the reception room in which a few guests had already assembled.

Sir Thomas clapped his hands and silence descended on the small gathering. "Gentlemen, before we dine, may I introduce Mr Charles and Mr James Cavendish from Ufton Manor in Derbyshire."

Drinks were offered and Charles and James began to circulate amongst the various guests.

"And how do you find our fine town?" a young gentleman who had introduced himself as Sir Francis Anderton asked James. "We call it Proud Preston."

"And rightly so," said James. "And is your estate in this area?"

"About ten miles away, a small manor estate that I inherited only because of the fact that my elder brother Lawrence, who succeeded to the baronetcy, relinquished his claim to the title when he took up holy orders in a Benedictine monastery in France. The estate is Lostock Hall."

In another part of the large room Charles was talking to Sir Henry Houghton. "I have received news that the Jacobite army that everyone was talking about are in fact already in Lancaster and it seems highly probable that they will be marching south to take Preston within the next few days."

"What will you do, Sir Henry?" Charles enquired. "You can hardly be expected to defend the town against such a superior force."

"You're quite correct, Charles. I have only two troops of Stanhope's dragoons plus my militia to defend the town," said Sir Henry. "I understand that General Wills who is garrisoned at Manchester is at this moment waiting for reinforcements before coming north to defend Preston, but I fear it may well be too late unless he can arrive in the next couple of days. If the rebels reach Preston first, I shall withdraw my militia and dragoons. I will not defend the town against hopeless odds."

Over dinner, conversation was pleasant with Charles and James making some useful contacts towards opening a trading house in Preston for the importing of goods into the county. But invariably the conversation turned to the subject of the Jacobite uprising and their invasion into the northern-most counties of England. Some speculated on the prospects for Preston if the highlanders reached the town within a few days. At the close of the evening Charles and James bade farewell to their hosts, little knowing that they would be seeing a lot more of them over the next week . . .

"I think that we should leave Preston as soon as possible," said James as the pair walked past the parish church to the Dog Inn. "We have no business here; the river is totally unsuitable for our ships from the Americas and the townsfolk seem more interested in farming and Catholicism. I don't think that it would be in our interests for the House of Cavendish to expand its trading links into Preston."

"I totally agree," said Charles. "But we may have a problem riding home the way we came. I was listening to Sir Henry Houghton and apparently we may encounter a government army on the move from Manchester coming up the Wigan road through Warrington; our journey home means we will be riding directly into its path. The roads were in a bad state on our ride here but with all those horsemen and foot soldiers on the move, the fields and lanes will be almost impassable."

The decision of when to leave was made for them when next morning news came that Sir Edward was withdrawing his militia and dragoons from the defence of Preston and was retreating south on the Wigan road hoping to join up with General Wills at Manchester.

"If Sir Edward is riding south to meet General Wills," said Charles, "I suggest we use him as an escort and join his cavalcade."

The pair quickly packed their travel bags, vacated their room, settled their account with the innkeeper and then with their horses saddled in the stable yard they rode off down London Road to catch up with Sir Edward's militia and the dragoons.

Flight from Preston

In contrast to the previous weeks, the cheese market on the ninth of November was poorly attended. Only a few of the outlying villages had sent their produce to town; some were possibly unaware of the approaching rebel army, while a few optimists had hopes of sales to the rebels. For the townsfolk the day was made even more sombre with torrential rain. The Jacobite cavalry arrived first; it had been a rough ride for them, with the roads from Garstang made almost impassable. The cavalry had ridden on ahead, leaving the foot soldiers to tramp the final ten miles through thick mud with the hope of arriving the following day.

Next morn, the first detachments of exhausted foot soldiers began to filter into the town and by ten o'clock large detachments were formed into regimental order and marched into the market square to the skirl of pipes and the beating of drums. At their head were Lord Kenmure and General Forster, followed by Brigadier William Mackintosh with his highland regiments. Leading the Clan Chattan regiment was Lieutenant Colonel John Farquharson.

At the rear of the highland regiments came the first of the local Jacobite militia led by Edward Tyldesley, who carried a silver-pommelled sword drawn and presented. At his side was his standard bearer, Cornet Shuttleworth carrying the Tyldesley green standard with its buff-coloured fringe fluttering in the breeze. A troop of armed men followed Tyldesley and Shuttleworth.

The officers halted in front of the market cross, the drums gave a final roll; the pipes ceased playing and a silence descended onto the market square. A tall young local man stepped forward to greet them; it was Sir Francis Anderton, the Jacobites had arrived in *Proud Preston . . .*

From the silenced multitude, a solitary trumpet sounded and William, Viscount of Kenmure, unrolled a proclamation, and in a commanding voice read to a hushed crowd,

"We the gathered assembly declare whereas, by the decease of the late King James the Seventh, the imperial crown of these realms did legally descend to his lawful heir and son, our sovereign James the Eighth; we, the Lords and this company, do declare him our lawful king by the Grace of God, of Scotland, England, France, and Ireland, Defender of the Faith and Most Mercifully for relieving this his ancient kingdom from the oppressions and grievances it lies under."

Cheering commenced, with caps and bonnets thrown into the air as celebrations began in earnest with the rebels realizing that the government troops had abandoned the town without a fight. Fraternising broke out as local girls swarmed around the brawny highlanders and as the day progressed the Jacobite ranks began to swell as supporting gentry accompanied by their tenants and servants joined the throng. A cry was repeated time and again that reverberated around the square, *"For King Jamie we march south."*

* * *

Meanwhile, an hour's march south of Preston on the road to Warrington, two dragoons posted to ride at the rear of the retreating column of militia caught sight of a pair of horsemen gaining on them. Twenty minutes later the riders caught up with the column and Sir Edward recognized them as Charles and James Cavendish whom he had met at Patten Manor a couple of evenings previously.

"Good morning, sirs; Mr Charles and Mr James Cavendish, is it not?"

"Good morning, Sir Edward," said Charles. "We heard you were riding south to join General Wills and we thought we could join you and have us escorted through the military lines so we can make our way south and home to Derbyshire."

"Nice to have you as a travelling companion, Charles, and you too, James." commented Sir Edward, "It is a sad day for England when we have to retreat from our towns before the ravages of these Jacobite highland savages." The three companions engaged in pleasant conversation as they rode on escorted by the militia and dragoons to intercept the government army lead by General Wills.

* * *

General Forster and Old Borlum had left the celebrations and withdrawn to the Mitre Inn where they were discussing tactics. "We now march on Manchester," said Forster. "All reports from the Lancashire supporters say General Carpenter is at least forty miles away and General Wills is at Manchester, so after two days of rest, we can march on Saturday. Let the lads enjoy the hospitality of this fair town for a couple of days; General Wills will never march against our numbers."

Mackintosh stood and gazed out of the window down into Fishergate and watched a band of new recruits being paraded by an officer.

"Look ye there, Forster, are yon fellows the men ye intend to fight Wills with? Never was a more uncouth and unsoldierly body to appear in the field. Just take a look, man, at these Lancashire rustics; some with rusty swords without muskets, others with muskets without swords, some with fowling pieces, others with pitchforks, others without weapons of any sort. Good faith, sir, had ye ten thousand of them, I'd fight them all with a thousand of Wills' dragoons, and that's a fact, sir."

Forster, who had joined him at the window, remained silent for a moment and then the pair sat down at the table in more sombre mood to plan.

* * *

Mr Robert Paul, the clergyman from Leicester, had initiated his ride to the north on the pretext of visiting his sister in Preston, but his intention was subversive. He planned to meet with the leaders of the Jacobites further north but his plan was thwarted by the swift southern advance of their army into England, an advance that alarmed the parliamentary forces in the Manchester area who were now stopping and questioning all travellers. On the afternoon of the ninth of November, Robert Paul had been in the saddle all day, he was tired and thirsty and as he approached Warrington Bridge he was stopped and questioned by an officer in charge of a troop of government dragoons. A nervous Mr Paul tried to remain calm as he recounted the story he had rehearsed but his manner aroused suspicions.

"Sorry, sir," said the officer, "but in these troubled times we cannot be too careful. I am not satisfied with your story. We shall have to escort you into town for you to be examined by a magistrate."

Mr Paul, now in fear of his life, began to sweat. If they searched him and found the letters hidden on his person, letters that offered support to the Catholic Jacobites from Catholic gentry in Leicestershire and Staffordshire, he, Robert Paul, would be tried for treason.

Under escort of two dragoons and accompanied by their officer, they presented Robert Paul before Colonel Noel the local magistrate, a military man whose active service days were long past and who now served as a justice of the peace for the crown.

"Mr Paul, can you explain to me the reason why you are travelling from Leicestershire to the north of England at this time when the country is in such turmoil with rebel forces on the march?"

Robert Paul tried to calm his nerves; his life was at stake, everything depended on his answer being presented in a calm manner. Taking a deep breath, he said, "Sir, I am travelling to visit my sister in Preston, who was widowed a few months back." The lies flowed from the clergyman's lip with skilful precision. "She is expecting her first child and I want to be with her for support."

Colonel Noel nodded. "And very commendable too," he said. Then addressing the dragoon officer: "I cannot find just cause for this man's detention; release him immediately and as dusk is falling, escort him back to the road where you arrested him and see him safely on his way."

The dragoon officer saluted, turned and escorted a drained and limp Robert Paul from the room.

Dusk was now falling as Reverend Paul turned the horse in the direction of Preston. The officer saluted, bade him a safe journey and wished his sister well with the baby. The clergyman nodded and rode off into the dusk, pressing on with as much speed as the dark would allow but the delay had cost him time and eventually he sought refuge at an inn for the night. It was late morning on the tenth of November when he finally rode over the Ribble Bridge and up the London Road lane into Preston. At first the town seemed deserted, and then in the distance he heard the beat of drums and the skirl of the pipes. Riding down the deserted street, past a church with a tall spire, the pipes and drums grew louder and then he saw the gathering in the market square. Remaining in the saddle, he watched the ceremony from the fringe as the proclamation was read. The Reverend Robert

Paul sat tall in the saddle. It was a proud moment in Proud Preston and it made the hazardous ride seem all worthwhile.

When the ceremonies were concluded, Mr Paul sought out a Jacobite officer. "Sir, I have travelled far with important papers. Please direct me to your headquarters."

The Jacobite officer pointed him in the direction of the Mitre Inn on Fishergate. Robert rode across the square to the inn, he dismounted and hurried inside and was shown into the presence of General Forster and Colonel Mackintosh, "Gentlemen, I have to inform you that the government forces at Manchester have moved north and are encamped at Warrington and ready to march north. Also I have letters offering you support from southern gentry."

While Forster read the letters of support, Old Borlum Mackintosh engaged Mr Paul in conversation, thanking him for risking so much on such a hazardous journey. Robert told of his arrest and how he had seen the government army that was encamped and guarding the Warrington bridgehead. Under Old Borlum's questioning, Robert described the type of weapons the government dragoons carried and how sturdy their horses seemed to be.

When General Forster had read the letters, he dismissed Mr Paul and began to fidget and pace the room.

"Good God, Brigadier, if General Wills is moving to attack from the south and General Carpenter coming from the east, we will have two armies to fight. What do we do?"

The incompetent Forster wrung his hands in anguish and continued pacing. Then, slapping his thigh, he cried, "Inform Lord Kenmure of the news, I shall take to my bed to mull over the situation."

* * *

Old Borlum Mackintosh was deep in thought as he sat in a high-backed chair in the room at the Mitre Inn. Evening was approaching; at his side sat his nephew Colonel Mackintosh and his aide, Lieutenant Colonel John Farquharson. Old Borlum was meditating, wondering what tomorrow would bring. In an adjacent room the general slept, while Lord William Widdrington had also taken to his bed with a severe bout of gout.

A sudden rap at the door brought Brigadier Mackintosh back to reality.

"Answer the door, John."

Farquharson jumped to his feet and opened the door only to be faced with all the Jacobite Lords who in their ranks as staff officers now proceeded to march into the room.

"This cannot continue, Borlum. Where is Forster?" Viscount Kenmure demanded.

Old Borlum Mackintosh remained calm. "John, rouse General Forster immediately. Inform him that their Lordships, the gentlemen officers await his presence for a council of war."

Colonel Farquharson hurried away to rouse Forster; the assembled staff officers took their seats around a large oak table and awaited their general, who, after another fifteen minutes, eventually made an appearance.

For over an hour the Jacobite general staff deliberated on what action was to be taken. Finally a decision was made to spend one more day in Preston to rest the troops and use the time to try to organize the new recruits into a fighting force; they would then march south to face General Wills on the Saturday.

* * *

It was early morning on Saturday the twelfth of November. Captain John Shaftoe who was the lookout in the church spire spotted a fast rider crossing the Ribble Bridge; for a few minutes the rider was hidden from view between the hedgerows as he galloped up the London road and into Church Street;

without halting he rode directly to the Mitre Inn, where he dismounted and ran inside to deliver his news. "Sirs, General Wills has left Wigan with six regiments of troops and is approaching Preston and will be in sight by noon."

Old Borlum was the first to grasp the seriousness of the situation and take command. "Plans to advance south are abandoned. Colonel Farquharson, select one hundred of your best, well-armed highlanders. March them down the lane to the Ribble Bridge. Guard that bridgehead and at all costs, prevent General Wills and his forces from crossing the river."

General Forster, who in reality had now let Brigadier Mackintosh take command, said, "I think I should ride at the head of the party to reconnoitre the position."

With General Forster followed by Colonel Farquharson and two other officers riding at the head of a column of Chattan Clan Jacobites, the group rode up Church Street and down the steep lane to the bottom of London Road. The column halted at the bridge; the only sound disturbing the air was the splashing of the water as it flowing around the two piers that supported the arches of the bridge that spanned the River Ribble.

From his elevated position in the saddle, Colonel Farquharson looked about then said, "If we bring two of the cannon down here, we could hold this bridge for days."

Forster, a general with no military experience, just nodded in bewilderment. "I shall ride up river to make sure there are no fordable points to cross," was all he could add to the situation and without further comment he turned his horse and rode off into the woodlands that skirted the river bank.

Colonel Farquharson watched Forster ride off and then he gave the order to his subaltern, "Report to headquarters and have two cannon dragged down here for the defence of this bridge."

By eleven the pair of cannon were mounted on the north bank of the river with their muzzles directed to fire across the bridge and into the ravine. Colonel Farquharson and his hundred picked highlanders were in position to hold the bridgehead: a key to the defence of Preston . . .

* * *

General Forster rode within sight of the river bank for an hour without finding a fordable crossing upstream of the bridge. After two hours of riding he was back in the stable yard at the Mitre Inn where he dismounted and in a despairing mood entered his headquarters and slumped into a chair near the bar.

"Innkeeper, bring me a glass and a bottle of cognac."

Forster poured himself a liberal amount into the glass. That was followed by another. *We are trapped and doomed to die traitors in this town.* Thoughts of himself being hanged, drawn and quartered ran through his mind as he drank a third glass of brandy, then rising to his feet he made his way up the stairs and entered the Jacobite staff headquarters.

"I have considered the situation," said Forster, addressing the attending officers, "and I think we should defend the town from barricades. Brigadier Mackintosh, issue orders for Colonel Farquharson to withdraw his men from defending the bridgehead and make necessary arrangements for building barricades and manning them for a defence of the town."

"But what about the two cannon we have dispatched to defend the bridge?" questioned Mackintosh.

"Dispatch a party with four horse to retrieve them immediately and drag them back up into town, we need them up here not down at that damn bridge," said Forster.

Brigadier Mackintosh and the other officers threw up their hands in exasperation at the ineptitude of their general and his lack of military knowledge.

"General," Mackintosh retorted, "General Wills and his army must not be allowed to cross that bridge; it is the key to defending Preston. Farquharson with his hundred picked men can hold that bridgehead all day."

"And how do we defend against General Carpenter and his army marching from Durham?" replied Forster. "He will attack Preston from the east and he will not have to cross the river. We will have lost two cannon and one hundred good men defending a bridge and all for nothing." Forster paused so that his words could sink in. Then he continued, "Now obey my orders, sir. Withdraw from that bridge. Now I am going back to bed," and General Forster left the room in a drunken huff.

The staff officers shook their heads in bewilderment while a frustrated Mackintosh thumped the table with a clenched fist.

"Damm the man," Old Borlum Mackintosh shouted as he lifted his fist from thumping the table. "It's up to us now, my wee laddies, let's build and defend the barricades."

* * *

The general was in pensive mood on the tenth of November as he paced the floor of his headquarters in Warrington. He was thinking of his past victories and failures, and his future. He had received news that the Jacobites had taken Preston and that they intended to march south towards Manchester and Liverpool.

General Wills had under his command four regiments of dragoons, one of horse, and Colonel Preston's regiment of foot, formerly known as the Cameronian regiment.

The general was pondering on whether to move to attack the Jacobites at Preston or wait; his dilemma being that with time, the Jacobites might get stronger with reinforcement sympathisers from Liverpool and Manchester. He was still reviewing the situation when Sir Edward Houghton, accompanied by Charles and James Cavendish and escorted by Stanhope's dragoons, rode into the camp.

Having ensured the comfort of his militia and the troop of dragoons, Sir Edward accompanied Charles and James and together they sought out General Wills at Ye Olde Lion.

"Welcome, Sir Edward," General Wills greeted the new arrivals. "I see you have brought a couple of guests to our mess. You are very welcome to join us for the evening, sirs, but then after supper, we must ask you to retire as we have battle plans to discuss in complete privacy. You do understand?"

"You have not introduced your guests, Sir Edward."

"How remiss of me, may I introduce Mr James Cavendish and his son Charles; they were introduced to me at Patten Manor in Preston by Sir Thomas Stanley and Lady Stanley. Sir Thomas hosted a dinner party in their honour just a few days before the rebellious events caused me to retreat from the town."

"Welcome to our mess, Mr Cavendish, and you, too, James. May I introduce you to my staff officers Colonels Philip Honeywood, Richard Munden and Lieutenant Colonel Richard Cavan and my adjutant Major Ward? Now please be seated. Can I get you some refreshments?"

"Three tankards of ale would be most welcome to wash the dust from our mouths after the long ride," said Sir Edward.

The innkeeper was called and took the orders for the refreshments. When he had departed, Major Ward rose from his seat and took the general by his arm and led him away from the table. "Sir, if I am not mistaken, these two guests are the alleged spies that I informed you about. The innkeeper reported them consorting with a Scotsman in this inn and then travelling up to Preston."

"Thank you, Major, I do remember you telling me, now let us remain seated and I shall get confirmation from the innkeeper when he serves the drinks."

The general and the major returned to their seats and listened as Sir Edward and Charles described the atmosphere in Preston.

The ruddy-faced innkeeper returned with the tankards of ale and set them down on the table. "Thank you." The general said, "But one moment innkeeper; before you depart, do you recognize these two gentlemen?" The general pointed at Charles and James.

"Indeed I dus, sir, them be the two spies wot met with the Scots fellow 'ere in this very room not ten day ago."

"Thank you and that will be all."

The innkeeper bowed nervously and left the room.

"So, Mr Cavendish, drink up. You and your son have some explaining to do and questions to answer before we decide whether to hang the pair of you."

"It's preposterous," protested James. "Assumptions made by an ignorant gossiping innkeeper. Are we still living in an age when wild accusations will get a man hanged?"

James took a long draught from his tankard and then trying to calm his agitation, he related to the general and the assembled staff officers how Charles and he were travelling to Preston to investigate the possibility of opening trading links in the port but had decided against the idea. James recounted how they had met James Gibbs who told them that he was an architect who had been tutored at the baroque architectural school of Carlo Fontana in Rome. Gibbs said that he happened to meet the Earl of Mar who became his patron and last year the Earl obtained for Gibbs his first important commission in London.

Charles hesitated as he tried to recall what Gibbs had said on that evening nearly two weeks ago. He realized their lives depended on his recounting the information accurately, so he paused for a little longer then continued, "I seem to recall that Mr Gibbs said he had been commissioned to design the church of St Mary-le-Strand, in the City of Westminster and that is how he happened to be in London. I forgot to mention that when we introduced ourselves to Mr Gibbs he said that last year he was visiting Sir Thomas Halton, who was a neighbour of ours when we lived in Newington Green, and he noticed a building nearby that is named Cavendish House. He asked if it was our family home."

General Wills had listened in silence while his aide made some notes. Now he said, "And that is all you can tell us about the Scottish gentleman that you met in this inn?"

James thought for a moment then added, "He did say he intended to travel up to Scotland on business and that he had only stopped in Warrington, as it may be a town for a future commission for him."

"And what were your plans, Mr Cavendish?"

"Well, next morning, when the London Flyer arrived with the news of the rebellion, we advised Mr Gibbs to return to London, which we think he did, and we thought we would have time to conclude our business in Preston and leave and get home to Derbyshire before any Jacobites reached the town."

General Wills now addressed Edward Houghton. "What is your opinion, Sir Edward? You met these two in Preston, are they really merchant traders, did they seem to be intent upon forging business links in the town?"

"They seemed genuine to me but I think that when we re-capture the town you should interrogate some of the Preston traders for more proof."

"I agree," said Wills. "I am not completely satisfied with your story, however, I am not a man to hang men without proof, so I am placing the pair of you under arrest and you will be escorted back to Preston so that I can ascertain the truth. Now, I can have you restrained and guarded or you can continue to enjoy the hospitality of Sir Edward in my headquarters if I have your word that you will not try to escape."

James looked at Charles. "We are most grateful for your patience in this matter, sir," said James, "and we know that when you retake Preston and question the appropriate persons, you will discover we are two innocent travellers caught up in circumstances over which we had no control. You have our word we will not attempt an escape."

"Very good; so that part of the incident is settled but we still have this Scot on the loose. What did you say his name was?"

"James Gibbs, an architect, who had the Earl of Mar as his patron," said James, "but he went back to London and I am sure he was a total innocent caught up in the events, the same as us."

"That may be so," said Wills, "but I shall send a dispatch to London requesting that he and any of his contacts be questioned."

Charles, who had listened to the conversation, thought of his friends William Halton and his wife who resided at Gloucester House in Woodford Green and how they might also be dragged into a net of interrogation.

Battle of Preston ~ Day One

The colonel's timepiece showed a quarter after noon as General Wills riding at the head of his dragoons came down the ravine and into the hamlet of Walton-le-Dale. The dragoons rode on past the Unicorn Inn. Thomas Cowpe had already vacated the premises for the last time to join the Jacobite rebels in Preston.

The general reined in at the bridgehead that spanned the river; silence pervaded the atmosphere. Followed by his escort, he rode slowly across the bridge. *Why haven't they defended this bridge?* he asked himself. *Was it a subtle trap, was the bridge mined?*

The general returned to the south side of the bridge and turning to his aide he said, "Order Grenadier Captain John Saunders to report to me immediately."

Wills dismounted and surveyed the hedge-lined lane leading up the hill into Preston. All was quiet, the lane was deserted. The general waited.

"Captain Saunders, sir, you ordered me to attend on you."

"Captain, uses ropes to lower two of your men and examine the piers under the bridge for evidence of gunpowder and fuses. I need to know the bridge is safe before my regiments attempt to cross."

"Yes, sir." Saunders saluted, then turned and ran back to his troop.

Twenty minutes later the captain reported that the bridge was safe and not mined.

General Wills gave the order for his four divisions to move forward. The dragoons rode over the bridge in columns of three. At their head was Colonel Philip Honeywell leading his own regiment of dragoons.

A Jacobite lookout in the spire of the parish church watched the deployment of the enemy troops and shouted a message down into the church. "Enemy crossing the bridge and are now formed up in ranks in the meadows at the bottom of the hill, sir."

The town was buzzing with the news.

* * *

General Wills and his aide and negotiator Colonel Cotton accompanied by Colonel Philip Honeywood and Sir Henry Houghton and escorted by a small troop of dragoons, rode up an embankment onto high ground to gain a better view of the town's defences.

The general could see a frenzy of activity at the junction of the lanes that led into the town.

"We have them, Honeywood. What do you think, Sir Henry?"

"Well, that large flat-roofed house at the top of the lane and at the corner of Church Street is my house and those damned Jacobites have built one barricade across the road and onto my land. I must admit it does have a commanding field of fire if marksmen are put up on the roof."

"You are correct. Gentlemen, I fear we are in for a bloody day. Do you recognize any of the tartans, Colonel Cotton?"

From his vantage point Cotton looked down the hill towards the Ribble Bridge and then at the lane leading to Sir Edward's house. "Well, sir, the lane out of the town to Sir Henry's house seems barricaded near the church. As far as I can see from here I can make out the Mackintosh standards and I think I just caught a glimpse of Old Borlum Mackintosh himself. It seems, sir, from the activity we must presume barricades have been erected to prevent entrance from the north along the Lancaster road."

"I think I have seen enough to determine my battle plan," General Wills said. "Now let us rejoin the other officers so we can discuss our tactics."

* * *

The general and Sir Henry, escorted by the other staff officers, gathered around a table in a tent at the Ribble bridgehead. The general produced some sketches of the town streets as advised by Henry Houghton.

"I plan to form the six regiments into three larger regiments," said Wills. "You, Colonel Honeywood, are promoted to Brigadier and will take command of the new regiment, but I still expect you to command your own dragoons as their Colonel-in-Chief. Now this battle will be no place for cavalry, so the attacks on the barricades must be done with the dragoons dismounted and fighting as infantry. Your new regiment, Brigadier, will also consist of Colonel Preston's Cameronian Regiment of Foot supported by two hundred and fifty dragoons taken in equal proportions from the four regiments of dragoons. Honeywood and Preston, you will be too exposed coming up that hill from the Ribble Bridge, you are to skirt eastwards then approach and attack the barricade positioned against the flat-topped house, which I believe is yours, Henry."

Sir Henry Houghton nodded and commented, "There are cellars with windows at street level. If Old Borlum is the general we think he is, he will have sharpshooters firing from that flat roof and from those basement and cellar windows."

"Thank you, Henry." The general turned to address his aide. "I hope you are noting all this down."

"Indeed, sir," Colonel Cotton replied.

The General now addressed Colonel James Dormer and Colonel Owen Wynne. "Gentlemen, I want your two regiments to merge to form the second large regiment. While

Brigadier Honeywood's regiment is attacking the barricade and the house and drawing fire and attention, I want your regiment to skirt through the fields towards the windmills to the north of the town, then circle round and approach Preston from behind the windmills. Have your men dismount and approach the town along the Lancaster road to attack the windmill barricades. Dormer, you are promoted to Brigadier and are in command."

The general paused while his aide made notes of the appointments, then Wills continued, "Brigadier Munden, I want you to command the mounted reserves to form a third regiment for reinforcing any weakened positions. You will command Pitt's Regiment of Horse and the remainder of Stanhope's division and take up position to the east of the town, ready to move cavalry to support Honeywood and Dormer's attacks and also to prevent any rebels slipping away behind our front line of attack. Good luck, gentlemen, and pray we see this day through."

* * *

Three hundred paces from Edward Houghton's flat-roofed house at the upper end of Church Street, Old Borlum was busy supervising the erection of barricades adjacent to the parish church. All that morning, the rebels had worked feverishly erecting barricades and defences in preparation for the oncoming onslaught.

The Earl of Derwentwater had just completed working on some entrenchments and he approached Old Borlum. "Is there anything I can do to help, Brigadier?" he asked.

Mackintosh took a rest and replied, "James, my boy, kenn'ya take some of the best marksmen to occupy yon flat roof and yon houses on both sides of Church Street. I suggest you take fifty of the best from Mar's regiment to occupy positions on the roof and in the windows."

"Consider it done, mon brave highlander," James Radclyffe said, and with a laugh ran to find the colonel in charge of Mar's battalion.

"Good morning, James," the colonel said. "Are the defences all prepared?"

"They are, sir, but I have a message from Old Borlum Mackintosh. He requests that you dispatch fifty of your finest marksmen to occupy the flat-roofed house and send another twenty-five men to occupy the street houses including Patten House."

"Captain Innes, Captain Wogan, over here."

Captain Innes ran across to the colonel and James Radclyffe.

"Captain, select fifty marksmen with expertise gained at stalking and deer shooting in the highlands. Take them and occupy the flat-roofed house. Captain Wogan, select another twenty-five marksmen and occupy the street houses. You will find that Captain Douglas is occupying the eastern houses so you take the western side. Captain Hunter already has men in Patten House. That's the large house with the iron railings and gates. I suggest you give him any support and assistance needed."

Captains Innes and Wogan both saluted, and then with hands holding the pommels of their swords, they ran to gather marksmen from within the ranks.

Radclyffe made his way to the parish church and flinging off his coat, he grabbed a spade and started again to help dig more entrenchments in the gardens of the church to provide covering fire for the troops manning the Church Street barricade. After an hour of digging, he picked up his coat and took out his purse. "Come on, you true sons of Scotland, dig, then stand firm for our King James," he said and distributed coins to the rebels. "The faster you work the sooner you can spend the coins in the ale house, so dig my fine lads, dig." And with a jaunty step he walked across Church Street and went the few yards towards Tythebarn Street where rebels were erecting a third barricade to protect the left flank of the defences erected in Church Street.

"Keep the lads busy," Radclyffe shouted to Lord Charles Murray who was supervising the barricade that was leaning onto the wall of the tythe barn.

Murray waved to James. "We will be ready, we have cut holes in the walls of the tythe barn and we shall be able to give good return musket fire. Good luck, James."

Radclyffe waved, turned and walked away; one fated to die under the headman's axe, the other to be pardoned . . .

* * *

Old Borlum, satisfied with the barricades to the north of the town, hurried to the market place to be met by Forster, who had now risen from his intoxicated slumber.

"Have you retrieved those two cannon from the bridge?" Forster asked.

"Yes, sir. I have positioned them at the Church Street barricades where I think the main attack will come. I have also put two cannon in support of the Fishergate barricade and the remaining two in support of the barricade on the road to Lancaster. All barricades are fully manned, sir, and within five hundred yards of each other so we can easily reinforce any weakened point during an attack."

"Let us stroll to your barricades," Forster said. "I want to show the men that we are not panicking, eh?" and the general nudged Old Borlum in the ribs.

"So what men have you allocated to the two barricades near the church and by the tythe barn?"

"I have taken command of the Church Street barricade. Lord Charles Murray is in command of the tythe barn barricade and reinforcing support from most of the gentlemen volunteers under the command of Viscount Kenmure and the Earls Derwentwater, Nithsdale, and Wintoun are mustered in the churchyard."

"Well, these barricades look firm enough and well manned; excellent job, well done," said Forster. "I heard talk that the Earl of Derwentwater actually got his coat off and was digging entrenchments up here. A most unusual gesture for an Earl but I suppose it gave some encouragement to the troops."

"Yes, sir, that's James Radclyffe for you, he likes to be popular and that's what's required, but then he can hold his liquor," Old Borlum muttered.

"And hold his tongue too; remember this Mackintosh, I am still in command here, and if I say I was indisposed, I was indisposed. Is that clear?"

"Yes, sir. Now, if we walk steadily to yon remaining two barricades," Mackintosh's sarcasm went unnoticed, "I have allocated the remaining gentlemen volunteers and a part of the Earl of Strathmore's regiment under the command of Major Miller and Mr Douglas to defend the lower end of Church Street at Fishergate with the intent of closing off the road to Liverpool. My nephew Colonel Mackintosh will command our own Mackintosh regiment at the barricade on the Lancaster road."

* * *

Just after midday on Saturday the twelfth of November, a pregnant hush settled over the town as the Jacobites waited for the first attack.

"Will they nae come and get at us?" a marksman on the roof of the Houghton house exclaimed.

"Calm yerself, laddie, there'll be plenty o' time for killing soon," replied James Innes.

Captain Innes knelt behind the balustrade on the flat roof peering down the London road, but failed to notice any movement between the hedgerows; he viewed the eastern lane that was the road leading to the Ribble Valley and

Clitheroe. All was quiet, too quiet. He looked again at his timepiece: it was nearly one.

The waiting was playing on the nerves of the highlanders; again Captain Innes gazed toward the east, and this time he saw a flash of red tunic amongst the hedgerows. James pulled out his timepiece again and noted it was five minutes to two.

"They're coming, laddies, he called to the men on the roof, hold your fire till they break cover and begin the charge."

* * *

Brigadier Honeywood gave the orders for two hundred Cameronians to attack the barricade at the side and rear of Henry Houghton's house. Colonel Preston led the charge and as they received the first volley, thirty redcoats fell around him under the fusillade.

The insurgents, from their position in the houses and behind the barricade, reloaded and took aim, again with devastating effect. From the houses on both sides of the road a withering crossfire of musket shot tore into the Cameronians and another twenty fell. Undaunted and unbelievably still on his feet, Preston waved his sword in the air as he encouraged his men.

"Forward, my braves," he shouted as he again rallied his depleted force. The man next to him fell backwards, a musket ball taking away half of his face. Again and again the redcoats charged the barricade and more fell under the withering musket fire coming from the Jacobite rebels holding the houses on both sides of the street and from Innes' marksmen occupying Henry Houghton's house. Realizing his initial attack had failed Colonel Preston finally gave the order to fall back and re-group.

"Sergeant, have someone tend to these men's needs; how many did we lose in that ten-minute skirmish?" a breathless Colonel Preston asked.

"One hundred and twenty dead, and of the eighty who came back with you, sir, there are some wounded."

The colonel turned to address General Wills. "Sir, we cannot sustain such losses, we need cannon to move the rebels."

At that moment a company messenger approached. "Sir, I have a message from Major Lawson. He says that he and your nephew Captain Preston have reconnoitred the back lanes behind the church. Apparently they lead behind the barricades and they are not guarded. The major also says that the houses on that side of the street are unoccupied and not defended by the rebels."

Colonel Preston turned to address his adjutant Lieutenant Colonel Lord George Forrester who had listened intently to the message from Major Lawson. "George, take two hundred men and infiltrate them down that unguarded lane that Lawson has spotted and which he says leads out into Church Street."

"Yes, sir." Forrester led his troop someway down the road and then back into the small lane that bypassed the barricades and the church.

"Colonel Preston, I know you have sustained heavy losses," General Wills said, "but another effort from your men is required. While Colonel Forrester is launching a flanking attack from that back lane, I want you to send a contingent of your men to fire the houses and barns on both sides of Church Street. The flames and smoke will cause confusion and a diversion."

Turning to his aide the General dispatched messages to Brigadiers Dormer and Munden ordering squads of men to fire the houses and barns at all the other roads into the town.

"That should set the town alight!" Wills said as he sat down on a chair that had been looted from a nearby house.

* * *

At the Church Street barricade the Jacobites were in high spirits; they had successfully beaten off an aggressive attack by the king's men. Old Borlum turned to address Captain James Dalziel, one of his aides. "You were formerly a commissioned officer in the king's service, what do you think General Wills' strategy will be now?"

"Well, sir, he has to take that flat-roofed house. I think he will try frontal and flanking attacks at the same time to divert your fire power, sir."

"I agree," Old Borlum said. "We can't hold that house much longer." Shouting to one of his captains he said, "Captain Farquharson, I want you to run to the flat-roofed house and command Captain Innes and Captain Wogan to withdraw their men to this barricade, then deliver the same message to Captain Douglas in the eastern houses and to Captain Hunter's men in Patten House. Order them all to withdraw and take up new positions in the houses alongside the church and behind the barricades."

Captain Peter Farquharson ran off to deliver the orders. He ran from door to door and made the safety of the large house; opening the front door, he climbed the stairs shouting orders as he went.

Captain Innes looked around the flat roof, and called for his sergeant to organize a slow withdrawal. The captain was the last to leave the roof; seeing the bodies of two dead Jacobites lying on the roof top, men who would never see Scotland again, he saluted them, then he descended the stairs into the hallway. He was the last man standing.

Peter Farquharson had already left. Running out of the front door after delivering his message to Captain Douglas, he ran across Church Street and opened the iron gates guarding the entrance to Patten House. Farquharson crossed the lawn and was about to enter the house occupied by Captain Hunter's men when a redcoat dragoon who had just occupied a house vacated by the retreating highlanders raised his musket and took a quick shot at the captain. At a range of about thirty yards the redcoat's aim was too low for his shot to hit the torso, instead, the musket ball shattered Farquharson's leg bone. As Peter fell to the ground, a fusillade of shots from the windows of Patten House sought out the sniper and the redcoat backed away from the wood chips that flew from the window frame. The dragoon ran out of the back door into the lane.

The Jacobites in Patten House ventured into the garden to assist the wounded officer, who lay gasping in pain as he delivered his final message: "Old Borlum says withdraw and take up new positions in the houses behind the barricade."

Farquharson lay back on the doorstep as the rebels began their retreat. Finally, with the house empty, the last four sturdy highlanders carried the wounded Farquharson down Church Street to safety behind the barricade. Brigadier Mackintosh ran over to the captain. "Yer a brave man, Captain, it took a most invincible spirit, and inimitable bravery to deliver those messages but you have probably saved the lives of the men in the houses 'cause we would'na have been able to hold them off in the next assault."

Old Borlum turned to one of the four highlanders who had carried the captain to safety.

"This gentleman is shot through his thigh bone; carry him down to the White Bull Inn just past the parish church; that's where all the wounded men are being sent. See that he gets treatment."

Brigadier Mackintosh knew it was hopeless; the shock of the amputation would probably kill the young officer.

Old Borlum saluted the departing captain.

The White Bull Inn, a large stone building with the usual coaching yard to the rear was a hive of activity with wounded men lying on the floor awaiting the services of a surgeon or a priest. The four highlanders carried the captain in a makeshift sling; Farquharson gritted his teeth and tried to suppress his groans as his body began to tremble with shock. The men gently laid the captain onto a table in the back room where a butcher with no medical skills was treating the wounded and performing amputations.

Peter Farquharson asked for a large glass of brandy and having consumed it, he had his glass refilled then addressing the four highlanders who had carried him, he raised his glass and said, "Come, lads, here is our master's health; though I can do no more, I wish you good success."

The butcher quickly got to work with his saw and butcher's knife. Within fifteen minutes Captain Peter Farquharson of Rochley was dead from shock and the loss of blood.

* * *

From his position in the lane behind Church Street, a dragoon reported to Colonel Forrester of the withdrawal of the rebel forces from Henry Houghton's house and from the houses in front of the barricades.

"Sir, I think the enemy is retreating from the houses. I saw an officer who was running across the street delivering commands but I managed to shoot him in the leg, sir," the dragoon said.

"Good man, that's one less we have to hang,"

The colonel now ordered his men to halt and take cover in the lane; he drew his sword and deliberately strode into the street to reconnoitre the position where he was met with a fusillade of bullets. Coolly he examined the barricade then slowly he turned and amidst another shower of musket shot, he returned to his troops in the lane and with adrenalin flowing George Forrester addressed his men. "Sergeant Major, I want one hundred and fifty men to follow me to attack the barricade while the remaining men occupy the houses vacated by those rebel marksmen."

The sergeant major selected fifty men and the two groups of men marched out into the withering fire from the Jacobites behind the barricade and those firmly entrenched in the church yard.

* * *

With Colonel Forrester leading the frontal attack on the Church Street barricade and the sergeant major with his fifty men giving flanking fire from the captured houses, Colonel Preston took command of two hundred dragoons and led them north to make a flanking attack on Church Street from the top of Tythebarn Street.

"Steady, lads, hold your fire," Charles Murray ordered from behind the tythe barn barricade.

With bayonets fixed to their muskets, Colonel Preston marched his dragoons down the street towards the barricade.

"Fire," Lord Murray shouted and a volley of musket balls hit the approaching redcoats. Six dragoons fell, five lay motionless, while the sixth, shot through the stomach, sat in a widening pool of blood, his hands trying to hold his intestines from spilling out of his torn breeches, a look of abject terror on his young face. Four wounded soldiers were retreating. A lull in the attack allowed the Jacobites time to reload before Colonel Preston with sword in hand ran forward once more screaming, "Charge, my brave boys, get in at them." Again the dragoons rallied and surged forward; half a dozen managed to reach the barricade and began to pull it apart with their bare hands but were met with bayonet thrusts from the Jacobite rebels standing on their makeshift platform behind the fortification. Two dragoons fell bayoneted and several more fell, caught in crossfire from rebels firing from windows and doorways of houses on both sides of the street.

The rebels behind the barricade reloaded and began firing at will as once more they drove off King George's men, now in full retreat to the safety of the unoccupied houses further up the street. Silence descended, only to be broken by the groans of the wounded lying before the barricade midst their dead comrades.

Lord Charles Murray breathed a sigh of relief: for the moment they were holding and secure but he hadn't sufficient men to hold the barricade if more prolonged attacks were pressed home. He addressed the Reverend Robert Patten, who was General Forster's chaplain, and was acting as a communications officer between the defensive positions.

"Mr Patten, would you hurry to the parish church and kindly inform Lord Derwentwater that I urgently require fifty reinforcements from the gentlemen volunteers that are held in reserve in the churchyard."

Drawing his chaplain's skirts around his legs with his left hand and with his right hand holding his hat in place, the chaplain ran down Tythebarn Street, across Church Street and entered the parish church to deliver the message.

* * *

General Forster opened the door of the Mitre Inn and strolled from the market place up Church Street towards the barricade; in the distance he saw Brigadier Mackintosh speaking with his men.

"How is the conflict going, Brigadier?" he asked Old Borlum.

"I've withdrawn from the houses and the first barricade and we are now defending from behind this main barricade, sir. We have just repelled a strong attack from the king's men who attacked from a lane behind the church. I have to admire their courage; their officer was leading each attack and wielding his sword to encourage his men. We managed to wound him several times but he kept coming back."

"Well, sally forth and attack," Forster said. "Attack, you're not going to win the battle sitting behind this pile of old wooden doors and logs."

"I willna obey you, sir, I willna sacrifice one brave Scottish soldier to run out into that street and I certainly will not send out cavalry; the temptation to desert the town on horseback may be a wee bit too much."

General Forster drew himself up to his full height, his face turning a shade of dark puce. "Damn you, sir," he said. "If you outlive this day and this conflict and when our King James comes I'll have you tried by court martial."

At that moment a defecting officer; Captain John Shaftoe, who had seen service in the king's pay and who was keeping lookout from the parish church steeple saw movement of government troops through the gardens to the rear of Henry Houghton's house, which was now in government hands.

The defecting officer, shouted to a Jacobite stationed at the foot of the bell tower. "A new attack is forming. Inform James Radclyffe."

The Jacobite ran into the churchyard to give the news to the Earl of Derwentwater who promptly went over to the base of the church tower. "Attack is forming up in Tythebarn Street," John Shaftoe shouted down the tower. I think you need to reinforce the tythe barn and its barricade, sir."

At that moment the Reverend Patten ran into the churchyard shouting for James Radclyffe. "A message from Lord Murray: he is in fear of being overrun and needs fifty men to reinforce him."

"Thank you, we were just about to do that when you arrived, our lookout in the tower spotted the danger and has seen houses burning. Will you return with us?" James Radclyffe asked as he turned; but before Robert Patten could reply James, Earl of Derwentwater had hurried away to marshal fifty gentlemen volunteers who were sitting in the churchyard.

"Gentlemen, put out your pipes, on your feet, form in two ranks and follow me; today we have redcoats to kill."

James marched them in double time across Church Street and up Tythebarn Street. At their rear followed the Reverend Robert Patten, his skirts still pulled high and still holding his hat in place with one hand.

A breathless James Radclyffe approached Lord Murray. "As requested, Charles, fifty reinforcements, how do you want their disposition?"

"Thank you, James. Send ten men into the tythe barn, find them suitable windows. They are to fire at will on sight of any redcoats." James Radclyffe led ten of the volunteers away to take up their positions.

Lord Charles Murray now addressed the remaining volunteers. "Gentlemen, come with me and find positions to fortify the barricade, we can expect further attacks at any moment. The enemy are burning the houses and barns as they approach so they may be hidden by the smoke, although you may occasionally glimpse a flash of a red coat through the smoke."

He spoke directly to the Reverend Patten. "Sir, you are a chaplain and dressed as such, so I doubt if government soldiers will fire on you. Will you go out in front of the barricade on the pretext of tending to the wounded, look about and report back to me as to the strength of the government force and their dispositions?"

The Reverend Robert Patten took a deep breath, nodded, then bravely stepped out of the front door of the house next to the barricade; a house that had miraculously escaped the flames and holding his clerical skirts tightly around his legs, Patten calmly walked up the street and into the smoke. As he walked he occasionally stumbled onto a fallen dragoon or highlander lying in the lane. Kneeling by each body he checked if that life was extinct. After examining fifteen corpses, he found a dragoon that was still alive.

Bending forward, he lifted the dying man and summoning all his strength, he carried the dragoon across the lane and into an area alongside a barn that flames had only partially consumed. Three dragoons who were taking cover behind the barn took their comrade and laid him on the grass, simultaneously nodding their appreciation. Mr Patten looked about, observing young recruits, some with sooty faces and others with blood-stained bandages binding their wounds. Dragoons sat on the soil or grass, some fidgeting with their muskets; one or two stood about with heads bowed in silence and in a subdued mood. Robert made a mental note that the government troops seemed to be young boys who were obviously newly recruited and inexperienced, then in pensive mood Patten walked back to the barricade. The silence was overpowering. Not a shot had been fired.

Charles Murray grasped Robert and embraced him. "A most heroic deed, sir, now how goes the disposition?"

"As far as I could see, the major part of the enemy seems to consist of raw, undisciplined young men who may have just enlisted. They seem to be led by experienced officers. I think there are probably about two hundred waiting to attack. But Charles, up to now you've held this barricade, well done," he said.

"Thank you, Reverend, and let us pray we can give another good account of ourselves if they come again."

And come they did. After the last withdrawal, and whilst Patten had reconnoitred the enemies position, silence had pervaded the killing field. That silence had continued for a few moments after the reverend had returned; then as Charles Murray stood sword in hand, the stillness was broken as eighteen dragoons rode into sight and began to canter, and then gallop towards the barricade.

Murray shouted, "They're testing us with cavalry this time, hold your fire; take careful aim, steady, men. Hold it."

The snorting horses were less than thirty yards away now. Charles could see the leading dragoons preparing to jump the barricade. He could see the flared nostrils of the horses.

"Fire!" A ragged volley rang out and seven horses went down throwing their riders to the ground; marksmen in the tythe barn now began to fire at the retreating enemy and another four horses went down.

The king's troops faltered, their spirit drained together with their blood that lay in small puddles around the bodies of the horses and their riders. A few redcoats began to hesitate and make moves to retreat, but urged on by their officers who rallied them by example, the dragoons attacked once more, striding over the bodies of their fallen comrades in a final assault and once again the assault failed. The thin red line began to waiver under the murderous fire from the defenders.

Colonel Preston finally called an end to the slaughter and gave the order for the bugler to sound a '*recall*'. The call of the trumpet echoed down the lane as the dragoons retreated, leaving twelve horses and forty-three dead to the chilling winter night air.

The orders to set on fire the houses at both ends of the town for the purpose of dislodging the Jacobites from their positions was taking effect; almost all the barns and houses in Tythebarn Street up to Lord Murray's barricade were ablaze and on the still evening air the smoke and flames spiralled to the sky. As he was about to leave the barricade, Robert Patten commented, "It is very fortuitous there is little wind or we may have seen the whole town burnt to ashes."

And once more all was silent as wraiths of smoke drifted up on the still autumn air . . .

* * *

After his excursion into enemy territory Robert made his way towards the market square were he unbridled his horse and rode the half a mile along Friargate towards Lancaster and the windmill barricades. Dismounting at the first barricade Robert tethered his horse and spoke to the officer in command. "How does it go with you and your men, Captain?"

"Aye, we be quite fine, sir, there may be only fifty of us here, the main force of three hundred is up at the first barricade but we'll give a good account of ourselves. We heard all the gunfire, sir, and we can see the smoke. Are the other defences holding?"

"For the moment, they are, and we have inflicted heavy losses on the government troops. From what I have seen, at least two hundred enemy troops have been killed and we have held firm at all the barricades."

From the Jacobites that were within hearing distance, a hearty cheer arose as by word of mouth the news spread. A piper pumped up his pipes and started to play. The wintry evening air lifted the skirl of the tune and filled the defenders' hearts with emotion. Robert listened for a moment then said, "I need to speak with Colonel Mackintosh and inform him of the state of the battle and events at the other barricades. Where will I find him?"

"He's up at the first barricade, sir; it's a further three hundred yards up Friargate."

* * *

While Honeywood and Forrester were engaging the Church Street barricades and Colonel Preston was unsuccessfully attacking Lord Charles Murray in Tythebarn Street, James Dormer's regiment of dragoons had ridden north, dismounted and formed up behind the windmills on the Lancaster road.

"Brigadier Wynne, form your squadrons into two columns of two ranks," Brigadier Dormer commanded. "I will do the same and I will take the left-hand hedgerows and houses, you take the right flank. Occupy and use the houses and barns for concealment then as we advance; set fire to them, the smoke and fire will cover our advance."

As Dormer was about to speak again, the faint skirl from a piper drifted on the afternoon breeze; Dormer remained silent and listened, then he looked at his timepiece: it was four o'clock and dusk was approaching. Calmly, he said, "Gentlemen, let us breach those barricades."

* * *

Robert Patten sat upright as he rode up Friargate from the first barricade. He saw the windmill barricade silhouetted against a north-western sky that was glowing orange from the fire of flaming barns and houses. In the distance came the faint sounds of shouting against a backdrop of musket fire. Robert spurred his horse on; he now bent double in the saddle and was twenty yards from the fortification when the mare faltered and went down on her forelocks, shot through the neck by a musket ball. The mare rolled onto her side, her hind legs kicking. Robert leapt from the saddle as her heart pumped blood in a fountain that spurted over his cassock; then the mare gave a final whimper, her head hit the cobblestones and she was dead.

Patten stood up and ran towards the barricade, a blood-stained hand holding his clerical hat firmly to his head.

"Keep your head down, Your Reverence," a rebel said as he reloaded his musket.

"Where is Colonel Mackintosh?" Patten enquired.

Removing his hand from his ramrod that had just been thrust down the barrel of his musket, the Jacobite pointed to the left-hand corner of the barricade. "That's him, Your Reverence, now can I get on with loading and fighting the enemy, sir?"

Reverend Patten nodded and bending double scurried across to the rear left corner of the barricade.

"Colonel Mackintosh, I have just come from Charles Murray at the tythe barn barricade and he is holding firm. Also Brigadier Mackintosh at the Church Street barricade sends his compliments and his condolences that you have missed most of the action and says he is holding the enemy. He asks if you need reinforcing."

* * *

Brigadier Dormer's squadron had found a local man who had been hiding at the rear of a house off Friargate. An officer was questioning the man as Brigadier Dormer approached.

"You say this lane at the back of your house is called Back Ween?"

"Yes, sir, and it leads up the hill at the back of Friargate and comes out behind the barricade."

Dormer turned to address the officer; at that moment the noise from cannon shot reverberated and a misdirected cannon ball knocked the chimney pot off one of the houses in Back Ween.

"God's truth," Dormer cried, "I didn't know they had cannon. Let us pray their gun captain is as bad with his next shot." To the officer, he said, "Captain, take twenty-five men and make a flanking attack on the windmill barricade from the lane and attack the barricade from the rear; when we hear the sound of your attack, we will do another frontal assault to divert their fire and we will have them like rats in a trap."

The captain saluted and ran off to summon his men just as second cannon shot fell short.

Behind the barricade a shot rang out towards the houses near the barricade quickly followed by three more from the houses and then a fusillade of fire from Dormer's infiltrators who had come up Back Ween and entered through the back door and occupied a couple of houses on Friargate.

"It looks like they are coming again," Mackintosh shouted. "Fire independently."

For over ten minutes the red-coated dragoons pressed home their attack supported by the twenty-five dragoons from Back Ween but each frontal assault was beaten off and the houses behind Friargate leading through to Back Ween were retaken by adopting General Wills' policy of house burning.

The fight for the Windmill barricade was over for the day; fifteen dragoons and three Jacobites lay dead. One of the Jacobites was a colonel.

* * *

"Take another horse and ride back and inform Old Borlum that it's almost five o'clock and getting dark. We can hold them off tonight and I will reinforce him with wine in the Mitre this evening."

At the Mitre Inn Old Borlum sat down to write a letter to the Earl of Mar stating how well the uprising was going.

Night had fallen and the glow from the fires still illuminated the streets. Against this backdrop the occasional figure from either side could be seen venturing out to deliver an urgent message. Often the messenger met with a sniper's musket ball.

"That's the third messenger I have lost in the last hour," said General Wills. "Major Ward, send orders for our men to light lamps and place them in the windows of the houses that they occupy, so the messengers and our men have an idea of where their comrades are positioned."

* * *

Brigadier Mackintosh roused his men at the barricade. "Look: yon stupid Georgie's men are lighting lamps for you to shoot at, my lads. Put a few wicks out, will yer?"

The Jacobites now had targets to shoot at, as in the darkness they began firing at the illuminated windows. Within ten minutes the whole of the top end of Church Street was under intense sniper fire.

"Put out your lights," called General Wills' officers and gradually the side streets of Preston became illuminated as the terrified populace who were hiding behind locked doors in their homes mistook the orders and began putting out lamps on their doorsteps and window sills.

Soon sounds of laughter could be heard from the government troops and from the Jacobites as both saw some humour amongst the carnage of the day.

But for Robert Patten his day was not yet over. From the relative safety of the market square he crossed Church Street and entered the White Bull Inn next to the parish church. As he entered he thought of the brave Captain Farquharson who had been carried there to die under the butcher's knife. The Reverend wandered amongst the wounded and dying, stopping and offering words of comfort; then he paused as he saw in a corner three wounded prisoners. Robert went over to them and kneeling by their side he said, "You may be our enemy but we have but one Lord, may I pray for your souls?"

In a whisper one Cameronian replied, "If you be a Protestant we desire your prayers, but name not the Pretender as King."

Robert prayed and departed.

Battle of Preston ~ Day Two

At dawn on that November Sunday, a misty haze lingered down by the river. Overhead a seagull, blown up the river estuary from the Irish Sea, screeched its mournful cry. In the dragoons' camp it was damp and miserable as Honeywood's regiment prepared to launch another attack against the rebel-held barricades.

"Here they come, wait for the order," shouted Old Borlum.

Leading from the front, Captain Ogleby, accompanied by Captain Preston, the nephew of Colonel Preston, charged down Church Street at the head of their men. Both officers, suffering minor wounds, reached the barricade and with swords in their hands began to climb it, followed by a dozen Cameronians who had survived the charge. Fourteen adrenalin-charged men grasped and tore to pull apart the barricade. As they climbed, they thrust their swords and bayonets into the defenders. A couple of redcoats fell. An officer received a musket shot above the breast; he slumped over the top of the barricade still clutching his sword in his hand. The survivors were over the top; they dropped down onto the street behind the barricade only to be encircled by thirty Jacobites armed with muskets and bayonets which they pointed at the attackers. For a moment silence reigned, it was a stand-off situation, ten Cameronians, some wounded, and one officer, facing thirty desperate rebels. Old Borlum stepped forward and broke the silence.

"Enough, yer brave sons a' bonny Scotland, we do'na wanna kill more, surrender with honour."

Captain Ogleby nodded and lowered his sword.

"Cameronians, lay down your weapons," Captain Ogleby ordered and the nine survivors from the assault laid their muskets on the ground. The captain reversed his sword and presented it to Brigadier Mackintosh.

Captain Wogan climbed up onto the barricade. "Sir, this officer is still alive." He lifted Captain Preston into his arms and carefully carried the wounded man down onto the street.

"Captain Wogan, exposing yourself to danger in the manner was a most composed and courageous act to help an enemy officer, and you yourself are not in the best of health," commented Old Borlum. He then turned to face a young Ensign and a group of Jacobites that had witnessed the surrender and the incident and said, "Ensign Erskine."

"Yes, sir."

"Take these six men, escort the prisoners to the White Bull where the wounded are being held or treated. Make sure these officers have there wounds treated. The rest of you, back to your posts on the barricade, they will attack again."

But Brigadier Mackintosh was wrong, that final charge led by Captains Ogleby and Preston was almost the last conflict in the battle.

* * *

As the prisoners and wounded were escorted away, the Jacobites were in high spirits, they had repelled everything General Wills and the king's dragoons had thrown at them and on the killing field the rebels had suffered only slight losses.

One of the escorting rebels jibed the prisoners, "Are ye nay going to fight for yer true king then? We wer' told you turncoats serving King George would flock to our cause. Will ye nay come over then?"

"Nay, man," said Captain Ogleby, be assured we would all rather die than take arms against his present Majesty and you canna' hold out much langer, we are expecting General

Carpenter with three regiments of dragoons to reinforce General Wills; then it will be over fer you lot."

The news of reinforcements for the government forces spread amongst the rebels and a mood of despair descended on the despondent Jacobites with the hardcore rebels in the town feeling betrayed.

During the night and in the early dawn hundreds of Jacobites and local militia deserted. They left, taking the road to freedom down Fishergate which was an extension of Church Street that wound down a long hill; crossing the marshes at two fords in the southern loop of the river that almost encircled the town. A loop from the Ribble Bridge in the east that the Jacobites had been prepared to defend so stoutly just twenty-four hours earlier.

A barricade on Fishergate under the command of Major Miller and Mr Douglas and guarded by the remaining gentlemen volunteers and part of the Earl of Strathmore's regiment hadn't prevented deserters slipping away in the dark. Some had deserted on horse, crossing the marsh and river at the two fords to take the lanes up into the village of Penwortham then on to Liverpool and safety, the only road that General Wills hadn't sealed.

Captain Preston also escaped on the Sunday night when he found his freedom in death.

* * *

General Wills was just sitting down to breakfast. He had given his orders for the dawn attack on the Church Street barricades, when a rider rode into his compound to deliver a message. Dismounting, the dragoon grasped the pommel of his sword as he ran to approach General Wills at table; saluting, he said, "Sir, I have to report that General Carpenter is fast approaching with three regiments of reinforcements. He left the town of Clitheroe at dawn and should be with you within the hour."

"Excellent news, Captain," Wills exclaimed. "Have you eaten this morning?"

"No, sir."

"Get a chair and sit down."

The general turned to his aide. "Get the cook to bring the captain some breakfast."

It was almost ten o'clock when Lieutenant-General George Carpenter arrived, escorted by the Earl of Carlisle and Lord Lumley, riding at the head of Churchill's, Molesworth's, and Cobham's regiments of seven hundred and fifty dragoons. Alongside them were local militia recruits bringing the total of reinforcements to two and a half thousand.

General Wills left his headquarters and went to greet Carpenter. Although there was no love lost between the two, the pair greeted each other amicably. The mutual dislike stemmed from a jealousy by Wills who had been continuously overlooked for promotion when the pair had served together in Spain. Both had fought well but Carpenter had gained a reputation for courage, good conduct and humanity and had been mentioned in dispatches and given honours by the Spanish monarch while General Charles Wills had served with little recognition.

General Carpenter dismounted and Charles Wills greeted his superior officer with a salute. "Thank the Lord you have arrived," Charles said. "We have contained the rebels within a small perimeter in the town centre; we sustained some losses but I think the Jacobites will surrender now they can see they are outnumbered and have no chance of escape. Now what is your plan of action, George?"

The pair walked back to Wills' headquarters talking amiably about past campaigns then Carpenter said, "You seem to have started the affair well, Charles, I think you should have the honour and glory of finishing it but I will do a tour of your deployments just to make sure you have everything secure."

"Thank you, George, I won't let you down." Then, escorted by twenty-four dragoons and two captains from Carpenter's reinforcements, the generals mounted their horses and rode to the west of the town to inspect Brigadier Dormer and Munden's displacements located forward of the windmill barricades.

"Very narrow lanes and streets, Charles, no place for horse," Carpenter said, "and I think there are far too many men, they are so closely packed, they cannot fight properly. I suggest you thin the ranks before the rebels do it for you. Now let's ride to the southern barricade."

Skirting to the south, Carpenter's cavalcade of dragoons halted at a ford and looked across the marsh towards the far bank of the river, on the hillside was perched the small village of Penwortham and below it the tidal waters of the River Ribble glistened as it ebbed towards the Irish Sea. Carpenter wheeled his party up the lane from the river ford and began to approach the Fishergate barricade; they were within two hundred yards of the barricade and had just breasted the hill from the ford when a couple of musket shots rang out from the gentlemen volunteers under the command of Major Miller and Mr Douglas.

"Very ill disciplined, eh, Charles?" General Carpenter commented as the party halted. "No one is going to hit anything at this range, however." Carpenter's voice now showed a tone of anger. "What I want to know is why the hell you haven't deployed troops to block this end of the town? God alone knows how many have escaped during the night."

General Wills remained silent at the rebuke. At that moment four rebels broke cover from the marsh grasses where they had been hiding and ran for the fords behind the backs of Carpenter's party.

"Look, sir, damn you, Wills, there go another four of them." Turning, Carpenter addressed Alexander Read, one of the two escorting officers. "Captain, I want you to ride post-haste to Brigadier Munden and order him to dispatch the men he has thinned from the lines to guard these fords across the river. After that I want you to ride over to Colonel Pitt and request that he moves the Earl of Londonderry's Second Dragoons down here to close off this escape route; and Captain, you are to stay with them at the fords. I wish to be informed of any attempted rebel escapes."

The captain saluted and galloped off to convey the orders.

General Carpenter now addressed Thomas Browne, the remaining captain. "Browne, you are to remain here in the meadow by the fords with twenty of your men and await Pitt's reinforcements. I want you to communicate with the other regiments if a large body of the rebels attempt to force a retreat this way. Our forces then will be all the more ready to hasten here to intercept them. General Wills and I will ride back under escort with the four remaining dragoons. Come, Charles."

The two generals and their four-man escort skirted the town to return to their field headquarters.

* * *

It was almost noon, and normally the market square would have been busy with townsfolk jostling with farm traders haggling over the price of cheese or some winter mutton from a Bleasdale sheep farm. Today, however, it was deserted except for the few horses that were tethered amidst the Jacobite baggage and the few disconsolate rebels that sat around talking about the hopeless situation in which they now found themselves. At the Mitre Inn, General Forster was addressing some of his senior officers to discuss the developments.

"Gentlemen, we are pent up within an ever decreasing narrow compass by the gradual encroachments of the royalist reinforcements; I am increasingly alarmed by the hour and think we should consider terms of surrender."

"As I see it, Mr Forster," Old Borlum began, deliberately dropping the general's rank due to his lack of respect of Forster's leadership during the campaign, "we Jacobites are now trapped in the town and are left with two choices: we can continue fighting or we can surrender. James Radclyffe is with me on this matter; we have no provision for a long siege but yesterday we inflicted heavy casualties on the attackers. We still hold the barricades and surrender will be a betrayal to our soldiers because we all know the fate that awaits rebels and, Mr Forster, it will be our fate as well."

"What do you say, Oxburgh?" said Forster.

"Well, I admit our situation is critical, sir, but the highlanders are fully aware of their situation, and after listening to Brigadier Mackintosh it only confirms what I must impress on you, sir: any idea of surrendering has never once entered their minds."

"I tend to agree," said Lord Widdrington. "Only an hour ago I heard a large group of Jacobites discussing the situation in the market square and three officers had to plead with them not to act hastily. The group of about thirty highlanders were advocating that they should sally out upon the royalists and attempt to cut their way through the enemy ranks. They all said they would rather die like men of honour with their swords in their hands than surrender, so I would suggest, sir, that you do not breathe that word whilst within hearing distance of a highlander."

General Forster thought for a few moments then said, "Gentlemen, I think we should try to seek honourable terms for surrender and Colonel Oxburgh is well received and respected in government circles so I propose that he goes to General Wills and requests his terms for our surrender."

Robert Patten, the Jacobite chaplain spoke up.

"I agree. Colonel Oxburgh is in my opinion better calculated from the strictness with which he performs his religious duties to be a priest than a field officer and we all know the negotiating skills the church teaches."

The group of officers laughed at Patten's attempt to bring a little humour into the tense situation.

"We agree then, we negotiate surrender terms?" Forster said.

Charles Murray, who had been listening but had not made any contribution, stood up and said, "Forster, you are a coward and a fool, sir," and drawing his pistol took aim at his general and pulled the trigger.

Forster was a dead man if it hadn't been for the reflex action of Patten who was standing next to Murray's chair; the pastor raised his hand and knocked Murray's arm upwards, deflecting the pistol ball into the wooden beam at the Mitre Inn. Visibly shaken by the attack, Forster turned his back on his assembled officers and in silence he retired to his room.

* * *

The rebel officers were still gathered discussing the situation when the door at the Mitre was flung open and a messenger rushed in. "Sir," he panted, "there has been an attempted breakout. About thirty men have slipped through the Fishergate barricade and are fording the river with a troop of cavalry charging them down."

Leaving General Forster in his room, Old Borlum, Radclyffe and Colonel Oxburgh ran down Fishergate to the barricade. In the distance they could see both fords where the lane crossed the river. In the shallow water and on the marsh banks lay Jacobite bodies. Dragoons rode amongst the corpses making sure all were dead.

"Search the bodies," the dragoon captain said, "then throw them back in the river. That's the way we deal with rebels. Cut the bastards down like rats."

"I found this on the body of a young officer, sir," a sergeant said, handing over a crumbled green tapestry with a buff-coloured fringe. "What do you make of it, sir?"

"I think you have captured one of the standards of the rebels, obviously the dead Cornet was trying to save the colours from falling into our hands. Look at the motto, Sergeant: *'Regis et patriae tantum valet amor'*, which I believe if my Latin serves me correctly means *'So much does love of King and country avail'* and that device above the motto on the colours of a pelican feeding its young seems to be the standard for a local Jacobite family. Anyway, well done, Sergeant, how many did we get?"

"Counted thirty-one, sir."

"Good man, leave them to rot, the river tide will take them for fish food or the gulls can have them. Form our men up and back to our lines, Sergeant." The captain rode at the head of his troop displaying the captured Jacobite colours as proud as if he were displaying a captured Roman Eagle.

At the barricade Old Borlum hung his head in sorrow while Colonel Oxburgh and Radclyffe strode purposefully back to the Mitre Inn.

* * *

General Forster emerged from his room seemingly calm after the attempt on his life.

"What has been happening? Have I missed something?" Forster said.

"Only the massacre of some of our deserters," Borlum said.

The general took hold of Lord Widdrington's arm and led him aside. "That settles it, you have to persuade Oxburgh to go and parley; he is very well connected at court and maybe he is our best chance to negotiate a surrender on favourable terms."

"I will have a word with the Earl of Derwentwater and see if we can prevail upon Oxburgh to go to General Wills, who is, I am told, a very reasonable man, and make an offer for our capitulation."

One hour later Colonel Henry Oxburgh prepared to leave the Mitre Inn; he selected Captain Philip Lockhart to accompany him and with a drummer boy, they walked up Church Street to the barricade. To allay their real intent Oxburgh explained to the Jacobites on the barricade that he was going to parley with General Wills who had sent an offer of surrender on honourable terms, if they would lay down their arms.

"Ah well, ye nay be givin' too much to them protestant bastards, ye kanna trust em," a Jacobite yelled from the barricade as Oxburgh and Lockhart, carrying a white flag of truce, and the drummer beating a chamade on his drum stepped in line abreast and approached Henry Houghton's flat-roofed house. The same house from which Captain Innes and fifty marksmen had inflicted such terrible carnage on Colonel Preston's dragoons twenty-four hours previously.

The ceasefire held. In silence, except for the beating of the drum, the three walked down the London Road towards the Ribble Bridge and the general headquarters of the king's dragoons. As they approached the headquarters, a sentry stood to attention and presented arms to the Jacobite senior officer. Colonel Oxburgh saluted and then the pair of rebel officers were escorted into the tent of General Wills and Carpenter. The generals remained seated.

Outside a dragoon strolled over to the drummer boy who was standing alone and spoke a few kind words to him.

Inside the tent Oxburgh said, "Sirs, I am empowered by my commander to make you an offer that we Jacobites presently under siege in the town of Preston will lay down our arms, provided you give us your word that you will recommend them to the mercy of the king."

General Wills went red in the face and restrained his inclination to respond in anger. He remained silent for a moment while he regained his composure, then said, "Now hear this, Colonel, I will not treat with rebels who have killed several of His Majesty's subjects, and who consequently must expect to undergo the same fate as required by the law."

Captain Lockhart, who had listened in silence, now said, "Sir, with due respect, Colonel Oxburgh came here today and said to me that he knew you as an officer and a man of honour, will you not listen?"

Oxburgh interrupted, "Sir, I do honestly believe you to be a man of honour who will show mercy to an enemy who is willing to submit and I beg you as an officer to treat us as prisoners of war."

General Wills spoke quietly to General Carpenter then he said, "Gentlemen, I have listened to you plead for favourable terms for surrender and all I will promise is that if the rebels lay down their arms and surrender themselves as 'prisoners at discretion', I will prevent my troops from cutting them to pieces. Now report back: I will allow this truce to continue for one hour for the consideration of my offer. Good afternoon, gentlemen."

A depressed Colonel Oxburgh saluted and with the drummer again beating a chamade and Captain Lockhart carrying the white flag, the three stepped out with heads held high and marched in line abreast back up London Road lane and into the besieged town.

* * *

Colonel Oxburgh had returned with the terms for surrender from General Wills. Rumours now began to spread amongst the Scottish Jacobites that the English Jacobites were contemplating surrender.

"Do you ken that Oxburgh has sought terms for the English?" Colonel Mackintosh said as he faced Old Borlum.

"I suspected Forster would do something like this," Brigadier Mackintosh replied. "Ask Captain James Dalziel to present himself here immediately."

When the captain arrived, Mackintosh said, "Captain, I want you to go down to General Wills' headquarters and enquire if you can obtain better terms of surrender for the highlanders."

Captain James Dalziel, who was a brother to the Earl of Carnwath and a close relative to Captain Philip Lockhart, passed discretely through the Church Street barricade and walked down to the headquarters of General Wills.

Entering the general's tent, he saluted then in an authoritative voice said, "Sir, I represent the highlander Jacobites. We would enquire what terms you will grant separately to the Scots?"

General Wills stood and eyeballed Captain Dalziel.

"Sir, I will not treat with rebels whether English or Scots, nor grant any other terms than those already offered to Colonel Oxburgh. Now the hour of the truce is almost over so I respectfully suggest you hurry back to your lines and convey that message to your fellow officers."

Fifteen minutes later General Wills addressed his aide. "What time is it on your timepiece, Colonel Cotton?"

Colonel Cotton took out his pocket watch and said, "Ten minutes past the hour of three, sir."

"Take a horse, Colonel," the general said, "and ride up into town with a white flag. Take a drummer to beat a chamade. Go to their headquarters and demand, no, rescind that, let us be diplomatic, and request that the Jacobite rebels give an answer to my offer for their surrender."

The colonel and the drummer rode up the hill, the beat of the chamade on the drum sending rhythmic sound across the fields. As the pair approached the flat-topped house that was now occupied by government troops, the drummer boy could sense eyes watching them, albeit friendly eyes. In nearby houses enemy eyes watched and waited.

Passing safely through the Church Street barricade the pair rode on and dismounted at the Mitre Inn.

"Wait here, boy," Cotton said; then he pushed open the door and stepped inside and saluted the Jacobite senior officers.

"Well, gentlemen," Colonel Cotton said, "General Wills would have your answer, will you surrender the entire Jacobite force as 'prisoners at discretion'?"

Colonel Mackintosh, an officer of equal rank, elected himself to answer. "There are differences to be settled between the English and Scottish officers on the terms of surrender and we request that General Wills will allow us till seven o'clock tomorrow morning to settle our differences and to decide upon the best method of laying down our arms."

"I will convey your request to the general." Cotton saluted and marched swiftly from the room.

"Come, boy, beat a chamade before the doors of those houses where our own men continue to fire. We must inform them to cease firing until they receive orders to the contrary from General Carpenter or General Wills on account that the cessation of hostilities has been agreed. Then we will report back."

The pair approached the houses, Colonel Cotton still had a white flag in his hand and the drummer was beating out the chamade when a single musket shot rang out. The beating of the drum ceased; the drumsticks slipped from the boy's grasp, for a moment or two he remained upright in the saddle as blood fanned like a fountain from his neck; then slowly the lifeless body of the drummer boy fell from the saddle to lie alongside his bloodstained drum at the side of the lane. Colonel Cotton spurred his horse to gallop the quarter of a mile down the lane to his headquarters.

Breathlessly Colonel Cotton presented himself before his general, saluted and said, "Sir, we were fired on from the flat-topped house, our own men shot the drummer boy,"

"I think that highly unlikely," the general replied. "Our troops must have certainly known him to have been one of our own men by his dress; more likely it was done by the rebels, who seem averse to all thoughts of surrender. My money is on a vengeful Jacobite who doesn't wish to parley. Anyway, no matter, it's a casualty of battle, what was their answer?"

"Sir, the English and Scots are divided on surrender; they request that they have until seven in the morning to decide on how to settle their differences."

General Wills paced up and down for a moment or two, his arms folded behind his back, he then faced Colonel Cotton. "Right, they shall have until seven to respond to my offer but the truce is on certain terms. I require two of their officers to surrender themselves as hostages, one to be Scottish the other English. Furthermore they must agree not to throw up any new barricades or dig entrenchments in the streets, nor allow any of their men to escape."

Colonel Cotton rode back into town; again he carried a white flag but this time his horse was galloping. Dismounting at the Mitre Inn he conveyed the terms offered by General Wills plus the demand for two hostages. "I will go," said the Earl of Derwentwater. "And I," volunteered Colonel Mackintosh.

Relieved to be in the company of Jacobite officers, Colonel Cotton and his two hostages rode down London Road towards the Ribble Bridge to bivouac at the government camp for the night.

* * *

Colonel Cotton escorted his two hostages to the tent and saluted. "General Wills, may I present your hostages, sir? This is James Radclyffe, Earl of Derwentwater, he is your English hostage and your Scottish hostage is Colonel Mackintosh."

The general thanked Colonel Cotton then said, "Gentlemen, we have a long night ahead of us and you are welcome to sit at my table and enjoy what meagre hospitality we can offer you on your last night of freedom."

* * *

The hour of seven on the Sunday evening was approaching; the government troops were on a final parade for the day and a roll call was taken. The dragoons were then dismissed to take their evening meals around the camp fires and sleep in the meadow alongside the river.

In the general headquarters a few tables were occupied for evening supper by Colonels Philip Honeywood, Richard Munden, Richard Cavan and Major Ward. Occupying a chair next to General Wills was the Earl of Derwentwater and Colonel Mackintosh who was speaking to Colonel Munden.

"Gentlemen, before we eat I have asked for two other 'guests' of His Majesty to join us on what may also be their last night."

General Wills nodded to the guard at the tent entrance and the guard escorted Henry and Charles Cavendish to the table.

The general watched the facial expressions of the hostages to see if there was any hint of recognition as the Cavendish prisoners were brought to table but he was out of luck. There was no acknowledgment by so much as a raised or twitching eyebrow; in fact nothing to indicate the four had ever previously met.

* * *

In the besieged town the Jacobites were on the rampage. In the market square a six-foot-seven broad-shouldered

121

highlander jumped onto the stocks and waved a basket-hilted sword above his head. He gave a shout, "I will na give in, I will na surrender to yon English followers of a protestant king."

Around him, others began shouting that they would sooner die than surrender.

The tall highlander leapt from the stocks, the basket-hilted sword still in his right hand and clutched in his left hand was a large key nearly a foot in length. The highlander had his huge left hand thrust through the key ring as he shouted again, "I will na give in, I will na surrender." He raised the key above his head. "This key, my bonny lads, is to open the lock to my lady's heart, for when I get back hame, I will wed the daughter of the laird and I have this key as her pledge. Tonight I will escape; will ye bonny lads join me?"

Six rebels yelled, "Aye."

* * *

The six Jacobite rebels and the tall highlander crept stealthily down the rear alleyways behind Friargate. They skirted the barricade that had been defended so stoutly by Colonel Mackintosh and his men but with the colonel a hostage, the barricade was almost deserted and in darkness, illuminated only by houses still on fire.

All was quiet as the seven deserters made their way into Back Ween, the lane that had allowed Drummer's dragoons to make a flanking attack on the windmill barricade. The tall highlander was leading, his sword in his hand, the key to his future clutched in his left hand.

The moon cast shadows that the seven used for cover as they moved furtively, then without warning a flash from the muzzle of a musket, and a shot hit one of the Jacobites in the chest. The remaining five led by the tall highlander ran forward, as more muskets fired. One by one the rebels fell until only the tall highlander was left standing. Finally with his sword held high he gave a mighty bellow and a final shout of, "This key will open the lock to my lady's heart, I'm gain' hame to my lady." And still clutching the large key, he ran to attack the dragoons who were firing from defensive positions.

A shot hit the gallant rebel and he fell to his knees, then clutching the key he raised it to his lips, kissed it and slumped onto his side, dead.

* * *

At the Church Street barricade a group of highlanders were also rampaging.

"If we can nay langer defend this post," one rebel was shouting, "then I say we should cut our way out through the enemy and make a retreat home to bonny Scotland."

Major Nairn, accompanied by the Earl of Wintoun and Captains Lockart and Shaftoe, now approached Old Borlum. "Sir, will you allow my foot soldiers to flank the hedgerows on the Lancaster road while the Scots gentry under the command of Lord Wintoun and Lord Derwentwater force an escape through the enemy lines?"

Old Borlum ceased drawing on his pipe said, "It's a wee bit late for that kinda talk, sirs. We've pledged our word and hostages, so we will have nay more talk of escapes."

"Well, it seems that somebody has made a run for freedom if that shooting from Friargate is anything to go by," Major Nairn replied.

All night the disturbances continued as furious highlanders paraded the streets, threatening all who even alluded to surrender. As dawn broke, calm settled on the town; twenty-five persons had been wounded during the rioting with several more killed.

Seven Jacobites lay unaccounted in Back Ween.

Battle of Preston ~ Day Three

"**M**onday the fourteenth of November in the year of our Lord seventeen hundred and fifteen," said General Forster as he addressed Lord Widdrington and Brigadier Mackintosh at the Mitre Inn, "a day that will be recorded in British history, the day when the Jacobites surrendered at Preston."

"Aye, a fateful day indeed," replied Old Borlum.

Colonel Oxburgh who was also in the room said, "Sir, I must tell you it is seven o'clock and an answer needs to be sent to General Wills immediately."

"Of course, Oxburgh, you are correct. Will you ride one more time to the general and inform him the insurgents are willing to surrender at discretion as he requires."

Old Borlum Mackintosh spoke up. "I've been a soldier for many years and I know what it means to be a prisoner at discretion. Don't ye forget that my highlanders are men of desperate fortunes and I will not be answerable for them surrendering without terms."

"Go, Oxburgh," Forster commanded, "inform General Wills that I accept his terms but inform him that Brigadier Mackintosh will not be answerable for his men surrendering without terms."

Colonel Oxburgh rode down London Road lane to the government headquarters and entered the general's tent.

"Good morning, Colonel Oxburgh, and what is the answer to my demands for the surrender of the town of Preston into government hands?"

Oxburgh drew himself up to his full height. "Sir, I have to report that the English insurgents are willing to surrender at discretion as you demand but Old Borlum

Mackintosh, who commands the highlanders, says he will not be answerable for his men surrendering without honourable terms."

"Then return to your people again," answered Wills, "and tell them this: I will attack the town, and the consequence will be that no one will be spared."

Colonel Mackintosh and James Radclyffe, who had been listening, looked aghast at the threat.

Colonel Mackintosh said, "Sir, we rendered ourselves as hostages but now it is over and after your comment to Colonel Oxburgh, neither I nor the Earl, James Radclyffe, can with good grace remain as hostages. We will return with Colonel Oxburgh to our comrades in the town."

Both colonels saluted the general. James Radclyffe nodded and said, "You may have sown a whirlwind and condemned hundreds to death, both yours and ours."

With the Earl of Derwentwater in the centre, flanked by two colonels, the three rode back up London Road to deliver the final ultimatum.

Thirty minutes later Colonel Mackintosh rode back to General Wills. "Sir, I have to inform you that on my return to our headquarters and after some brief discussions, it was agreed that Lord Kenmure and Old Borlum plus the rest of the Scottish noblemen will surrender on the same conditions as the English."

"I am pleased they have seen sense," Wills said. "Thank you, Colonel, you may return to your men and inform your commanders that I will immediately dispatch Colonel Cotton with a contingent of two hundred dragoons to take possession of the town."

Colonel Cotton rode up London Road at the head of his squadron of dragoons.

All was now quiet in the town; the barricade on Church Street had been partially demolished to allow the dragoons to pass unhindered. Colonel Cotton dismounted at the Mitre Inn and gave the orders for the dragoons to form up to prevent ingress or egress from the headquarters.

Colonel Cotton then stood to attention sword in hand and waited.

* * *

In the market square, the armed Jacobites were lined up in their regiments, their officers standing in attendance for the official surrender of weapons. To the ear came the sound of trumpets accompanied by the beating of drums. Generals Wills rode his black stallion at the head of his dragoons up Friargate towards the market place. Simultaneously a cacophony of drum beats coupled with trumpet calls echoed from the area of Church Street as General Carpenter and Brigadier Honeywood approached with the remainder of the king's men. Both groups halted with flags flying and the drums beating; they then formed into ranks of three to encircle the Jacobites.

General Wills addressed the Jacobites. "Men, your leaders have agreed your surrender. Lord Kenmure will now give you the command to peacefully lay down your arms, and that order will be repeated to you by Mr Forster, your appointed English General. The officers and gentlemen will stand fast and surrender their arms later."

Lord Kenmure and General Forster stepped forward and issued the commands to the rank and file rebels. There was a clatter of metal and wood as swords, pikes and muskets were laid on the cobbled floor of the market square.

"Colonel Cotton, give the command for the rank and file prisoners to be marched by their junior officers under close escort to the parish church. I want a count of their numbers then lock the other ranks inside the church and make it secure and escort the junior officers into the custody of Colonel Preston. Have the numbers reported back to me."

The colonel saluted General Wills and issued orders to his captains.

"Brigadier Honeywood, escort Lord Kenmure and the rest of the Jacobite Lords to the Mitre Inn for them to surrender their arms in private. Colonel Preston, you will escort General Forster and the senior officers to the Mitre, the White Bull, and the Windmill Inns. Make arrangement to accommodate them and also let them surrender their weapons in private. Also arrange accommodation for the remaining subaltern rebel officers who will have marched their troops to the church, those junior officers will surrender their weapons in the churchyard."

Brigadier Honeywood and Colonel Preston saluted their General and ran off to organize their respective duties.

General Carpenter, who had remained in his saddle alongside General Wills and until now had remained silent, said, "Well, General, it's over, I will retire and let you have your moment of glory; although I must repeat it has been an unnecessary loss of English lives, you should have waited for me to reinforce you. However, it's over and you need to get the dead buried and the town back to normality. There is not enough accommodation for my officers nor room to manoeuvre my three regiments and considering my three regiments have been extremely harassed with a month's continual marching, I shall send them this day to Wigan, to rest for a day or two, and then I shall move them on by gentle marches to their new quarters. I will leave the care of the prisoners to you."

General Carpenter addressed his adjutant, Philip Carpenter. "Make the necessary arrangement for conveying my orders to the colonels to march their regiments out of this square and proceed on the road to Wigan. I shall follow."

Around the square voices reverberated as orders were shouted by Colonels Humphrey Gore, Thomas Sydney and Joshua Guest of Cobham's, Molesworth's and Churchill's regiments respectively. The three regiments quickly formed up into ranks of three. Drums began to beat and with flags flying the king's regiments marched out of the market place.

General Carpenter turned his horse; General Wills saluted his senior officer, the salute was returned in silence, then with a flick of the reins Carpenter and his horse followed his dragoons into history.

* * *

The Mitre Inn now became the headquarters for General Will's and his aides and the general wasted little time in calling a meeting of his staff officers. "Gentlemen, there is a need to organize burial parties and to get the streets cleared of all debris and bodies. Also we must convene a court martial for the serving officers who still held a king's commission but defected to the rebels and there is the case of the Cavendish spies to be resolved; we might as well shoot them all."

Brigadier Honeywood interrupted, "That is if they are found guilty, sir?"

"Of course, Brigadier Honeywood, and as you are the most senior officer, will you organize the convening of a court martial as soon as possible; we don't want this unpleasant situation to linger on, and finally, Colonel Cotton, organize the burial parties."

The general now addressed Colonel Forester. "I hope your wounds are only slight and you will be able to organize the feeding of the prisoners. The Lords and gentry are in various inns but the rank and file that are locked in the church should be fed by the townspeople; after all, they welcomed them into their community. The final task falls to you, Colonel Preston, order the subalterns to organize their men to demolish the barricades and clear the streets? Now attend to your duties, gentlemen."

The officers all saluted and left General Wills to mull over his intended report to His Majesty King George I. In the report he intended to include the map he had before him that one of his cartographers had sketched of the taking of Preston and the deployment of the king's forces.

* * *

Colonel Cotton took Major Ward aside and said, "I need to get the dead buried quickly, I want you to take two lieutenants and twenty dragoons and organize the burials for those killed at the Church Street and Tythebarn Street barricades. I will command the burial parties at the windmill barricades on the Lancaster Road."

Major Ward saluted and taking Lieutenants Roper and Rothwell, he gave the orders to delegate twenty dragoons for burial duties.

Colonel Cotton summoned Lieutenants Stow and Thompson. "Gentlemen," he said, "we have work to do. You are to command the burial party at the windmill barricade; select twenty dragoons and you can take those Cavendish gentlemen that are under arrest to help get this task done quickly before any disease can spread. They may as well help pay for their keep."

The burial party had been digging since midday and it was now almost three. They had dug three large pits in the meadow behind Back Ween. In the first pit the dragoons had used horse power to drag the carcass of Reverend Patten's horse along with other dead horses killed at the barricade and dispose of them into the pit. Lime was shovelled onto

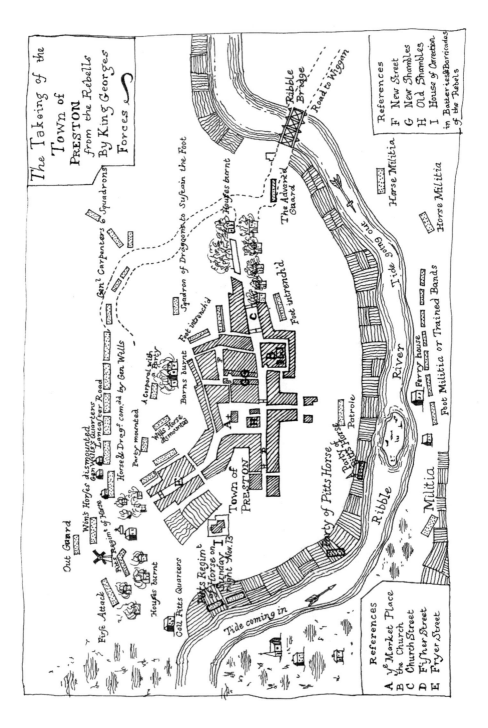

The Takeing of the Town of PRESTON from the Rebells By King Georges Forces

References
F New Street
G New Shambles
H Old Shambles
I House of Correction
   in Batteries & Barricades
   of the Rebels

References
A ye Market Place
B the Church
C Church Street
D Fisher Street
E Fryer Street

the carcasses and the pit quickly filled with soil. Henry and Charles helped carry the bodies of the fifteen dragoons and laid them in the second pit. It was then time to bury the rebels; first the body of the Colonel and the two Jacobites from the barricade were interred alongside six of the seven rebel escapees. "Have we got the names of the dead?" Colonel Cotton asked.

"The rebel colonel was named Brereton, and as far as possible we have listed the names of the other ranks, sir," said Lieutenant Stow. "We don't know the name of this giant of a man though."

Just as Charles and Henry were about to place the huge highlander in the pit with the rest of the rebels, a dragoon in the burial party who had witnessed the attempted escape spoke up.

"Sir, this man died a hero. He ran at us waving that basket-hilted sword and that huge key, shouting something about, *'this will open my lady's heart and I'm going home to my lady.'* We shot him dead, sir, but he was a brave man."

Colonel Cotton ordered the sepulchral pit to be filled with the six rebels then being a romantic at heart, he ordered two dragoons to dig a separate grave about two feet deep. He gave the orders for the body of the highlander to be placed into the ground still clutching his sword and key. Lime was scattered over the corpse and the grave filled.

Colonel Cotton saluted the grave and whispered, 'Go to your lady, gallant soldier,'

* * *

"Sir, the burial parties have completed their work and I have my report of the total number of prisoners taken and of the casualties. However, there was one disturbing factor afforded to the burial party at the windmill barricade. They had buried all the dead and identified and listed as many as possible; sir, when one of our commanding officers examined the lists and could not be persuaded that one interred gentleman of military rank was a secret Jacobite and part of the rebellion. He ordered them to take him out of his grave to satisfy his curiosity that the dead man whose name he recognized had in fact defected and gone over to the rebels. The rebel was Colonel Brereton with connections to the Cheshire family."

"And was he?" General Wills asked.

"Apparently so," replied Colonel Cotton. "They found that the body of the colonel had several wounds, one of which had caused a vast flux of blood that had not been discovered until too late by his surgeon. Mind you sir, had he lived; his fate would probably have meant him facing a firing squad."

"Saved us the time and a musket ball, I suppose," said General Wills. The general took the report from Colonel Cotton and scanned it,

To General Wills.

At the Battle of Preston Lancashire in which the final surrender took place on Monday the fourteenth of November in the year of our Lord 1715 I submit my report in which the casualties and prisoners stated are listed as true and factual.

Kings Men

Officers	Killed		3
	Wounded		15
Soldiers	Killed		142
	Wounded		116
	Total casualties		276
Jacobites	Killed		17
	Wounded		25
	Total casualties		42

Prisoners

Scottish Lords, officers and gentlemen	143

English Lords, officers and gentlemen	75
Scottish soldiers	879
English soldiers	388
	1,485

I remain sir.

Your obedient servant

Colonel Cotton

"One thousand four hundred and eighty-five," General Wills said, as he laid the report aside. "Damn it, Honeywood, it would appear from the small number of prisoners we have taken, that most of the local people who joined the rebels when they took Preston escaped during the Saturday and Sunday nights. Still it is of little consequence; the local militia know who they are and will round them up in the next few weeks. Now, Brigadier, I want you to check the names of the seventy-five English Lords, officers and gentlemen, and make a list of any officers on the half-pay lists. Colonel Cotton my aide will assist you."

Next day Colonel Cotton presented the list to Brigadier Honeywood. "Sir, there are seven half-pay officers: Lord Charles Murray, Major John Nairn, Captains Lockart, Shaftoe, Fraser, Dalziel and a young ensign named John Erskine. Six of the officers are in custody but one officer, Captain Simon Fraser, was injured with a musket-ball in the thigh and was with the wounded in the White Bull Inn but last night he escaped and is in hiding. I have organized search parties but we have not been able to apprehend the rebel officer."

"The general will not be pleased with that news, but never mind, Colonel, continue with the searches."

Brigadier Honeywood presented himself and the report at the Mitre Inn. "So what have you done to set the proceedings in place for the courts martial of the six officers?" Wills asked.

"I have sent Colonel Nassau to London to request a judge advocate be sent for the trials but initially I have convened a preliminary court martial to sit in four days on the seventeenth of November, sir . . ." Brigadier Honeywood paused. "And about the other matter, I took the liberty to have my aide make enquiries in the town about Mr Charles and Mr James Cavendish, sir, and apparently numerous townsfolk vouch for them, all saying that they are honest traders who were visiting Preston to view the prospect of opening trading links here in the town. I think you should let them go, sir."

"Very well, Honeywood, release them, make sure their horses are fed and watered and wish them well and give them my apologies, but one cannot be too careful."

* * *

For a final time, Charles and James Cavendish rode down London Road. As they crossed over the river, Charles let his gaze wander once more over the shimmering waters that flowed so peacefully between the sandy banks. "You know, Father, it's not just the quicksand that is a danger here . . ."

Executions

The door of the courtroom opened and armed red-coats escorted the six prisoners to face charges of desertion by the formal proceedings of courts martial. For this initial hearing and standing behind a solid oak table were Brigadier Honeywood and Colonel Cotton and to his left was Colonel Cobham.

"The courts martial are in session," shouted Captain James Baker who was adjutant to General Wills and delegated to duties as court adjutant.

"Halt," Baker commanded. The prisoners stood to attention. "Officers on parade." Lord Charles Murray, Major John Nairn, Captain Philip Lockart, Captain John Shaftoe, Captain James Dalziel and Ensign John Erskine remained rigidly to attention while the tribunal took their seats.

"The prisoners may be seated," James Baker said. There were a few moments of noise as chairs scraped noisily on the floor.

Brigadier Honeywood looked up from the paperwork on his table and addressed the six defendants. "The charges against each of you are the same, that you held a military commission from His Majesty King George and that you did dishonour and betray that commission between the eleventh and the fourteenth of November seventeen fifteen in that you did bear arms against His Majesty's lawful forces in the town of Preston Lancashire. How do you plead, guilty or not guilty?"

Each of the defendants rose to give his name and rank and answered, "Not guilty."

"Captain Baker, you are court adjutant, are their pleas noted?" Honeywood asked.

"They are, sir."

"Very well, I shall adjourn these courts martial until twenty-eighth of November to give the defendants time to prepare their cases and for the court to request the services of a judge advocate to be sent from London. The accused are to be held under lock and key, given access to their needs and fed well. This court is now adjourned."

The prisoners rose and were led away.

* * *

The days following the battle were cold and the nights even colder. Martial law was imposed on the populace of Preston but with many of their houses destroyed or damaged by fire and their normal rural lives ruined, the order to feed the rank and file prisoners locked in the church was not accepted with enthusiasm. Each day groups of women brought bread and buckets of water to the prisoners but with no hot food the rebels began to fall sick. Many had no blankets and to survive they had to keep warm. The hapless captives ripped the linings from the seats and pews to give them extra clothing as they sought additional protection from the inclemency of the November cold, but that was not all; the days dragged by in endless boredom.

With the courts marshal adjourned on the seventeenth of November, General Wills gave orders for one hundred of the Lords, higher ranking officers and gentlemen to be assembled in the market square, each alongside his horse. Amongst those selected for the long humiliating journey was Old Borlum Mackintosh, Colonel Macintosh, and Lieutenant Colonel Farquharson and to prevent any escapes, each prisoner had his arms tied behind his back.

"They're in for an uncomfortable ride to London, with them not being able to hold the reins," a soldier commented to his companion as the foot soldiers helped the bound prisoners into the saddles

"Aye, and it's also a long walk, just think of my feet, never mind their Lordships' arses," replied the foot soldier.

Day after day during the harsh rigors of the November winter, the horses were led through the snow by a foot soldier while the prisoners, cold and hungry, rode in abject misery. In town after town innumerable crowds of spectators lined the streets, not to shout abuse for the detestation of their crime, but most to stand in silence, although some sympathizers stepped out of the crowds and kissed the cloaks of the prisoners as the passed. Eventually the cavalcade arrived in London on the ninth of December seventeen fifteen.

* * *

At the Mitre Inn General Wills was in close conversation with Philip Honeywood. "I am in a quandary, Philip. If the prisoners are found guilty of desertion and mutiny at their courts marshal, and I fear it is a forgone conclusion, then I am loath to be the tool that implements the order to execute a relative to the Duke of Athol, and yet Charles Murray is a rebel. I have written to His Majesty recommending clemency for I am sure he will not want a loyal nobleman like the Duke to be antagonized by the shooting of one of his nephews."

"And if the king does not send through the clemency in time, what will you do?" said the colonel.

"Then I shall delay Colonel Murray's execution and send him to London for him to be executed in the Tower. That way we buy time for the Duke of Athol's relatives to rally and send their pleas to the king."

Brigadier Honeywood took a sip from a glass of wine that the general had poured. "In the meantime, Honeywood, the military cannot administer civil justice to the rebels, but I do want an example made very quickly of some of the local ringleaders. Send a dispatch to London requesting a commission of oyer and terminer to establish a court to try the rebels. Meanwhile the Preston people can continue to feed them."

* * *

The courts martial reconvened on the twenty-seventh of November. Edward Hughes the judge advocate in London had sent an assistant judge advocate accompanied by Colonel Nassau to apply judgement at the courts martial.

As the charges were read out, the prisoners stood before the judge advocate and a tribunal of military officers.

"Lord Charles Murray, you were conspicuous at the defence of the Preston barricades. You were apprehended wearing highland dress and are charged with mutiny against the crown. Captain Philip Lockhart, you are charged with desertion from the half-pay contingent of Mark Kerr's regiment. Captain John Shaftoe, you are charged with aiding and abetting the enemy in that you were a courier used by government spies to send messages to the northern Jacobites planning the rebellion. Major John Nairn, Captain James Dalziel and Ensign John Erskine, each of you were on the lists as half-pay officers and therefore you are charged with desertion. You have all entered a plea of not guilty at your preliminary hearing. Do you wish to change those pleas?"

Lord Murray was the first speak. "Sir, I Lord Charles Murray, wish to change my plea. I now plead guilty and throw myself on the king's mercy."

The judge advocate noted the plea. "And how say the rest of you?"

One by one the other five officers repeated their pleas of not guilty and in their defence they all claimed that although serving as half-pay officers under the previous monarch, none of them had sworn allegiance to King George.

"Before sentences are passed, have you anything more to say, gentlemen, in your defence and in repentance for the rebellious acts for which you are charged?"

Major Nairn said, "Sirs, we the accused can only repeat that as half-pay officers we swore an oath of allegiance to Queen Ann who sadly died last August in seventeen fourteen and none of us has renewed that oath of allegiance to King George, therefore we hold that these courts martial and the charges are unlawful in English law."

"Thank you, Major Nairn, your comments are noted and the court will now pass sentences in order of seniority. Colonel Charles Murray, we accept your plea of guilty of mutiny against the crown and this court recommends that His Majesty shows mercy. The sentence of these courts martial is that you shall be taken to a place of execution and shot; the sentence to be adjourned for one month. Major Nairn, we find you guilty of desertion. The sentence of these courts martial is that you shall be taken to a place of execution and shot."

The same sentences were prescribed for Captain Philip Lockhart, Captain John Shaftoe and Ensign Erskine.

"Captain James Dalziel, formerly in King George's service; you continued as a half-pay officer until the rebellion; the fact that you threw up your commission before joining the rebels leads this court to acquit you of charges of desertion and you are released into the hands of the courts at Liverpool for civil justice to be applied. His Majesty to confirm the sentences, these courts martial are now closed."

The judge advocate and the tribunal of military officers rose and left the court. The escorts led the prisoners away to await the king's pleasure.

* * *

The slow beat of a solitary drum heralded the cold winter dawn on the second of December as the four condemned officers escorted by a troop of dragoons slowly marched up Tythbarn Street, passing the burnt-out houses and the barricade that two weeks previously they had so bravely defended. The column marched in time to the slow beat of the drum winding its way up a slight hill, then on a command the party halted.

Major David Ward read out the charges to each of the accused officers and each confirmed his name and rank. Francis Gore the regimental chaplain spoke a few words to each of the condemned men asking them to repent.

Major Nairn spoke. "Sir, we are all sinners in the sight of God and for that we repent and trust in the merits of Christ to obtain pardon, but we have done no more than our duty and since that was the will of God then we are happy to seal it with our blood."

Captain Hugh Palliser had been selected to command the firing party; he now approached Major Nairn and said, "Sir, please step forward, the time has come, and as the senior prisoner you must show an example to the others."

Major David Ward, escorted by Captain Palliser and two dragoons, marched Major Nairn to a large post that had been entrenched into the ground. Captain Palliser supervised the binding of the major's arms to the post and the attachment of a white handkerchief to his left breast.

The Major asked, "Do you wish a blindfold?"

"No, thank you, Major Ward, I wish to see the light of day before I meet my God, but I have a final request. May I give my last military command to 'fire'?"

Colonel Cotton who was witnessing the executions said to Major Ward, "Deny that request, Major."

"Request denied, Major Nairn."

Major Ward retired to stand by Colonel Cotton. Captain Palliser saluted them both, turned and gave the order, "Firing party, take one step forward."

From the ranks of the dragoons, six men who had been selected by lots for the unsavoury task of executioners, stepped forward, and lined up fifteen paces in front of the execution post.

"Squad, present muskets, take aim . . ." Captain Palliser's sword arm was raised in the air. He made a downward stroke with his sword arm and simultaneously commanded, "FIRE."

A volley of musket fire rang out. Wraiths of smoke from the muskets drifted skyward and the smell of the gunpowder lingered on the air as Captain Lockhart stepped forward. "Sir, my friend died an officer and a gentleman and I request that no common soldier touches his body but me and our two other condemned gentlemen."

Colonel Cotton nodded his approval and Captain Lockhart strode over to the execution post where he would meet a similar fate in a few minutes' time. Gently he untied the cords that bound John Nairn to the post and gently laid the major in one of two coffins that had been provided. Then with the greatest composure he performed the last duties to a fellow officer.

Captain Palliser saluted Captain Lockhart. "Please sir, the time has come, and I hope you die as bravely as the major. We do not want the common soldiers that are witnessing this day to think officers have no stiff upper lip or backbone, do we, sir?"

Major Ward and Captain Palliser and the two dragoons marched Captain Lockhart over to the bloodstained post and again supervised the binding of the prisoner's arms and the attachment of a white handkerchief to his left breast.

"Do you wish a blindfold?"

"No, thank you, Captain, I will also go to my God with the winter sun in my eyes, knowing I am innocent."

Captain Palliser turned and gave the order. 'Firing squad, reload; present muskets, take aim . . ." Captain Palliser's sword arm dropped as he shouted, "FIRE." Captain Lockhart's body jerked and twitched in response to the impact of the musket balls.

Captain John Shaftoe and Ensign Erskine stepped forward without making a request; Colonel Cotton and Major Ward watched in silence as the remaining two prisoners released their comrade from the post and placed his body in the second coffin.

It was then the turn of Captain John Shaftoe to face the firing squad. Ensign Erskine cut his bindings and with the assistance of Captain Pallister, the shot-through corpse of John Shaftoe was placed in a woollen winding sheet.

"Thank you, sir," Erskine said, "I realize that no coffins have been provided for John nor myself but please will you lay my shrouded body next to his in the ground?"

"I will, my boy, now be brave," Pallister said, and led young John Erskine to the execution post that was standing like a sentinel rooted in the bloodstained ground. The captain saluted and took up his post to command the last execution of the day.

Major Ward checked the bindings then asked, "Ensign John Erskine, do you want a blindfold?" "No, sir, but I would like to pray for a moment."

As Major Ward marched back to take up position next to Colonel Cotton the strains of the voice of Erskine's voice drifted softly across the air.

"Squad, present your muskets. Take aim." Major Ward raised his hand to silence Captain Pallister's next command and the place grew silent as Erskine's words from the Scottish Psalter filled the air:

> *"The Lord's my shepherd, I'll not want.*
> *He makes me down to lie*
> *In pastures green: he leadeth me*
> *the quiet waters by.*
> *My soul he doth restore again;*
> *and me to walk doth make*
> *Within the paths of righteousness,*

ev'n for his own name's sake.
Yea, though I walk in death's dark vale,
yet will I fear none ill:
For thou art with me; and thy rod
and staff me comfort still.
My table thou hast furnished
in presence of my foes;
My head thou dost with oil anoint,
and my cup overflows.
Goodness and mercy all my life
shall surely follow me:
And in God's house for evermore
my dwelling-place shall be.
Amen"

Major Ward nodded as the word Amen was uttered and Captain Pallister's sword dropped to the command "FIRE." Ensign Erskine breathed his last.

Amidst the smell of gunpowder and blood, three graves were dug, a coffin placed in two of them and the shrouded bodies of Shaftoe and Erskine were laid side by side in the third grave.

* * *

General Wills and Brigadier Honeywood were mulling over the situation of the civil trials of the rebels, and the general finally said, "It's a week since we shot the officers, and we still have no response from parliament on my request for the civil commissioners at Westminster to examine our rebel prisoners by grand jury on the lawful principle of oyer and terminer. I know that the commissioners travel the county circuits twice a year during the vacations of the royal courts and we are well into the winter recession. I should have had a response by now."

Brigadier Honeywood failed to respond, he just sat and gazed out of the window of the Mitre Inn and thought of the long cold months ahead before the military could finally discharge its duties that martial law had brought to the market town.

It was the middle of December before General Wills received a communiqué from Westminster that the Royal Commission of Oyer and Terminer had appointed three judges who would be leaving London on the fourth of January and travelling to Liverpool to set up assizes for the trials of the accused prisoners. The communiqué ordered that General Wills should disperse the prisoners to prisons in the area of Lancashire and Cheshire to await their trials.

"Well, Honeywood, that relieves us of the problem of guarding the rebels. Make suitable arrangements for batches of those held in the church to be sent under escort to the prisons of Wigan, Chester, Manchester and Liverpool to await trial at the Liverpool assizes."

* * *

The wind had drifted the winter snow along the banks of the Mersey. The streets of Liverpool were filled with slush when the three judges, Mr Baron Burry, Mr Justice Eyre and Mr Baron Montague, arrived in the city and immediately took up the invitation of Richard Molyneux for temporary residence at Woolton Hall, which allowed them to meet social peers and also to have easy access to the court rooms in the city. The day was the eleventh of January seventeen sixteen.

One day later, and travelling into the city by coach, the three judges opened the assizes. A grand jury heard the bills of indictment against forty-eight of the rebels charged with insurrection and plotting against the state and the church and the prisoners were given seven days in which to prepare their defence.

That evening before supper, the judges were discussing the task they had in giving judgment on so many prisoners.

"We are in for a very busy assizes, and I don't want to be up here in this northern wilderness for too long," Judge Burry commented as he sat twirling a glass of sherry in his hand in the library at Woolton Hall.

"So what do you propose? There are hundreds of rebels to be indicted and as you say, we could be here for weeks all through the winter," said Justice Eyre.

"What I suggest is that when we have held the indictments for these forty-eight prisoners, we then propose that the remaining prisoners be put into batches of twenty, and lots are drawn to select one in every twenty to stand trial. We can respite the other nineteen in each batch for hearings at later assizes when the weather is more clement."

"Excellent proposal and we should be back in London to witness the trial and judgements on the nobility," added Mr Baron Burry.

For the next week the judges enjoyed the hospitality of their hosts at the Hall then on the twentieth of January the county sheriff arranged for the Liverpool sanguinary assizes to reconvene.

On the first day of the court hearing Judges Burry, Eyre and Montague sat in judgment as the verdicts of guilty were announced by the grand jury finding five men from the Preston area guilty of plotting against the state and the church.

Judge Eyre looked down on the five hapless prisoners and said, "You have been found guilty of high treason in so much as you did make insurrection and plot against the state and the church. It is the sentence of this court is that you be taken to the town of Preston were you will be hanged drawn and quartered. Take the prisoners away."

* * *

On the morning of the twenty-eighth of January the crowds lined Church Street heard the slow beat of a solitary drum as three wicker sledges passed by dragged by horses.

Tied to the first sledge was the rebel Richard Shuttleworth, to the second sledge Roger Moncaster, the town clerk of Garstang, and to the third sledge was tied Thomas Cowpe.

The crowds pressed forward; those at the back stood on tiptoe to take a look at the hapless prisoners who, only a few weeks before, had been jubilant and seemed certain of a victory; now they were being dragged backwards on hurdles to their place of execution. The drummer leading the procession passed the parish church where so many had been confined; then the cavalcade turned left and headed up Tythbarn Street passing the burnt-out houses where Charles Murray had commanded the barricade. The street gave way to a lane and fields. The procession now went up a slight hill where a scaffold had been erected near to a shot damaged blood stained wooden post. Alongside the scaffold the executioner had stacked a pile of faggots which had been lit to provide a hot fire for the burning of the heart and entrails of each of the prisoners.

Richard Shuttleworth was the first to suffer. He was assisted up onto a horse drawn cart where he made a very short speech proclaiming his loyalty to the king but to the Catholic faith. Because of his family connections a huge amount of local sympathizers were in attendance as the noose was placed around his neck and the horse and cart were drawn away to leave Richard dangling at the end of a short rope. For a few minutes Shuttleworth's legs kicked and twitched before the executioner cut the body down but did not attempt to revive the unconscious man with cold water as was the custom with traitors. Swiftly he cut open Richard's stomach and removed his intestines. With a thrust of his knife he mercifully opened the chest cavity and removed the beating heart. Lifting the still-pulsating organ high, he proclaimed to the crowd, "See the heart of a traitor."

The executioner's assistant took the entrails and heart and threw them onto the embers of the fire; there was a sizzling noise and then the smell of burnt offal filled the air. The corpse lay on the scaffold as the executioner severed the head from the trunk and placed it on a spike for it to be displayed in front of the town hall. The axe of the executioner now began to fall rapidly as he severed the arms and legs from the trunk. With his bloody job done, his assistant threw the severed body parts onto a cart for display at strategic points around the town as a warning to others of the fate that awaited traitors. The next to suffer execution was Thomas Cowpe, the innkeeper of the Unicorn Inn in Walton-le-Dale, a meeting place for the Preston Jacobites. The executioner disembowelled the rebel and removed the heart but did not quarter the remains and allowed the relatives of Thomas to claim the mutilated corpse. The body was placed in a coffin and taken by cart to St. Leonard's church for burial.

Finally Roger Moncaster, an attorney and town clerk from Garstang, was untied from his sledge and with shaking legs he mounted the horse drawn cart beneath the scaffold and addressed the crowd:

"Dear Friends, I am a Protestant and I beg forgiveness from my Church. I am brought hither to be a miserable and dismal spectator to you all. The crime I am accused of, condemned, and brought hither to be executed for, bears no manner or less infamous title than rebellion; a crime prohibited both by the Laws of God and Man, and though I be not the only person to suffer for it, yet, I declare that from my heart, I do detest and abhor the very principles of rebellion, and look upon the promoters and abettors thereof to be men without any principles, and enemies, in the highest degree, to the Lawful Sovereign King George, and country. I shall not trouble you any further with this, but

acquaint you, that upon serious recollection into my wicked course of life, those very sins that I have wretchedly committed, have brought the deserved vengeance of God upon me. I heartily, and, with the utmost sincerity repent my sins of what ever nature, and I hope through faith, and the merits and intercession of my Blessed Saviour and Redeemer to obtain remission thereof. And I, in perfect charity with all men, and freely from my heart, forgive all, particularly every one concerned in my execution, desiring forgiveness of all persons, here present or else where, whom I have otherwise offended."

The executioner placed the noose around Moncaster's neck and swiftly the horse and cart were drawn away to leave Roger hanging at the end of the rope. A few minutes later the executioner cried to the crowd for a third time that day, "Behold the heart of a traitor."

In the afternoon, another two prisoners, William Arkwright and William Butler, also had their hearts exposed and burnt.

On the ninth of February the crowds again lined Church Street, the sound of a solitary drum beating out a slow beat as horses dragged seven more rebels tied to wicker sledges to their executions. Tied to the first sledge was the rebel James Drummond. Leading the procession as it passed the parish church was a drummer beating out a slow march. The procession turned into a lane and the drummer boy led them across a field and halted alongside the scaffold at Gallows Hill where the executioner was in wait.

The drum ceased its beat and the gathered crowd grew silent as the charges of treason were read out. The first to suffer was James Drummond and as he confirmed his named the drum began to beat again. James was assisted up onto a horse-drawn cart; the noose was placed around his neck and the horse and cart were drawn away to leave him dangling at the end of a short rope. For a few minutes his legs kicked and twitched, then the executioner cut the body down and gave him the full treatment of being hanged drawn and quartered. The executioner now impaled James Drummond's head on a spike for display on the portals of the town hall.

The remaining six prisoners, Richard Chorley, William Black, Donald McDonald, Rorie Kennodie, John Ord and John Robotham were all hanged, disembowelled and their hearts burnt; but by now the Preston populace were sickened by the savage retributions of the Crown and sympathy had turned again to favour the Jacobites.

Home and Away

Charles and James had ridden with little thought of stopping; they were putting as much distance between them and Preston as they could. They were on the way home but they were also on a mission, a mission that took them to Warrington and into the cobbled courtyard of the inn where four weeks earlier they had stayed overnight and met the Scottish architect James Gibbs. Standing in the doorway of Ye Olde Lion they saw the ruddy-faced inn keeper, looking shocked and nervous.

Father and son stomped into the premises and sat down. "Remember us, innkeeper?" James asked the man as he approached to question their needs. The innkeeper nodded nervously. "And do you remember saying to General Wills that we were," James mimicked the innkeeper's voice, "the two spies wot met with the Scots fellow?"

The innkeeper nodded nervously, clearly embarrassed.

"Well, my man," said James, "as you can see, we have been released, we are not spies but your gossip could have cost us our necks."

The innkeeper gulped and offered his humble apologies.

Charles said, "It is obvious the contrition you feel is genuine and to make some amends from your pocket, we shall have refreshments as some recompense for the inexcusable bearing of false witness."

The innkeeper nodded, bowed and retreated into his back room.

An hour later, rested and refreshed, father and son left an innkeeper still apologizing and wringing his hands at the thought of how much worse the pair could have treated him.

Two days later, when the saddle-sore pair rode into the courtyard at Ufton Manor, Constance, Annabel and Charity were there to greet their loved ones . . .

"Was it a successful journey?" Constance asked as she embraced James.

Don't even ask about it, Mother," said Charles, "we have so much to tell you."

As the five strolled toward the manor house, Annabel twittered, "When I was over at Wingfield Hall, David Halton was telling me all about rebel highlanders fighting to restore the Stuarts to the throne, it's the talk of the neighbourhood. Did you see any rebel highlanders?"

"Yes, Annabel, but we will tell you all later," said a tired and weary Charles.

* * *

It was the following evening when the family gathered at supper before Charity and Constance extracted the entire story from Charles about their ill-fated journey to Preston. Annabel sat at the table and listened in silence. The version of the events relayed to her by David was forgotten when she heard of the exploits of her father and her brother Charles.

"I am overcome with the vapours," said Charity, "you could have been hung or shot as spies and we would probably never have heard of your fate."

"Stay calm, my dear," said Constance, "I am sure James and Charles were able to settle all the doubts in that general's mind and the matter is now ended."

"Not exactly, Mother," said Charles. "I fear that our dear friends in Woodford Green may be in some danger."

"I agree," added James. "When we met that Scottish architect James Gibbs, he did mention that he had met William Halton and his wife Frances when he visited Sir Thomas at Gloucester House in Woodford Green. The danger to Sir

Thomas Halton and to William may arise because that architect is a friend of the Jacobite rebel John Erskine, the Earl of Mar. I do think that Charles should travel to London to warn Sir Thomas and William that investigations are being done and that the Halton family may be in danger. I am sure they are entirely innocent; but in these troubled times, the authorities are arresting all persons with links to the Jacobites."

"Oh, Charles, don't leave again," whispered Charity, grasping his arm. "I could not bear it if anything were to happen to you." Tears began to well into her eyes. "Charles, my love, I am too young to be a widow."

Charles and James tried to console their wives as they explained that they were duty bound to go to London to warn Sir Thomas of his architect's associations with Bobbin John, the Earl of Mar.

"I have a suggestion," said Constance. "It is almost two years since we left London and Charity has not visited her parents; and in all that time they have not seen their granddaughter Elizabeth. Why don't we all travel up to visit the Clarke household and we could stay for the Christmas and the New Year celebrations."

"Oh, can we, Charles?" Charity exclaimed in excitement. "Please say yes, I would love to have a festive season again in our old family house and I know Mother and Father will be overjoyed at having us all as guests."

"I think that suggestion is admirable," said James, "but Annabel has beseeched me to let her stay at Wingfield Hall for the festivities and I said I would consider it. Now it's three weeks to Christmas; if I send an express rider to Samuel Clarke's home informing him of our plans, we should get a response in a week. If we go, we can travel in our coach, Ben can drive us and we should be in London about the twentieth of December."

Constance glanced at Annabel and saw the pleading look in her eyes. "And you should speak with David Halton's family," she said, "to make sure that if we allow Annabel to stay with them, she is properly chaperoned."

"Yes, dear," said James.

* * *

An apprehensive Vivien stood in the courtyard of Ufton Manor. Her husband had carefully loaded the coach with the family's baggage ready for their departure. Ben placed the steps against the coach and aided by Charles and James the two wives took their seats with Charity carefully holding a slumbering baby Elizabeth.

"Are you sure you understood all that you have to do while we are away?" James asked Vivien.

"Everything will be fine, sir, now don't you go worrying about me and the house," she replied.

Then bidding her farewell, father and son climbed aboard the coach and Ben stowed the steps under his driver's seat. Finding himself alone with Vivien in the cobbled yard, where he understood James' grandparents, Robert and Elizabeth Cavendish, had waved farewell to their son when he left to seek his fortune in London more than a century earlier, Ben gave a final embrace to Vivien and bade her farewell.

"You keep the fires going and stay warm. I shall miss you, Viv," he said. Then giving her an extra hug, Ben climbed up onto his driver's seat and with a flick of his whip the horses took the first steps on the three-day journey to London.

* * *

Once settled into the Clarke household, Charles and James wasted little time in ordering Ben to drive them out to Woodford Green.

"There, Father, as I told you, our old residence still has Cavendish House above the portal." Charles then gazed from the south-west corner of the Green towards Gloucester House where Sir Thomas Halton lived with his wife

Elizabeth, the parents of his friend William and wife Frances.

From inside the coach, James slid open the small communication window and called up to Ben, "Drive us over to Gloucester House,"

The coach circled the green and entered a small lane that led to a large mansion house that stood in elm-lined grounds.

"Drive up to the front door," called up James.

The carriage halted and Ben retrieved the mounting steps from under his seat and placed them against the carriage door. The pair stepped down. "Wait here, Ben, we will be about an hour," said James as he grasped the knocker on the front door and rapped twice. In response the front door was opened by a footman.

"We have an urgent desire to speak with Sir Thomas if he will receive us," James said and he placed his calling card on the silver tray that the footman held in his extended hand.

The man opened the door wider and invited them into the large hall, he then closed the door and took the tray and visiting card into a side room.

"Sir Thomas, there are two gentlemen in the hall who say they have an urgent desire to speak with you," the footman said.

Thomas Halton took the calling card and recognized the name *James Cavendish*. For a moment his thoughts flew back to his youth when he and James were two young men sowing their wild oats around the capital. In particular he recalled the Christmas of 'eighty-seven when his father had allowed him to hold a festive dance at Gloucester House and amongst his guests he had invited James. His father had invited the eligible daughters of several friends but as the evening drew to a close James had departed without being attracted to any of the ladies. Thomas remembered all too clearly when, later that night when all his guests had left, he had taken advantage of one of the serving girls in his father's house. For Thomas, the memory of that night was etched into his brain. Of course the girl had been willing; there had been no difficulty in seducing her. He didn't think he was her first, but as events proved, he was probably the last. Two months later, she informed him she was with child. Thomas was sent on a grand tour and the girl was given several guineas to buy her silence and sent to the country residence of Winfield Halton in Derbyshire. Seven months later, after a long labour, the girl had died giving birth to a boy and the Haltons of Wingfield Hall; who were distant relatives, informed Sir William that although they had two sons of their own they would adopt the boy and name him David. When he was old enough, he would be informed of his adoption but not of the details of his biological father. In London, Sir Thomas was forever haunted by the wrong he had done to the girl.

Still holding the calling card in his hand as all those memories flashed through his mind as Sir Thomas said to the footman, "George, please show in the two gentlemen."

"Welcome to my house," Sir Thomas said, rising to meet the pair and extending his hand. "Hallo, James, how are you? It's been a long time since we saw you at Gloucester House and what is this important information that causes such an urgent desire for you to speak with me?"

James was about to recount the events of the Jacobite rebellion and their arrest by General Wills when Charles said, "Sir Thomas, what we have to tell you may affect your son, my friend William, and I think he should be present to hear what my father has to tell you."

Sir Thomas pulled at a cord hanging by the fireplace and the footman entered the room. "George, please request that William join us."

For the next two hours, Charles and James recounted the events that led to their arrest on the accusation of them being Jacobite spies.

"And you say all that came about because of your chance meeting with James Gibbs the architect?"

"That's correct," said James, "and although General Wills released us and accepted us as bona fide merchants visiting Preston to establish trading links, the general will send orders to London for the authorities to investigate your connections with James Gibbs."

"It's all totally innocent," replied Sir Thomas. "I wanted an architect to redesign the interior of this house and I heard that Mr Gibbs was a new architect in the city. I was looking to commission someone and Mr Gibbs visited our house on two or three occasions but then he informed me that he was very busy with other work and did not think he would be able to work on this house, but he recommended the work of another architect. Anyway, thank you for your concerns but I don't think we have anything to worry about."

William Halton said, "Well, I'm pleased the explanation has allayed your concerns, James. Now, Charles, how long are you and your delightful wife Charity going to be in town?"

"We intend staying for the Christmas festivities and we may stay on at my father-in-law's home for a couple of weeks into the New Year. As Father just explained, we saw the Jacobites at Preston after they had surrendered and the nobility are being tried for treason here in London, so we may stay on to witness the executions," said Charles.

"A bloody day that will be; however enough of that, can we meet and have an evening together?" said William.

Sir Thomas said, "William has told me that your father-in-law and his wife are very agreeable persons. Apparently he met them, Charles, when he shared a table with you at the Albion on Aldersgate Street. We would be pleased to see them at Gloucester House. I think that Elizabeth and I should invite you all to supper at Gloucester House on the twenty-sixth of December."

"That's very gracious of you," said James, "and we look forward to the evening with anticipation."

James and Charles rose from their chairs and shook the hands of Sir Thomas and William Halton. William escorted Charles to the front door while Sir Thomas engaged James in reminiscing.

"I hope we don't have a repeat of that Christmas celebration all those years ago," Thomas said humorously. "Those were the days of our youth, eh, James? I know I did that poor girl wrong and David; the crop of those wild oats, is now a young man. I understand he still lives at Wingfield Hall, which is very near to your Derbyshire estate at Ufton Manor. Tell me, James, do you ever see him?"

"Not yet," said James, "but my eldest daughter Annabel seems to be suited with his company so I think we shall have to meet soon, for I think we may hear wedding bells in the near future. Annabel asked her mother to persuade me to let her spend the festive time with David and your relations at Wingfield Hall. I have made sure that she is chaperoned of course. That is why she hasn't come to London with us for Christmas."

"Splendid news," said Sir Thomas, "so until the twenty-sixth, William, I bid you and your family a very peaceful Christmas.

They entered the coach and with a flick of his whip, Ben drove the horse and carriage back to the Clarke residence at Bunhill Row. He cleaned the coach and then with the horses safely stabled in Aldersgate he walked back to his room in the servants' quarters.

* * *

After the party at Gloucester House, the cold was so severe that for days the Clarke household and the Cavendish family failed to venture out. Instead they huddled around the fireside to keep warm. The Thames froze and after three days the ice grew thick enough that it was deemed safe to have a Frost Fair on the frozen river.

The New Year was already in its fourteenth day and the Cavendish and Clarke family had gathered for warmth in the library. A large log fire blazed in the grate as Samuel read the news sheet that a runner had delivered. Looking up he exclaimed, "You won't have to wait long for the execution of those Jacobites, it says that parliament impeached the rebel leaders on the ninth of January."

"I fear it will be a bloody business on Tower Hill in the near future," replied James. "Does it say when the impeachment trials will begin?"

"Wait a minute . . ." Summarising, Samuel said, "It seems that the Lord Chancellor William Cowper presided as Lord High Steward at the trials of the peers Lord Widdrington; James, Earl of Derwentwater; William, Earl of Nithsdale; George, Earl of Wintoun; Robert, Earl of Carnwath; William, Viscount Kenmure; and William, Lord Nairn. The accused were brought to the Bar of The House of Commons, to have the Articles of Impeachment of High Treason read to them and the trials will take place on the nineteenth of January. The accused are charged with conspiracy against church and state to incite the people to raise rebellion in Northumberland, Durham, Cumberland and Lancashire."

"Well, that's true enough," said Charles.

"The paper goes on to say that the Lord Chancellor asked them individually what they had to say to the charges and if they had any requests, that was the proper time to make them."

"It seems Cowper was being very fair to them to give them an opportunity to defend themselves," said Charity.

"Ah, but it seems it was only because the accused were ignorant of the legal proceedings and justice would not seem to have been done," said Samuel. "Anyway, to continue, it goes on to say that the Earl of Derwentwater said to the House that he was unprepared, and very ignorant of the Articles and Forms of their Lordships' judicature, and desired to have a copy of the said Articles, and such time to answer as the House should think fit. He also requested that Counsel might be assigned to assist him. The paper says that the other Lords all made the same requests."

Samuel read a little more in silence then said, "Apparently William Cowper agreed to the prisoners' requests. The House then requested the prisoners name their desired counsel but the Jacobite Lords said that as they were in solitary confinement and strangers in the city, they desired help and time to name their counsel."

"Can I read the remaining report?" said Charles.

"Certainly," answered Samuel and he handed the news sheet to Charles.

Charles read in silence whilst James and Samuel conversed with the women, who by this time were completely bored with the whole subject.

Charles perused what Samuel had told them. He read that the accused had been allowed a counsel and a solicitor until Saturday to help them nominate legal representations at their trials. The report went on to say that all witnesses called upon at the trials would have the protection of the House, for safe coming and going, during the time of the said trials. Finally the news sheet gave a list of the counsels that the accused had selected.

Impeached	Advisors & Counsels	Solicitors
Earl of Derwentwater	Duke of Richmond,	Mr Henry Eyre of Gray's Inn
	Duke of St. Albans,	
	Lord Viscount Longueville,	
	Lord Lumley,	

Lord Widdrington	*Duke of Richmond,*	*Mr Neville Ridley,*
	Lord Lumley	*Mr Henry Eyre of Gray's Inn*
	Nathaniel Piggott Counsel	
Earl of Nithsdale	*Duke of Roxburgh,*	*Mr Henry Eyre of Gray's Inn*
	Earl of Orkney,	
Earl of Wintoun	*Mr Heriot a Clergyman,*	*Mr George Lesley Lawyer:*
	Mr Menzies,	
	Major Sinclair,	
Robert Earl of Carnwath	*Duke of Montrose,*	*Doctor Wellwood*
	Mr Bailie of Gervase Wood,	*Mr Llewellin*
	Mr Mead Counsel	
	Mr Kettelbey Counsel	
Viscount Kenmure	*Duke of Montrose,*	*Doctor Wellwood*
	Mr Bailie of Gervase Wood,	*Mr Llewellin solicitor*
	Mr Mead Counsel	
	Mr Kettelbey Counsel	
Lord Nairn	*Duke of Montrose,*	*Doctor James Gray a Divine*
	Earl of Orford,	*Mr Llewellin solicitor*
	Sir Thomas Powys Counsel	
	Mr Mead Counsel	

"I say, Father, you will find this interesting," said Charles.

"What's that, my boy?" said James turning away from his conversation with the women.

"Do you remember when some years ago we made a twenty-mile coach ride from Ufton Manor to visit Hassop Hall near Bakewell?"

"Yes, I seem to recall the visit, to meet Thomas Eyre, if I recall,"

"That's correct, Father. Well, it seems that the Lords Derwentwater, Nithsdale and Widdrington have all chosen a Mr Henry Eyre of Gray's Inn, one of the three Inns of Court that can legally call counsel to the Bar, and Henry Eyre is the third son of Thomas Eyre from Hassop."

At that moment Samuel, having tired of the chatter of the women, returned to the conversation. "So, Charles, does the news sheet say how the Lords pleaded at their initial hearing?"

"All except Lord Wintoun pleaded guilty," said Charles.

"Isn't William Cowper related to Sir William Asshurst, who was a former Lord Mayor of London?" said James.

"That's correct," Samuel confirmed. "He married into the Asshurst family when in early July of 'eighty-six he wed William Asshurst's granddaughter Judith Booth. You remember old George Booth the merchant trader, don't you, James?"

"Now you mention it, I do recall the name. In fact, I remember my father said that when his father, Robert Cavendish, founded Cavendish House, he had many contacts at court and it was said that James the First had sold titles to merchants to raise money for the exchequer. Father said that he was acquainted with one of them named George Booth and also his son-in-law, Henry Brereton of Handforth in Cheshire, and he knew for a fact that they both bought a baronetcy."

"Well, Judith Booth, the daughter of wealthy George Booth, married Cowper at the church of Saint Nicholas Cole Abbey. I don't know if you can remember the church, it's not too far from here? It was the first one to be rebuilt by Sir Christopher Wren when the old one was destroyed in the great fire."

Constance had been listening and said, "James dearest, when you were telling us of your exploits in Preston and when that awful colonel made you and Charles dig those graves to help bury the dead, didn't you say that an officer demanded that you dig up one of the Jacobite bodies so he could identify it as Colonel Brereton?"

"You are so right, Constance," exclaimed James.

"And," Charles added, "Colonel Cotton wrote on his report that the dead colonel came from a Cheshire family."

"I wonder if the Jacobite sympathies within the Booth family secretly extend through to the Lord High Steward William Cowper," James said.

"That we will never know," said Samuel, "but the man certainly has a dark past."

Ann Clarke, Samuel's wife, had remained silent, but she now entered the conversation. "Don't you go spreading rumours, Samuel."

"I wasn't about to, dear, I was only repeating what is common knowledge in the coffee houses and may be news to our Derbyshire visitors," responded Samuel. "You see, Judith Cowper died about ten years ago but during their marriage he seduced a young woman named Elizabeth Culling and married her bigamously. Within months of Judith's death, William Cowper married another woman named Mary Clavering. He tried to keep that wedding secret because rumours started that his mistress, Elizabeth Culling, whom he had bigamously married, had born him two children during Judith's lifetime."

"Well, I hope all this dark side doesn't cloud his judgments, but if he has Jacobite sympathies he may be harsh in his sentencing just to absolve all connections to himself and family and surely there has been enough blood spilled already in the lost cause of the Stuarts," said James.

"I think my bed calls and to keep awake any longer is also a lost cause," said Charity.

Next morning, Samuel and James were discussing what to do with the day. Outside the snow glistened on the ground and sunlight sparkled on the icicles dangling from the neighbouring houses. At that moment Elizabeth and Constance joined their husbands at table.

"Where are Charles and Charity this morning?" James enquired.

"They are sleeping late; young Elizabeth has kept them awake for most of the night. I looked into their bedroom earlier and they were in a deep sleep," said Constance.

It was near the hour of noon when James and Charity came downstairs to join the family in the drawing room.

"It is such a lovely day," said Charity. "Can we go and see the Frost Fair? I believe it's like a small village out on the ice."

"I think we can take a look but perhaps young Elizabeth should stay here if Grandma Elizabeth will look after her," said James.

James summoned Ben. "Drive the coach up to the front door on the hour of two, Ben. We want you to take us into the city."

On the appointed hour, the Cavendish family mounted the coach and on instructions from James, Ben headed the coach and horses in the direction of Whitehall to drive across the bridge. As they were approaching the London Bridge, James pointed to the right and said, "That is Westminster Hall where the impeachment charges of the rebel leaders were read."

"I have never had the honour to be invited into Westminster," said James, "but I am told that it is like the inside of a church with family pews surrounded by wood partitions a few feet high. There are even stalls that sell books, spectacles, mathematical instruments, legal stationery, coffee and ale."

"Why are those men all standing outside the Hall?" said Constance.

163

"I believe they are the *Men of Straw*," answered James. "They are people offering to sell their service as witnesses."

Charles laughed. "Father, you jest, why would they be called men of straw and surely it's against God's law to bear false witness?"

"I jest not," countered James. "They place a straw in one of their shoes so that they can be identified."

The coach crossed London Bridge, slowly meandering through the crowds and on the way passing nearly two hundred shops that lined both sides of the bridge that made it look like a narrow street. To aid the illiterate, respective business owners had hung signs over their shops depicting their trades. Ben continued to drive the coach slowly as the dismal light filtered between shops and houses that spanned the street. Suddenly Charity exclaimed from inside the coach, "This is like driving through a tunnel."

"I notice there are no ale houses on the bridge," said Charles

"That's because ale and beer beverages require cellars, and that's not possible on a bridge over a river," said James, "but the merchants do live above their shops and sell their goods at street level."

Eventually the light grew stronger as the coach emerged on the south bank of the river.

"How amazing, just look at the frozen river with the fair against the backdrop of St Paul's Cathedral," said Charles.

James looked towards St Paul's, where a street of booths had been erected on the ice in front of the Temple stairs, and to their left, another street of booths ran parallel to London Bridge. The iced-up river had become a carnival, with drinking booths, and stalls selling toys, pots and pans and cutlery.

"Can we go down onto the ice?" said Charity. "I want to have a look at those people playing skittles."

For two hours the four wandered amongst the booths; Constance stopped at one where the shopkeeper was selling toys.

"I am buying this cup and ball toy for Elizabeth," she said, but Charles and James were not listening; they had wandered to a booth that had a gaming table.

"I think it is time we got our men and headed for home," said Constance.

Charity wasn't listening, she had just caught sight of her cousin Thomas and his wife Fiona; accompanying them was William who had been pageboy at both Fiona's and her wedding. Waving her hand in the air, Charity left her mother's side and occasionally slipping on the ice she made her way across the frozen river. "Hallo, Thomas," she said before embracing Fiona. "Isn't William growing tall?"

Looking at William she said," How old are you now, young man?"

"Eleven, ma'am."

At that moment James, Charles and Constance joined them and began exchanging family news.

Thomas took Charles to one side and said discretely, "Fiona is with child, she is not telling anyone yet because it is very early days but she is concerned that news of a new baby in the home may upset William. As you know Sarah, William's mother, died in childbirth and Fiona is worried that William will begin to panic when he knows Fiona's condition. Do you think that when you go back to Derbyshire you could take William for the year until Fiona's confinement is over?"

"Of course we will, Thomas."

"What are you men whispering about now?" enquired Charity.

"Men's talk, my dear, just men's talk," said Charles . . .

Trials and Tribulations

After the long trek from Preston, James Radclyffe, the Earl of Derwentwater, was escorted and lodged in the Devereux tower, one of the twenty towers in the Tower of London. On the ninth of January seventeen sixteen the prisoners were given three days to nominate the counsels for their defence and on Sunday the twelfth of January orders were again sent to the Lieutenant of the Tower to escort the Jacobite peers to The House for them to enter their pleas.

Countess Mary Cowper was attending the trials to witness her husband's triumph and his conduct at court. She intended writing a diary of the proceedings against the peers on the charges of high treason. Commoners Forster, John Clavering, William Shaftoe and Thomas Errington were also charged, the latter being of particular interest to the Countess as he was a relative. Eight others who had made the long pinioned trek from Lancashire were also impeached.

* * *

"The charges are that you did conspire against church and state and incite the people to raise rebellion in Northumberland, Durham, Cumberland and Lancashire. How do you plead?" Lord High Steward William Cowper asked the assembled peers.

Lord Wintoun remained silent but George Lesley his defending counsel said, "Your Lordship, the Earl is unfit to plead or stand trial due to his insanity. I am entering a plea of not guilty on his behalf."

"We have all heard of the madness of your client," Cowper said. "It is common knowledge in the counties that the Earl was considered completely mad when he ran away to join the gypsies, but I consider his feigned madness is but an excuse. However, your plea of not guilty is noted and the Earl is remanded to stand trial on the fifteenth of March."

The chamber of the House erupted in laughter as Wintoun was led away leaving the remaining prisoners to enter pleas of guilty.

"The court will rise," Lord High Steward William Cowper said. "The prisoners are to be held in custody until the nineteenth of January to give them time to prepare their mitigations for their defence."

* * *

Lord High Steward William Cowper sat at the head of the judicial bench; it was the nineteenth of January and before him stood arraigned William Lord Widdrington, James Earl of Derwentwater, William Earl of Nithsdale, Robert Earl of Carnworth, William Viscount Kenmure and William Lord Nairn.

Cowper said, "My Lords, be seated. To this impeachment you have all pleaded and acknowledged yourselves guilty of the high treason therein contained. In mitigation have you anything you wish to say?"

"We were never involved in plotting and only learned of the Jacobite plans when we were called upon to ride and join the rising," said James Radclyffe, Earl of Derwentwater.

"And what mitigation do you offer, Earl Widdrington?" said Cowper.

"The same as James Radclyffe, my Lord."

Lord Nairn and Earl Nithsdale offered similar pleas.

"And have you nothing to say, William Gordon, Lord of Kenmure and Earl Carnwath?

Neither peer offered any mitigation for their crimes.

"James Radclyffe, Earl of Derwentwater added a final plea. "My Lord Cowper, I ask you to consider my wife and children and I give you and the king a strong assurance of my future loyalty."

"Enough," shouted William Cowper, "I have listened to your protestations of ignorance about Jacobite plotting, and I am unmoved by them. Even if they were true, it only adds to your guilt, because you convinced your friends and neighbours to ride with you and everyone needs good friends and neighbours. Furthermore, at your own surrender you made a plea for His Majesty to show mercy, but to that plea you have shown no remorse to the rebellious act, therefore it is not proper for me to take notice of it in mitigation. Your Lordships will likewise do well to consider what an additional burden your treason has made it necessary to impose on the people of this kingdom, who wanted, and were about to enjoy some respite. To this end, 'tis well known, that an increase of taxes for the last year was carefully avoided, and His Majesty was contented to have no more armed forces than were sufficient to attend his person. He closed a few garrisons but what His Majesty did for his people, you ungratefully turned to your advantage by taking encouragement to endanger the kingdom's safety, and to bring oppression on your fellow subjects."

William Cowper paused and took a sip from a glass before continuing. "As to your Lordships who profess the religion of the Church of Rome was the temptation. Success on your part would forever have established Popery in this kingdom, and to that aim you probably could never again have so fair an opportunity, but how your Protestant rebels must be confused, for they rebelled without giving any thought of capitulation of their religion. It is my duty to exhort your Lordships thus to think of the aggravations, as well as the mitigations, if there be any, of your offences, but I would beg you not to rely any longer upon those pious and learned divines of the church of England, who have constantly borne that infallible mark of sincere Christians towards universal charity."

Before continuing with the sentencing William Cowper requested for the prisoners to stand.

"And now, my Lords, nothing remains but that I pronounce upon you; and sorry I am that it falls to my lot to pronounce the terrible sentence of the law, which must be the same that is given against the meanest offender for treason. The most ignominious and painful parts of it are usually remitted, by the grace of the crown, to persons of your quality; but the law, in this case, being deaf to all distinctions of persons, requires I should pronounce it, and accordingly it is adjudged by this court, that you, James Earl of Derwentwater, William Lord Widdrington, William Earl of Nithsdale, Robert Earl of Carnwarth, William Viscount Kenmure, and William Lord Nairn, be returned to the prison of the Tower, from whence you came; from thence you must be drawn to the place of execution; when you come there, you must be hanged by the neck, but not till you be dead; you must be cut down alive; then your bowels must be removed and burnt before your eyes; your heads severed from your bodies, and your bodies divided into four quarters; and these must be at the king's disposal and God Almighty have mercy to your souls."

The rebel Peers were remanded into custody at the Tower to await their fates . . .

* * *

When the news came of the defeat of the Jacobites at Preston and the long trek the rebels had made to London, Lady Winifred, Countess of Nithsdale realized at once that her husband could expect no mercy, and that his execution would follow his imprisonment. At the age of twenty-six, she was an attractive young woman with reddish hair and pale blue eyes, and was determined to be at her Lord's side. Lady Winifred first burnt all incriminating papers linking the family to the Jacobites then accompanied by her maid Grace Evans and two armed grooms she rode in the Niths-dales' coach to Newcastle. At Newcastle the party took the stage down to York, but due to the depth of the January snow on the countryside, the stage could not depart for London.

Lady Nithsdale was now desperate. "Evans, I shall take horses and ride from here, I will have the two grooms with me for safety but you may stay here in York."

"My Lady," Grace replied, "I am given to serve you and his Lordship and I shall ride with you."

So began the long hard ride though the snow, which, on long stretches was above the horses' girths.

The four travellers arrived safely in London on the six-teenth of February and Lady Nithsdale on the recommen-dations of her maid, Grace Evans, sought out a lady named Mrs Morgan who was the mistress of Lord Dorset and Mas-ter of the king's bedchamber. Mrs Morgan quickly arranged lodgings for Evans and the grooms.

"You are so kind, Mrs Morgan," said Lady Nithsdale. "Now all that remains is for me to find suitable lodgings."

Mrs Morgan thought for a moment than said, "My Lady, I can recommend a very discreet and good friend who will help you in all your needs. The woman is named Mrs Mills; she is pregnant but with her husband away, she will be pleased to have your company."

* * *

A hackney coach driver drove Lady Nithsdale to the home of Mrs Mills on Drury Lane. The driver climbed down from his seat and knocked on the door, which was opened by a tall red-headed woman.

"Mrs Mills?" the coachman enquired. The woman nod-ded. "I have Lady Nithsdale, my passenger for you." And the coachman turned, opened the coach door and Lady

Nithsdale stepped down from the coach; immediately noticing the woman's swollen stomach that gave her a similar girth to Lord Nithsdale.

"Mrs Morgan recommended you to give me lodgings for my short stay in London."

"Welcome, my Lady, and I hope you find my house comfortable."

Lady Nithsdale paid the coachman and entered the safe house.

* * *

Next day Lady Nithsdale began to canvass persons at court for support to petition for the pardoning of her husband but she found very little to give her hope of a reprieve.

Later that morning she spoke to the Countess of Derwentwater. "Countess, I know that some of the Lords pleaded guilty and some may be pardoned but it is said that neither yours nor mine will be of that number. Do you know of any reason why they are excluded?"

The Countess replied, "It is rumoured my Lady, because my husband was one of the leading insurrectionists and actually fought at the barricades in Preston but the reason for your husband's fate is different. Your husband has estates on the borders of Scotland that have always been a problem to the English, and because his family proclaims strong Roman Catholic links that have always pledged themselves to the House of Stuart, His Majesty is persuaded by parliament to show no clemency to such a prominent Scottish peer; they are determined not to let him escape, Lady Nithsdale, I fear your Lord will suffer the same extreme penalty as mine."

* * *

Lady Nithsdale took a coach to Tower Hamlets and sought out the residence of the Lieutenant of the Tower.

171

"Sir," she said, "I seek permission to visit my husband whenever I wish. May I have that permission?"

"I am sorry, my Lady, but my orders are that prisoners can have family members reside with them in the Tower but not to visit. You may see and converse freely with Lord Nithsdale if you agree to reside in the Tower with him," said the Lieutenant.

"I cannot undertake to stay confined in such damp conditions," said Lady Nithsdale. "My health will not permit me to undergo the confinement."

"Then I am sorry," said the Lieutenant. "Then I am afraid, permission is denied."

"I bid you good day, sir." She left and boarded the coach but before driving back to her lodgings in Drury Lane, she sought out and made contact with a guard at the Tower, a man who could be bribed to smuggle forbidden items into the prisoners.

Lady Nithsdale approached the guard and held a whispered conversation with him before instructing her coachman to drive her back to Mrs Mills' lodgings. Two days later; after several bribes, Lady Nithsdale eventually gained access to her husband's chamber.

She now had one idea in her head: to obtain her husband's freedom by any method possible.

* * *

Lord Nithsdale embraced his wife for a few moments before saying, "My dear courageous Winifred, how it cheers my heart in this place and in these circumstances to have you at my side for just a few moments."

"William my love," she replied, "I intend to get you out of here."

She then looked round the room; the first thing she noticed was one barred window, which was high and looked out onto the ramparts and Water Lane. Strolling over to see the view from the barred window she saw that there was no chance of an escape that way. Even if the bars could be removed a guard was posted on the ramparts. If her husband was to escape he must exit via the door and passageway and that was strongly guarded by two sentries with fixed bayonets and a halberdier stood outside the door. The stairs and the outer door were also well guarded. She now realized her Lord would have to escape by her planned ingenuity. In Winifred's head was forming the foundation for an escape plan but that plan necessitated the help of her maid.

On her next visit, the guard opened the door and let Lady Nithsdale and her maid Grace Evans pass into the prisoner's room.

After Winifred embraced her husband she said, "William, I intend to get you out of here, and I have a plan."

For ten minutes she spoke quietly outlining the plan but Lord Nithsdale's response was not what she expected, "You intend to paint out my thick black eyebrows and tint them a sandy colour to match the colour of Mrs Mills your friend. Then you want to shave my chin and rouge my cheeks and dress me as a woman and you expect me to walk out of here in disguise? It's madness, how do you expect a soldier with a rugged face and a martial stride to pose as a woman? Give me a sword in my hand and I might do something but dressed as a painted lady, I would be a laughing stock. No, dear Winifred, I know you mean well but my best hope is for you to place a petition for clemency in the hand of the king; at least there might be some hope in that. Now that is the end of the matter."

With pretence Lady Nithsdale agreed, although she knew full well that King George had given strict orders that no petition from Lord Nithsdale should be received and she knew that none of her friends at court were willing to disobey the king and act as intermediary.

* * *

On the 18th of February Hatton Compton the Lieutenant of the Tower received orders for the executions to take place in six days, time enough for Lady Nithsdale to engineer a daring plot to aid her husband's escape.

The King's Bedchamber

Charles Lennox, the illegitimate son of Charles II and now titled Duke of Richmond, was in the king's bedchamber at St James Palace and was waiting on George I whilst the king ate in private. Charles Lennox had already aided His Majesty to robe while other gentlemen of the bedchamber guarded the doors. Although King George was Germanic, Charles addressed him in French, the language of European courts.

"Your Majesty, there are several petitioners craving an audience, namely the Countess of Derwentwater, together with several of her family and influential friends who crave your clemency for the Lords Derwentwater, Kenmure, Nithsdale, Widdrington, Carnwath, and Nairn, who are under sentence of death for treason but plead for your Majesty's pardon. Will you grant them an audience?"

"I suppose we must appear to be merciful and listen to their pleas," the king replied, "and I pray I will not be subjected to the tearful pleas and near assault on my person that I was subjected to yesterday by Lady Nithsdale; I endeavoured to escape out of her clutches, but she kept such a strong hold that I dragged her from the centre of the drawing room to the door. At last, one of the guards who attended me grasped her around the waist, whilst another wrested my coat out of her hands. It was awful and so pointless. The petition, which she had endeavoured to thrust into my pocket, fell down onto the floor. A gentleman-in-waiting picked it up and gave it to Lord Dorset the Lord of the Bedchamber. I was out of the bedchamber and safe from that wretched woman but she wrote a note to Dorset entreating him to approach me on her behalf to read the petition."

"How awful for your Majesty," said Charles Lennox, then in an attempt to change the subject Lennox said, "I understand my Lord Dorset has a new mistress, a Mrs Morgan, I hear?"

"Apparently so," the king replied, "and a very charming lady she is; however, I fear that neither her charms nor those of the Countess of Derwentwater will prevail, for I have also seen petitions that were brought before both Houses. One motion in the House questioned whether I have the power in cases of impeachment to actually grant a reprieve. Apparently I do and the House sent me an address desiring me to reprieve such of the condemned Lords as deserve my mercy with the time of the respite for the executions left to my discretion. To that address I replied that on this and other occasions, I would do what I think most consistent with the dignity of the crown, and the safety of my people."

"A very diplomatic response, sire," the Duke of Richmond replied as he backed away to summon the Countess to enter the bedchamber.

The Countess accompanied by her family entered, and curtseyed before the king. Speaking in French, she begged His Majesty for clemency for the condemned peers.

Hugh Walpole, who had entered with the Countess and was the king's first minister in parliament, reminded him of the offer of sixty thousand pounds that the King had already received to show clemency to the Earl of Derwentwater.

"Countess," the king said, "I have earlier today been merciful and granted clemency to Lords Widdrington, Carnwath, and Nairn but I remain unmoved on the Lord Nithsdale, the Earl of Derwentwater and Viscount Kenmure. I offered clemency to your husband on condition that he renounce his faith and conform to the established Protestant faith of England but I am afraid your husband has declined the offer on the grounds of his honour and conscience. Forgetting and irrespective of religious matters, your Lords Nithsdale,

Derwentwater and Kenmure were the principal leaders in Northumberland and the Borders; they were the most influential of the rebels and therefore they must pay the supreme penalty of the law. I have been most merciful, Countess, and they will only face the axe on Tower Hill. I am sorry but the severity of the sentences will stand. Not even bribes will sway me."

The King signalled the audience was over. It was Saturday the twenty-second of February.

* * *

Lord Nithsdale's counsel had failed to present any petition to His Majesty for clemency and Winifred knew her husband's life and fate now lay in her hands. Taking a coach she drove to the Tower and with a pretence of joy and excitement she told the guards and keepers and those wives of the guards who were in the council chamber that her husband's last petition to the House of Lords had been received favourably and His Majesty was about to grant clemency.

"Congratulations, Countess, we hope that all goes well for your husband," commented a guard as well-wishers gathered around to congratulate her. Giving a cheerful wave, she hastily took her leave and climbed the stairs to William's room, where she told him the truth.

"My dearest William, the time has come to face reality. Tomorrow is Sunday and King George must answer the petition I forced on him. I am informed that it will be refused, and it is certain that you, together with Derwentwater and Kenmure, will go to the scaffold on Monday morning. Now listen carefully; this is my plan."

For two hours Lord Nithsdale and his wife discussed the details and although he had little hope of its success, he acknowledged that it was probably his last hope.

Sunday Escapades

At the Clarke home, Samuel was conveying the latest new to James and Charles. "It is Sunday and I have just heard that the king has pardoned Lords Widdrington, Carnwath, and Nairn but tomorrow, Derwentwater, Nithsdale and Viscount Kenmure go to the block on Tower Hill."

"Can you get us seats to witness the event?" said James. "I have been told that for such public spectacles of prominent persons they erect stands and I would imagine that there will be hundreds of witnesses tomorrow."

"Well, I do have a merchant friend who has a house in George Yard and I could write him a request that he grants us the privilege to enter his home to witness the event from his upstairs room. I will send a runner to his home. Would Charity and Constance wish to attend, Charles?"

"What do you think, Samuel? You know your daughter better than I."

"We can ask the ladies later today," replied Samuel.

* * *

At the Tower, the guards were expecting the families and friends of the condemned men to pay final visits and say their farewells but on Sunday morning at the home of Mrs Mills on Drury Lane, Lady Nithsdale was going over her plans again and discussing them with her landlady and Grace Evans. At about two in the afternoon, Mrs Morgan joined the plotters to go over the final details.

"All three of us will drive in a coach to the Tower with Evans, my maid. You, Mrs Morgan, will be introduced to the guards as a friend, and I shall call you Mrs Catherine," said Lady Nithsdale. "Mrs Mills, you will be introduced as Mrs Betty, another friend. Now, Mrs Morgan, as you are slim the plan is for you to wear an additional skirt and your own hooded cloak plus the one belonging to Mrs Mills. When we get into my husband's room, you are to take off the extra clothes and then leave and go home. Everything depends upon you being able to slip away quietly, is that clear?" said the Countess.

Mrs Morgan nodded. "Now, Mrs Mills," said Winifred, "I want you to sit in the coach with Evans while Mrs Morgan and I go in for the first visit. When you see Mrs Morgan come out of the Tower I want you to come in as Mrs Betty, wearing that hooded cloak, which will fit Lord Nithsdale." The Countess pointed to a large hooded cape on the table. "When you come up the stairs to my Lord's room, I want you to pretend to be weeping bitterly and holding a hand-kerchief to your face."

Then addressing all of her companions Winifred said, "The important part of the plan is to confuse the guards as to who has entered and gone out and bearing that in mind my dear friends, it is almost four and time for us to take the coach to the Tower.

* * *

As soon as they were all seated in the coach, Lady Niths-dale began a constant stream of chatter to allay the fears of her companions so that they had no time to reflect on the danger and magnitude of the task that lay before them. "La-dies," she said, "each of you has extra garments and I have a spare wig in my bag. As I can only take one visitor in at a time, when the coach stops, you, Mrs Morgan, will accom-pany me on the first entry."

The coach finally came to a halt near the Lieutenant's door to the Tower and Lady Nithsdale and Mrs Morgan alighted and were met with blasts of chilling cold air blowing in from the frozen river. Inside the coach, Mrs Mills and Grace Evans huddled together for warmth.

Entering the gate at the Middle Tower, the first pair of plotters walked over the bridge to the Byward Tower. The guards on duty knew the Countess well but she introduced her friend Mrs Morgan by her alias as Mrs Catherine. The first stage of the plot was going to plan as the guards let them pass unhindered at both gates.

"Come this way, my Lady," the guard said as he escorted her and Mrs Catherine up the stairs to the room where William Maxwell, Lord Nithsdale was held prisoner. On the way they passed a council chamber where several curious women had come to observe Lady Nithsdale as she passed through for they had a suspicion that tonight was the last occasion on which the Countess would see her husband alive. The presence of these women, who were all talking together, lifted the heart of Winifred, for she realized it would help to confuse the guards even more.

The escort opened the door to Lord Nithsdale's room and let the two women enter then closing the door he left the family in peace.

"William, we have gone over the plan," said Winifred, "and I know you are still reluctant to involve us and you think there is no chance of success, but if we fail the authorities will not harm us ladies and you will be in no worse a situation. If our plan succeeds, you will be safe in France tomorrow. Now we shall wait for a short time while Mrs Morgan takes off the extra garments and her own hooded cloak."

After fifteen minutes Lady Nithsdale accompanied Mrs Catherine to the top of staircase and Mrs Catherine descended. Winifred cried, "Send my maid to me at once. I must be dressed without delay or I shall be too late for my petition to go to the king."

Mrs Morgan, alias Mrs Catherine, swiftly departed wearing the hooded cloak of Mrs Mills.

Seeing her depart, the pregnant Mrs Mills, her girth enlarged further with the extra skirt, stepped out of the coach.

Lady Nithsdale came down the stairs and introduced the grief-stricken and sobbing woman as Mrs Betty. Taking her by the hand she led her up the stairs and into Lord Nithsdale's room.

"This is like a comedy," said William. "You have me totally confused as to the comings and goings."

"That is the plan," said Winifred. "Now, Mrs Betty, or should I call you Mrs Mills, remove that extra skirt and bodice." Mrs Mills quickly dried her tears and discarded the extra clothing then donning the cloak that Mrs Morgan had left behind, a slimmer and diminished figure vacated the room dressed as Mrs Morgan alias Mrs Catherine.

"Farewell, my dear Mrs Catherine," the Countess cried after her. "Don't forget to send my maid. She is so late but cannot have forgotten that I am to visit the king tonight to present my petition."

From the council chamber the gathering of noisy women watched Mrs Catherine depart. At the exit, the sentry opened the door; the blast of cold air caused her to gather her cloak around her and as he let her pass, Mrs Mills, who had entered as a grief stricken Mrs Betty, exited as Mrs Catherine with her head held high and walking with a spring in her step.

In Lord Nithsdale's chamber Winifred sat with her husband; the whole plot now depended on the guards thinking that Mrs Betty was still in the room with them.

They waited . . .

* * *

Winifred removed three of her four petticoats and tied them round William's waist. "Now step into this skirt," she said. "Be quick, it is almost dark and time is of the essence, any moment lamps will be brought into the room and even a single candle will betray us. I fear there is no time for you to shave." Her instructions became staccato, "faster," she said, "We have not much time, wrap this muffler round your chin." she paused for breath, "I will apply this rouge to your cheeks then put the wig on and the hooded cape."

Two minutes later, Lady Nithsdale cautiously opened the door and led William by the hand. In his other hand he clutched a handkerchief to his eyes. "For the love of God," she cried, her voice impatient with anxiety, "go to my lodgings, Mrs Betty, make haste and find my maid, bring her with you and if ever you hurried in your life, hurry now. You know I am driven to despair with this delay."

The light from the windows was failing and it was growing dark on the passageway as the Countess slipped behind her husband. Anyone peering after them in the gloom would not see his gait which was unlike that of a woman. The unsuspicious guards let them pass; one of them even opened a door for them. "Make haste, make haste," the Countess cried once more and then, almost before she realized it, they had passed through the last door and past the last guard. They were outside the lieutenant's door; Grace Evans was waiting and William was safe in her custody.

Taking a firm hold of the arm of the disguised Lord Nithsdale, alias Mrs Betty, Grace said, "Come, Mrs Betty, we must hurry to Drury Lane." And the couple entered the coach leaving Lady Nithsdale alone outside the Tower.

The Countess's heart was racing with the adrenalin now coursing through her body; taking a few deep breaths she calmed herself before re-entering the Tower. Assuming an appearance of distress she rushed back to her husband's room and slammed the door shut dreading some keeper should enter the room and find him gone.

For some minutes she stomped about with the step of a heavy man whilst indulging in an imaginary conversation. Occasionally she interspersed her own voice with imitating gruff replies. Finally she was ready for the final stage of her plan and she calmly walked to the door, raised the latch and standing in the doorway so that all in the crowded council chamber could hear her, she addressed her Lord's empty room. "Sleep well, my dearest, I must flee now as something must have delayed Evans. I fear I must find her myself but have heart; know that you are all I live for and I will see the king tonight and I will get you a reprieve. If the Tower is still open I will return tonight but failing that I will be with you early in the morn with good news."

Winifred drew the latch string through the hole into the room so the heavy studded door could only be opened from inside. Then she closed it firmly and walked away. As she passed a servant in the passageway, she said, "I pray you, do not disturb my Lord for he is at his prayers. Do not take him candles till he calls for them." Lady Nithsdale calmly walked across the council chamber to an exit door were the unsuspecting guard opened it for her, saluted and bade her goodnight.

Winifred hurried along the passageways, guards courteously opened doors for her until finally she was once more outside the Tower.

Approaching the row of hackney coaches waiting on the stand she summoned a coach. "Take me to Drury Lane," she said. "I have to meet somebody so drive to the theatre and I will wait."

Winifred had arranged for a certain Mr McKenzie to carry the petition to the king in case the escape plot failed. After paying and discharging the coachman outside the theatre, the Countess walked to her lodgings.

"Mr McKenzie, thank you for waiting but we have no need to present a petition, as my Lord is now safe and out of the Tower."

"I am so pleased, Countess. Is there anything else I can do?" McKenzie said.

"You could send for a sedan chair for me. I discharged the coach at the theatre so it could not be traced to this address."

Mr McKenzie stepped out into Drury Lane and quickly found two carriers and a sedan chair. Taking them back to Mrs Mills' house, he bade the Countess farewell and good-night and left.

With a cool head, Lady Nithsdale had final tasks to do to tidy up the loose ends of the plot. First she was carried in the sedan chair to the home of the Duchess of Buccleuch who had promised to petition the king if the escape plot failed.

The sedan halted and Lady Nithsdale discharged the two carriers, then braving the cold winter air once more and drawing her skirts around her legs she mounted the steps to the front door and rapped on the knocker.

The door was eventually opened by a footman. "The Duchess is expecting me," said the Countess. "I am not in any condition to see her in any company and I beg you to show me into a chamber below stairs and then please send her Grace's maid to me as I have an urgent message for the Duchess."

The footman bowed and retired. Almost immediately the maid presented herself and said, "The Duchess has company with her."

"I understand and that was my reason for not coming up-stairs," replied Lady Nithsdale. "Will you convey my sincer-est thanks for her kind offer to accompany me later tonight to present my petition? To spare her any further trouble, I have been advised it is more advantageous to present one general petition in the name of all the condemned prisoners. Please inform her Grace that I will not forget my obligation to her for her kindness."

The Countess exited the downstairs chamber and re-quested the footman to send for a sedan chair.

"Take me to the home of the Duchess of Montrose," she said to the leading carrier.

When the Duchess heard Winifred's news she said, "I ad-vise you to go into hiding. When I was at court today His

Majesty was still highly displeased and still enraged at your assault on his person when you tried to present the petition yourself. Lord knows how the news of your husband's escape will affect him but I will go to court immediately to see how the news is received and I shall keep you informed."

Lady Nithsdale sent for another chair as she had discharged the previous carriers for fear of pursuit and set off to go to the address of the safe house that Grace Evans had found for her and Lord Nithsdale.

* * *

Dawn was breaking; the ground was still white from the night's hoar frost. It was Monday morning, the day set for the executions, when Mr Mills arrived by coach at the safe house. Lord Nithsdale had changed out of the disguise and into men's clothes and he and the Countess now boarded the coach with Mr Mills who escorted them to the Venetian Ambassador's residence.

"Does his Excellency know of the plot?" said Lord Nithsdale.

"Certainly not," replied Winifred. "The fewer that know the safer it is. Only Mr Michel the Ambassador's servant knows. He has promised to shelter us in his room till Wednesday when the Ambassador's coach and six go down to Dover to meet his brother. Mr Michel has a servant's livery to fit you. I will travel in the coach with both of you."

For three days Winifred and her husband hid in the Ambassador's residence. Mr Michel secreted them in an unused attic room and supplied them with food and drink. Rising before dawn on the Wednesday the fugitives crept down to the waiting coach in the courtyard and with Mr Michel for company they started out on the final part of the escape

Two hours later the Ambassador's coach halted on the quayside at Dover and Mr Michel left the coach for a few minutes. When he returned he said, "Senor, I have hired a small boat to take you and your lady to Calais. The captain will set sail immediately."

Mr Michel helped the Countess step down from the coach.

"Our everlasting thanks Mr Michel, we shall never forget you." said Lord Nithsdale

"Farewell, I am pleased to have been of assistance," said Mr Michel and escorted by her husband disguised as a servant Winifred boarded the vessel and the captain cast off.

Mr Michel in his servant's livery stood waving on the quay . . .

* * *

The fugitive peer leaned on the deck rail breathing in the air of freedom. The passage seemed remarkably short with the wind perfect for a fast crossing and with the French coast in sight the captain said, "The wind was perfect; it could not have served you better if you had been fleeing for your lives."

The Countess giggled and squeezed her husband's hand. "Many a fine word is spoken in jest," she whispered.

* * *

It was first light on the dawn of the executions; at St. James Palace the king flew into a passionate rage when he heard the news of Lord Nithsdale's escape.

"I have been betrayed, this escape could not have been done without complicity from within," the monarch roared. "Dispatch two of my Earls to the Tower immediately to make sure that the other prisoners are well secured. I will not have them attempting to escape and cheat the block."

"Yes, sire," replied Charles Lennox, the Duke of Richmond and a gentleman of the bedchamber. Lennox hurried away to issue the necessary instructions to the captain of the guard. On his return the wrath of the king had subdued and in a calmer manner he instructed the Duke to draft a reprieve granting clemency for Lord Nithsdale.

"I know the man has escaped but we cannot let my subjects think that I was going to let him go to the block. A show of clemency may stop my subjects from making heroes of Nithsdale and his damned wife," said the king.

Inside the court, however, furore raged as accusations of complicity were bandied about, but the Duchess of Montrose kept her counsel, for she alone knew the truth.

In the city, faithful Grace Evans quietly disappeared and made her own way to France, then on to Rome to join Lord and Lady Nithsdale in service.

Tower Hill

Monday morning the twenty-fourth of February seventeen sixteen had yet to dawn, it was still dark, icicles hung from the trees and the ground was covered in the night's hoar frost. In the Clarke house on Bunhill Row, Samuel and Ann had risen early. James had arranged for Ben to have the coach at the door on the hour of seven in preparation for the two-mile drive to Tower Hill.

As the coach was nearing its destination Charles pointed to Charity and Constance and said, "Look, we are just passing Seething Lane, where our family benefactor the inimitable Samuel Pepys lived. Apparently next door to his house is the Navy Office where he worked."

"That's correct' said James, "I remember him telling me that he lived there when the Fire of London broke out and he said that he put his head out of his window as the church bells began sounding an alarm but then went back to sleep again. Apparently at about two in the morning, his wife woke him again to inform him of new cries of fire coming from Barking Church at the bottom of Seething Lane, so he dressed and grasping his block of Parmesan cheese as it was so valuable, he ran into the garden and buried it."

The coach trundled on for a few more minutes and then drew to a halt at the south-west corner of Tower Hill where a disguised Sir Walter Raleigh had taken a boat for Tilbury after his escape from the Tower in sixteen eighteen. Already crowds were gathering and people were taking their seats in the temporary stands.

"Ben, stay with the coach on the river embankment. When the executions are over, we will walk down the hill and find you," said James. "Now, Samuel, lead us to your friend's house."

Samuel had hold of Ann's arm as he guided her through the crowds, followed by Charles and Charity and James and Constance. Meanwhile baby Elizabeth slept soundly in the Clarkes' home in the care of the housekeeper.

It was towards the hour of nine; the sun was glistening on the ice as three troops of the lifeguards led by their colonel, rode from Whitehall to Tower Hill and took up their stations around the scaffold.

Inside the Tower two of the Jacobite peers made their farewells to family and friends, then on the hour of ten the Lieutenant of the Tower said, "My Lords, it is time to escort you to the Hill."

Amidst tears from their wives the two Peers left the Tower for the last time.

"Is Lord Nithsdale not joining us?" enquired James Radclyffe.

"I am pleased to say that this morning the king granted him a clemency," said the Lieutenant.

"God is merciful," James replied.

Unknown to them and what the Lieutenant of the Tower failed to say was that during the night Lord Nithsdale, aided by his wife and her maid, had escaped from the tower, unaware that a reprieve had been partially granted.

From the window of the merchant's house, the Cavendish and Clarke family watched the procession as the two condemned men slowly walked under escort up towards the scaffold where they were received by the sheriffs at the bar who conducted them into the privacy of a small room so they could prepare for their ordeal. At the expiration of about an hour, the Earl of Derwentwater sent word that he was ready.

* * *

From their window Charles said to Constance, "Something is happening now. The door to that house where they took the prisoners is opening."

Charity and Constance stood on tiptoe to get a better view.

* * *

From the privacy of the room James Radclyffe, Earl of Derwentwater stepped forth led by Sir John Fryer the sheriff. "I shall walk with you, sir," said Sir John.

The condemned Earl and his escort climbed the steps of the wooden scaffold, the floor of which was covered in sawdust. The earl noticed that the block had been partially covered with red baize.

The sheriff said, "Sir, you may have what time it so pleases you to prepare yourself."

"Thank you, Sir John. I have written a speech that I desire to read."

Sir John, the sheriff in charge of the execution, gave his permission and the Earl began to speak in an unfaltering voice, "My Lords and Ladies and friends that are here gathered today to witness my demise, I say to you that I now regret that I pleaded guilty at my trial for I acknowledge no King but James the Third, for whom I have an inviolable affection. In my heart I know that these kingdoms will never be happy and settled until the ancient constitution is restored, and I hope that my death will contribute to that desirable end. I now die a Roman Catholic, but if that prince who now governs this country had granted clemency in my faith, I would never more have taken up arms against him."

Sir John Fryer took the paper from the Earl. "I will have copies made and send them to your friends."

"Thank you, now I wish to read some prayers." The Earl produced two small books and lowered his head to pray in silence. The Earl raised his head, and handed the books to Sir John then kneeling he tested the block to see how it would fit his neck and found a rough place which hurt his chin. The earl raised his head and quietly asked the headsman to chip off the projection with his axe before he knelt down to receive the final blow. The executioner obliged and now satisfied James Radclyffe stood up and told the executioner that he forgave him, and likewise he forgave all his enemies. Finally the Earl of Derwentwater knelt down and placing his head on the block directed the executioner to strike when he repeated the words "Sweet Jesus" for the third time.

James Radclyffe then said, "Sweet Jesus, receive my spirit. Sweet Jesus be merciful to me; Sweet Jesus . . ."

The axe fell, striking the head off at one blow. The executioner exhibited it at the four corners of the scaffold and shouted, "Behold the head of a traitor. God save King George."

From a prominent witness stand the three circuit judges from Liverpool, Mr Baron Burry, Mr Justice Eyre, and Mr Baron Montague sat in judgement and watched in silence.

* * *

"What a gruesome spectacle," said Charles as he tried to release himself from Charity's clutching grasp on his arm.

"How brave of the Earl to speak like that," said Ann.

James and Constance stood in silence, both shocked at what they had witnessed.

"Look," said Samuel to James, "they are wrapping the Earl's headless body in black baize and carrying it to a coach."

"I presume it will be delivered to his family for burial," replied James.

Charity, who had now regained her composure, again looked out of the window. "Oh, see, Charles," she said, "how thoughtful, they have put fresh baize on the block, and they have strewed clean sawdust all over the scaffold so that Lord Kenmure will not see the blood of his friend."

At that moment the house door of the privacy room behind the scaffold opened and Lord Kenmure attended by

191

two Protestant clergymen and a surgeon mounted the steps onto the scaffold.

Sir John Fryer again led the procession. "Do you wish to say a few word to the assembly?" he asked the Viscount.

"No, thank you, sir, I come here to die, not to make speeches, but I will take a few moments in contemplation and prayer."

Lord Kenmure, having finished his devotions, said to the executioner, "I forgive you for what you have to do, please accept this gift of eight guineas to make a swift cut."

Lord Kenmure then knelt and laid his head on the block. His surgeon who was in attendance drew his finger over the part of the neck where the blow was to be struck and stepped back. The axe fell.

Viscount Kenmure's head joined that of James Radclyffe in the basket on the scaffold.

* * *

At the ancestral home in Scotland Lady Kenmure wept, reminiscing of the day three months previously when she had whispered, "Now ride, never look back."

He never looked back, he never came back . . .

* * *

The executions over, Samuel thanked his friend for allowing them to have access to his upper rooms for viewing the dispatch of the rebel peers.

"Oh, that's all right," said the man. "Living in George Yard on Tower Hill; it becomes a common occurrence on execution days."

Samuel and James escorted their families down Tower Hill to the embankment, where the coach waited to drive them home to Bunhill Row.

The women were in sombre and silent mood, a mood that was carried into the Clarke house. The following day the women were still in shock after witnessing the beheading of two young men. Charles took his father to one side and said, "We only came to London for the Christmas festivities, we have left Annabel with the Haltons' at Wingfield Hall and it is now the end of February. I realize the roads will be bad with snow but I think it is time we went home."

"I tend to agree," said James. "I shall inform Samuel we shall pack and leave by the end of the week."

"There is something I must tell you; we will have an additional passenger travelling back to Ufton Manor," said Charles. "I told Charity about it last night and she has no objection."

"And who is this additional passenger?" James asked.

"It's young William Clarke, the pageboy at our wedding six years ago. You met him when we talked with Thomas and Fiona at the Frost Fair three weeks ago. The problem is that Fiona is with child and Thomas fears that it may upset William because he lost his mother at his birth, so Thomas asked if we would take William to the country until the confinement was over. Naturally I said yes."

"Of course it's all right," said James. "The boy is most welcome; what harm can an extra mouth do? And he is family, though not a blood relative."

It was a decision that would eventually bring down the House of Cavendish and result in the ruin of Ufton Manor . . .

Samuel was informed that they would leave on Friday. "I will tell Thomas and Fiona to bring young William round here on Thursday so he can sleep over," said Samuel.

Exodus from London

James and Charles made sure that Ben had packed all the baggage safely on the rear of the coach. Samuel and Ann Clarke said their tearful farewells to their granddaughter Elizabeth.

William, who had slept overnight, watched apprehensively as the family said their farewells. With a look of consternation, Ann took hold of his hand and said, "This is a big adventure for you, William. Not many young men of eleven get the chance to go and live in a big manor house; you must take care of young Elizabeth, because she is only three and needs a big strong young man like you to look after her on the journey. Will you do that for Aunty Ann?"

William nodded and gave his aunt a hug then he turned and held out his hand to Samuel. "Goodbye, sir, thank you for letting me stay here last night and I will write letters to you and also to Father and Fiona."

Charity gave Ann a final embrace and said, "It will be a long cold drive home, Mother, but at least the family warehouse keeps us well supplied with quality furs to keep us warm in the coach, and Ben is well provided up on top."

Finally, with the farewells over, the Cavendish family departed with an addition member, young William Clarke, the stepson of the pregnant Fiona Clarke. On the steps of the Clarke residence Anne and Samuel waved as the coach slowly gathered momentum on its three-day journey back to Ufton Manor . . .

* * *

Mrs McQuire had large fires blazing in all the rooms as her ageing husband Ben drove the coach into the cobbled yard at the manor. Excitedly, Vivien ran out into the court-yard and as Ben climbed down from the coach she embraced him almost before he had time to stretch his weary stiff legs. He placed steps at the coach door and in her eagerness Vivien opened it to allow James and Charles to step down into the yard.

"Welcome home," said Vivienne as Charity handed young Elizabeth down into her arms. Finally James assisted Constance and young William to descend and Ben closed the coach door.

"Leave the baggage till morning," said James. "Just stable the horses, Ben, then go into the house and get warm."

"Yes, sir." Ben walked the pair of stallions across the yard and backed the coach into the carriage room. Unhitching the horses, he led the pair into their stalls and covered them with woollen blankets. Then making sure the horses had water and hay at hand he slapped them both on their flanks; gave their muzzles a pat and whispered, "Good lads," before closing the stable doors and returning to the servants' quarters and to Vivien; who had arranged for the cook to prepare hot meals for them all; after which she expected the travellers to all retire for an early night so that she could catch up on all the London news from her husband.

* * *

James and Charles were the first to rise next day. An early March copy of the *London Gazette* lay on the table in the hall. James picked it up and he strolled into the breakfast room commenting, "We must send Ben over to Wingfield Hall to bring Annabel home."

Sitting down he began to scan the paper.

As Charles also sat down, he said, "Not necessary Father, Mrs Mcquire informed us this morning, Annabel returned home three weeks ago. Apparently David used the Halton coach to bring her home and Vivien has been looking after her needs."

"We shall hear all about it when Annabel graces us with her presence. I expect she is still in bed, is she, Charles?" James didn't expect an answer and continued to read the *Gazette*. "I see they still haven't recaptured Lord Nithsdale," he said eventually. "There is a large reward offered but I doubt if he is in England now, I expect he made it on a boat to the continent. All the city is still talking about the bravery of Lady Nithsdale. It says that the other rebel peer George Seton, Earl of Wintoun who pleaded not guilty at the trials in January and who was remanded, is now going to be brought to his trial before the House of Lords on the fifteenth of March."

"That will end in another bloody day on Tower Hill," remarked Charles.

* * *

On the appointed day, Earl Wintoun remained silent as George Lesley his defending counsel repeated his previous plea that his Lordship, the Earl was still unfit to plead or stand trial due to his insanity and furthermore he had witnesses in his favour who were delayed by the inclement weather and the impassability of the roads from Scotland, therefore his counsel re-confirmed the plea of not guilty on his behalf.

"Enough of this talk of insanity," cried the Earl. "I dismiss my counsel and I shall defend myself to the best of my ability considering my enfeebled mind."

The House of Lords erupted in laughter.

"My Lords, I say this to you in my defence: I object to the article of my indictment for when I surrendered my person at Preston it was in consequence of a promise from General Wills to grant me my life."

The High Steward, Lord Cowper, replied, "We have it on oath that General Wills has sworn, that no promise of mercy was made and that the rebels surrendered at discretion.

Therefore I overrule your objections to the indictment with some harshness."

"I hope," Earl Wintoun replied, "you will do me justice, and not implement 'Cowper-law', as we say in Scotland: hang a man first and judge him later."

One or two of the Scottish peers erupted in laughter.

"I fail to see any humour in that remark," said the High Steward. "Explain yourself."

"Ah," said the Earl to Lord Cowper. "It is a play on Scottish words. In Fife, there is a famous sanctuary with an old cross of MacDuff. Those claiming the privilege of the Law of Clan MacDuff are required to appear after sanctuary before judges assembled at Cupar in Fife, but the accused that have run to the cross do not always live to reach Cupar to have a fair trial. They were usually hanged on the way. And my Lord Cowper, since you will not allow my objection to be heard by counsel, nor await my witnesses, I have nothing more to say."

The court adjourned whilst the peers considered their verdict.

"George, Earl of Wintoun, I have acquainted you with the fact that your Peers have found you guilty," said the High Steward. "By the terms of the law, you are convicted of the high treason whereof you stand impeached and the next step is to proceed to judgment."

The Lord High Steward Cowper rambled on, giving the same speech verbatim that he had given in January before the other convicted Lords; he then sentenced the Earl of Wintoun to be remanded in custody to await his execution on Tower Hill . . .

George Seton, the fifth Earl of Wintoun began to plan his escape . . .

* * *

The winds blew, spring seemed a long way away; the snow had gone but there was a chill in the March air at Ufton

Manor as James and Charles waited eagerly for the weekly delivery of three issues of the *Gazette*, which was the main source of London news.

"I see the House of Lords found Lord Wintoun guilty," said James as he perused the paper. "He is languishing in the Tower awaiting the king's approval for his sentence to be carried out."

"Imagine languishing in the cold confines of the Tower in this weather knowing you may never see another spring," replied a sympathetic Charles.

At that moment Charity entered the drawing room. "I do wish you would stop spending all your time discussing the London news," she exclaimed. "We have marriage plans to discuss and we only have a few more weeks before Annabel's wedding day."

"You are quite right," agreed James. "Charles, you retire to a quiet room and discuss the guests list with Charity and then I suggest the pair of you get Ben to drive you over to Wingfield Hall to finalize the arrangements with David's family."

Charity turned and left the room expecting Charles to follow but James took hold of his arm and said in a low voice, "Does Charity know that David is the illegitimate son of our London neighbour, Sir Thomas Halton?"

"Indeed she does not, Father, and if Winfield Halton at the Manor wishes to keep the matter of their adopted son a secret then I think we should respect that secret. In fact, there is no reason why they would think we have any knowledge of the affair."

In transpired that David knew he was adopted but he did not know the name of his biological father.

* * *

The April sun was giving a little warmth as it shone through the windows into the drawing room. Charles and

James gazed out onto the trees in early bud. "A lovely time of the year for a wedding," said James, "and the ceremony at our church in our grounds should be perfect." In philosophical mood, he continued, "Every spring I am filled with hope that the year will be better than the last; usually it is a false hope but one must be optimistic."

Attempting to divert the thoughts of Charles from the wedding and his duty to give Annabel's hand in matrimony, James said, "I see you have read the *Gazette* today, what do you think of the news about the South Sea investments that seem to be the talk of the city?"

"That is something I wanted to talk to you about, I should have mentioned it to you earlier, Father. When I was in London, Samuel Clarke told me that he was investing heavily into that company and it seems he is making a lot of money. I know Granddad Henry vowed never to deal in slavery again after he received that letter from the ship's doctor but that was some years ago when we all agreed to avoid the slave trade. However, surely now that His Majesty's government has issued more shares in that South Sea Company with its monopoly on slave trading, the conditions on the slave ships must have improved since those bad days. Should we invest some money into the venture?"

"Sorry, Charles, but I am still against participating in the trafficking in human cargoes," said James, "and I think the whole idea of paying off the government debts with the profits from such a scheme is a bad idea and doomed to failure. Take my advice, Charles: avoid investing."

Through the glazed window the sound of the bell at Limbury church began calling personages to witness the marriage ceremony but there was plenty of time for James to escort Constance to the church and he continued to converse with Charles.

"What else does the *Gazette* say?"

"Well, there is a full column devoted to the escape of the Thomas Forster the Jacobite general who was a prisoner at Newgate gaol. It says Thomas Forster is about thirty-five years of age and late of the county of Northumberland. He is a person of middle stature, inclined to be fat, well shaped, except he stoops at the shoulders, fair complexioned with grey eyes. His mouth is wide, his nose is large. He speaks in a northern dialect. He was lately apprehended and committed to Newgate jail for high treason for levying war against the realm; last Tuesday he escaped. We therefore have sought fit, with the advice of our Privy Council, to issue this royal proclamation, hereby requiring and commanding our loving subjects to use their best endeavour to discover and apprehend the said Thomas Forster. And for the encouragement of all persons to be diligent and artful in discovering him, we do hereby further declare that whosoever shall apprehend and bring Thomas Forster before a Justice of the Peace shall have and receive as reward the sum of one thousand pounds which the Lord Chancellor is hereby required and ordered to pay accordingly."

"Good heavens," exclaimed James, "all these escapes makes one wonder if His Majesty really wants more executions or is some conspiracy at work to aid the prisoners to escape?"

"Let me pour us a port before Constance and I leave you to your fatherly duties. I hope you have told her of her duties, eh, Charles?"

"I've left all that to Charity, all that about lying back and thinking of England seems better coming from a mother," said Charles.

Moments later Charity and Constance escorted Annabel and her flower girl, Mary Tristram, down the stairway of the manor house and into the hallway.

James kissed his granddaughter and wished her good luck then he opened the door of Ufton Manor to escort his wife and daughter-in-law to the church.

* * *

David Halton left Wingfield Hall and got in the Halton coach with Peter Kendall his best man to drive the few miles to the church. As the coach approached the Peacock Inn it slowed and finally came to rest. "Come in and let us have a final drink," said Peter, "We've been friends since the days we shared the same tutor and we've consumed a few flagons of my ale in the Peacock over the years but today I have arranged for a friend to serve us at the bar."

Peter Kendall opened the door to his inn and escorted David inside, then with two tankards of ale before them, Peter raised his and before drinking deeply said, "Today I drink to wish you and Annabel good health and many years of happiness and when you are allowed, come down and visit your old friend Peter."

David thanked him and drained his own tankard. They had both consumed a flagon of Peter's ale before the pair re-entered the coach to drive the short distance to Ufton Manor and its associated Limbury Church.

The coachman drew rein alongside the lichen-covered churchyard wall. From the church tower the solitary bell rang out. David and Peter dismounted and opened the old gate and walked the path that led across unlevelled and hummocky ground adorned with a mix of old grave slabs, chests and crosses. Two large ancient yews at the southeast corner of the church provided cover and foliage to the ancestral graves of the Cavendish family. Along the northern boundary wall stood a row of yew trees, and although younger than the ancient yews, that row, planted by Robert Cavendish when Silvia Leach the mistress of Henry Cavendish had died in sixteen fifty-four, was now eighty years old.

Dividing the path leading to the church door was an octagonal stone plinth beneath a churchyard cross constructed from a slender octagonal shaft of red sandstone. The groom and best man parted for a moment as they passed the cross then came together to enter Limbury church. The spring blossoms that adorned the interior failed to hide the faint dank odour of an old cold building that was illuminated with dozens of candles.

* * *

James, Charity and Constance had left Ufton Manor some fifteen minutes previously, leaving Charles in the entrance hall to engage his daughter Annabel and Mary in small talk before the trio walked the few hundred yards to the church.

Finally it was time to depart and Mary Tristram, Annabel's flower girl, stepped forward to open the front door to let the bride pass. Charles tilted his head; nodded it in appreciation, then he closed the door of Ufton Manor and Annabel the virgin escorted by Mary carrying a posy of orange blossom stepped off the premises for the last time. She would return a bride.

* * *

Annabel and David were well ensconced in Wingfield Hall, but after the wedding, it was a week before James found time to visit Chatsworth House to learn the full account of Forster's escape which he in turn related to an attentive family audience as he held court over supper at Ufton Manor.

"My contact at Chatsworth says the story the authorities are issuing about Forster's escape is that he was carousing with Mr Pitts, the prison governor. Apparently his custodian liberated too much wine from the bottle," James said as he paused between courses. "Charles, I think we should liberate another bottle of claret."

Charles rang for the footman to serve another bottle, then James continued, "Well, at some point having liberated too much wine from the bottle, Forster made the excuse to go to the toilet and when the governor awoke from his stupor he noticed Forster had been absent for some time. Mr Pitts staggered off to investigate and found the night garments of the prisoner lying on the stairs. Apparently Forster had been wearing them over his day clothes. A search revealed that the governor's own servant had been locked in a small room downstairs by Forster's servant. On the outside of the side door was a false key that had been left in the lock so the door could not be opened from the inside. Charles, it seems you were correct after all and this story of the governor being drunk seems to confirm collusion and bribery did take place. Of course the governor was arrested and put in the Tower. He has been tried for his neglect of duties and been acquitted on conspiracy charges but he has lost his job because an investigation revealed that Forster's sister Dorothy had befriended Mr Pitts. Dorothy had made a journey down from Northumberland accompanied by the village blacksmith; a journey that took them three or four weeks on horseback in atrocious conditions of deep snow and ice and when she arrived in London they sought out and stayed at the Salutation Tavern, which is situated behind Newgate gaol and she began her association with the governor."

"Forster will be long gone and in France by now, so that ends that trial. I wonder who will be the next to make a run for it?" said Charles.

They didn't have long to wait . . .

* * *

With a new governor in place, the attempt to tighten up security at Newgate was only partially successful. Some guards were new and unfamiliar with all the routines, which now generated a certain degree of confusion, and Old Borlum Mackintosh and his fellow prisoners began to exploit any avenue of escape.

"We can tunnel out of this old gaol," said Borlum to his nephew Colonel Mackintosh. "The walls are decaying and yon sturdy hands on our highlanders will soon be through that mortar."

For three nights six highlanders scraped at the crumbling brickwork and eventually forced a hole through the outer wall of their cell that overlooked the street below.

Directly across the street William Collett, a corn chandler, had a residence and he employed a maid with anti-Jacobite sympathies. Unfortunately the hole in the wall made by the Jacobites was directly facing the maid's room and on the night of the escape a full moon illuminated the prison wall. As the girl lay in bed thinking amorous thoughts of her beau, she saw the head and shoulders of a man attempting to push his torso through the dark shadow of the hole in the prison wall. Suddenly a body of a man scrambled free and dropped into the street and a second man appeared in the shadow of the hole. All amorous thoughts now erased from the mind of the maid, she leapt from her bed and ran downstairs to raise the alarm with her employer.

In the prison, guards rushed into the cell and grasped hold of Old Borlum's legs as he was half way out through the hole in the wall.

"Clap him in irons," the governor ordered and Brigadier Mackintosh found himself severely restrained after his first escape attempt.

The Duke of Marlborough; an old friend of the brigadier, visited him a few days later and remarked, "If you and your companions stay fettered in this place for long amongst these felons and persons with infectious diseases, your deaths will soon exclude the need for trials and executions."

"Then, sir, I think we must escape," Borlum replied.

Within days a loyal Jacobite supporter smuggled a file into the prison and for two nights, Old Borlum and eight of the fettered prisoners quietly and carefully cut through their chains. On the third night Mackintosh accompanied by Charles Wogan, James Mackintosh and the rest of the rebel prisoners in their cell crept out into the passageway. As they passed another cell where more Jacobites were confined, they handed the file through the bars and the nine moved on.

The midnight hour was approaching. Old Borlum held a finger to his lips to indicate silence; they heard a soft shuffling noise from down the passageway, suddenly the silhouette of a man loomed out of the gloom, it was a servant; before he could raise the alarm, the man was quietly and quickly overpowered.

Old Borlum and the nine rebel escapees surged silently forward towards the watch house gate.

"What can you see at the gate?" Old Borlum whispered to Wogan.

There's one guard and inside I can see the movement of two shadowy figures," replied Charles Wogan.

"We shall have to rush the guard and hope for the best," whispered Borlum.

As quietly as possible the nine Jacobites moved across the yard; the leading escapee was within yards of the sentinel when the guard turned and saw them converging onto him. A swift blow to his jaw and the guard was out cold. Inside the watch house nothing indicated that an assault had been overheard.

Brigadier Mackintosh brazenly opened the door of the watch house and stepped inside, quickly followed by his eight comrades. A look of astonishment froze the faces of the Keeper and the Turnkey; quickly and silently they were overpowered and the keys to the door of Newgate gaol confiscated.

Opening the prison door, the brigadier and his companions slipped out and disappeared like the mist in the glens into the dark alleyways of London by night. Moments later six more Jacobites who had managed to use the file to sever their chains fled into the unknown streets of the capital.

* * *

The fourth of May dawned; servants that had risen early to prepare Westminster Hall for the trials of the next batch of rebels were at a loss. The streets of London were awash with news of a mass escape. The Lords at Westminster met immediately and adjourned the court proceedings until the escaped prisoners were recaptured. James Talbot was the first, quickly followed by seven others who were unacquainted with the streets of London and quickly fell prey to the locals who turned them in for the large rewards being offered.

The government had a full column published in the *London Gazette* offering the rewards for the apprehension of the remaining escaped Jacobites but it was to no avail; Old Borlum had made it safely to France with the help of his brother-in-law and with a price of one thousand pound on his head he was immediately a public hero in England as well as Scotland.

In due course the *Gazette* was read at Ufton Manor.

For Apprehending William Mackintosh commonly called Brigadier Mackintosh, who is fair complexioned with grey eyes beneath a beetle-brow. Mackintosh is a tall raw boned man, about sixty years of age. and speaks broad Scot, and For Apprehending Charles Wogan, James Talbot, Robert Hepburne,

*William Delmahoy, Alexander Delmahoy, John
Tasker, and John Mackintosh, who were lately Committed to the Gaol of Newgate for High Treason, in
Levying War against Us within this Realm, did, on
Friday the Fourth Instant, make their Escape out
of the said Gaol; We have therefore sought fit, with
the Advice of our Privy-Council, to issue this Our
Royal Proclamation, hereby Requiring and Commanding all Our Loving Subjects whatsoever, to
use all their utmost Endeavour to Discover and Apprehend the said persons and to Carry them before
One to Our justices of the Peace, who is hereby
required to Commit them to the next Gaol for the
said High Treason, there to remain till they shall be
discharged by due Course of Law ; of which such
justice of the Peace is hereby required to give immediate Notice to One of Our Principal Secretar-
ies of State. And for the encouragement of all Persons to be Diligent and Careful in endeavouring
to Discover and Apprehend the said Persons, We
do hereby further declare, That whoever shall Apprehend and bring before such justice of the Peace,
the said respective Persons, or any of them, shall
have and receive for each of them, so to be apprehended and brought before a Justice of the Peace,
the following rewards to pay, for the said William
Mackintosh, the Sum of One thousand Pound; and
for each of those others so apprehended the Sum of
Five hundred Pounds. The Lords Commissioners'
of Our Treasury are hereby required and ordered
to pay the rewards accordingly.*

"Heavens above, London is leaking prisoners like a sieve,"
said James after reading the report.

"Fifteen escaped this time plus Lord Nithsdale and General Forster who are already at large. Let's see, that means seventeen fugitives have escaped," said Charles. "What an embarrassment for the government."

"Yes, but eight of the escapers from the fourth of May have been re-captured which means that there are only nine at large," replied James as he quickly calculated.

"Only nine," said Charles, "that's more than enough. The *Gazette* also reports that Colonel John Farquharson has been acquitted because he proved he joined the Jacobites under pressure. The paper says he was in prison with Old Borlum and was his personal aide at Preston but did not attempt to escape with the Brigadier."

"I'll wager there is skulduggery at work," said James. "I seem to remember a report about the Preston battle that said that Colonel Farquharson took one hundred well armed highlanders down to the Ribble Bridge to hold the bridgehead at all costs and prevent General Wills and his forces from crossing the river but he was withdrawn by General Forster."

"Well, it does seem that parliament finally has had enough retribution," said Charles.

* * *

George Seton, Earl of Wintoun sat in his room in the Tower and contemplated his situation. Unlike Lord Nithsdale he had little hope of family assistance and any escape would be reliant on the Earl's own ingenuity. The Earl studied his assets. A trusted servant had managed to smuggle in a small file, he had a large pocket watch that he had made whilst working in France, he had cutlery, a pewter plate plus two wine glasses and a daily supply of wine and food. Time was what he didn't have . . .

The solution came to him as he meditated. The Earl removed the back of his pocket watch and using the sharpened end of his table knife he managed to remove the high tensile steel spring that he had personally manufactured as a blacksmith.

Taking care to avoid any noise, hour after hour he sat by the window with the pretence of gazing out at freedom whilst slowly his two fingers drew the tensile steel spring across the soft iron bar. Occasionally he used the small file to open the cut.

The month of May slipped into June followed by July and still the king had not signed the death warrant. The Earl was now desperate; his watch spring was very near to breaking although the iron bar was almost cut through. On the afternoon of Wednesday the first of August a knock by a warder on the Earl's door announced the arrival of an unexpected visitor; in the portal of Seton's room stood a tall sun-tanned man.

"*Sastimos,*" said the man, uttering the Romanic greeting for good health.

The warder closed the door and left the Earl and his visitor in peace.

"My name is John Gunn, my Lord, and I lead a group of Romanic gypsies. We heard of your estranged circumstances and I am here to offer you, our brother and friend, any help that we can."

The Earl and John Gunn sat in conversation during which George Seton told John about the bar on the window and how it was nearly ready for removal.

"And then what will you do? There are the battlements to cross and guards posted. I have a simpler and surer way to get you out of here," said John.

And so the pair discussed the plan . . .

* * *

That August day dawned as any other day except that the guards on the battlements reported that they had seen the Earl sitting in the window of his room for weeks, hour after hour, day after day. They were suspicious that he was signalling for help.

The Lieutenant of the Tower ordered an examination of the Earl's room and it soon revealed what had been happening and all chance of escape for the Earl via the window was gone.

"My Lord, we are moving you to another room. This room seems to have become unsecure with somebody attempting to cut through the bars on your window. We are moving you for your own safety, sir," said the Lieutenant of the Tower.

"Very diplomatically worded," the Earl responded, "however, I do have a minor request. Soon I face execution and I would like to put my family estates in order and to do so I have requested old charters and papers. I have asked servants from my estate to deliver the important ones; I expect them any day now, will you make sure they are sent up to my new room immediately?"

"Certainly and now let us escort you to your new quarters."

Late on Saturday evening the fourth of August, John Gunn and two Romanies dressed as servants carried a large hamper of old charters and papers into the Tower and were escorted to Lord Wintoun's new room.

"So they discovered your escape plan via the window? It was good that I came along and we now have this new plan or you would soon be headless, my Lord."

The four conspirators emptied the hamper of the papers and charters and made a pile of them in the corner of the Earl's room. It was approaching nine o'clock when the Earl climbed into the empty hamper; a few papers were placed over his inert body and a couple of charters complete with their wax seals laid on the top, then the lid of the hamper was closed and John Gunn and his two daring accomplices opened the door of the Earl's room and carried the hamper out onto the passage.

John looked back into Earl's empty room and shouted, "Good night, my Lord, sleep well, we shall see you soon."

The two men carried the hamper whilst John Gunn led the way out of the Tower to freedom for Lord Wintoun. Another bird had flown the nest to escape to France and to join Lord Nithsdale in Rome.

The Bubble Bursts

The year began with a flourish of executions and escapes followed by Annabel's wedding and in the autumn came news from Samuel and Ann that Fiona had safely delivered a son whom they named Joseph. Mother and child were both doing well. But as William had settled into the country life it was decided he would stay at Ufton Manor until the spring.

The Christmas festivities were perfect; Annabel and David Halton presented Charles and Charity with Amelia their first granddaughter. "A new year, a new life," said Charles.

"Talking of a new life," said James, "Fiona's baby must be about three months old; I suppose in a few weeks when the weather improves, William can now return home?"

"I was thinking exactly the same," said Charles. "I will have to visit the Clarkes in London to check on the profits from the spring imports and arrange the shipping departures. I will take the opportunity to discuss William's future with Thomas and Fiona."

The condition of the road to London in March was good due to a very dry spring; consequently, Charles made an uneventful ride to Samuel's home within two days.

"Everything is going well, the winter furs that arrived this spring were of the finest quality and the profits for the House of Cavendish are better than they have ever been," said Samuel.

"You are doing an excellent job," said Charles. "Incidentally, do you remember, two years ago we wanted to expand our trade and we made that fateful journey to Preston? We never did find new markets in which to invest."

"All my friends and traders are investing as much as they can in the South Sea Company," said Samuel. "We are so excited, they have issued more bonds for payment of a further two million pounds of government debt, and I personally am buying as much as I can."

"Even if I believed in this company, Father is totally against investing in it with its slave-trading connections and its exclusive right to sell slaves in all of the American colonies. So as much as I want to expand our business we cannot invest in what you believe to be a most profitable prospect. But, Samuel, beware," said Charles, "all this promise of profit does seem too good to be true."

"It's a pity," said Samuel. "I have doubled my investments and so has Thomas. He says it will make a fortune for William when he grows up and comes back home. Incidentally, how is the boy?"

"Oh, he seems very content and he dotes on young Elizabeth. It will be a wrench for him when he comes back to London. I have to visit Thomas and Fiona before I leave to give them all the news about William."

"Well, why not leave the boy at Ufton Manor till the summer is out? We are all sure that the country air will do the boy good and when he returns, Fiona's baby will be six months old and the household will have settled down," suggested Samuel and when Charles broached the subject with Fiona and Thomas they both tended to agree.

* * *

Charles left Bunhill Row and the Clarkes' home with the intention of driving directly back to Ufton Manor but on an impulse he said to Ben, "First drive me over to Gloucester House at Newington Green." An hour later, the coach finally came to a halt in the lane that led to the familiar large mansion house.

Charles alighted, walked up to the front door, rapped the knocker and presented his card to the footman who had opened the door.

Inviting Charles into the hall, the footman excused himself and entered a side room only to return a few moments later to invite Charles to enter the drawing room.

"Good day, Charles," said Sir Thomas Halton. "Is this a social call or have you come to warn me of another impending disaster?" he joked.

"On the contrary, I come to inform you of news about which you may not be aware. The information would be better coming from James; my father, but he is in Derbyshire. Last April my daughter Annabel married David Halton, who I know is your illegitimate son. They now have a daughter. Congratulations, Sir Thomas, you are a grandfather, although I do not think you wish to inform society of the fact."

A tear glistened in Thomas's eye as he grasped Charles and gave him an uncharacteristic embrace.

"That is the best news you could have brought me," said Thomas, "You have to know that my conscience has troubled me for many years and now I can see a way of making amends. Recently I have been investing a lot of money in the South Sea Company and at the moment the stock price is rising. When I feel the time is right and a good time to sell, I will make an anonymous donation of the profits to David and Annabel."

In that summer twelve-year-old William Clarke returned home to Thomas and Fiona; but Annabel and David had to wait unsuspectingly for two more years until the July of seventeen twenty for the promise to be fulfilled . . .

* * *

Christmas saw the first decade of the eighteenth century come to a close with an economic disaster looming on the horizon.

In the July a letter addressed to Mr David Halton was delivered to Wingfield Hall, it was from the only bank in

Derby. In the drawing room, David read it slowly and could scarcely contain himself from revealing its contents to his adopted father, Winfield Halton.

Leaving a curious Winfield in the room, David discretely excused himself and sought Annabel. "My love," he said, "we have received a letter that says we have been given a large sum of money. You and I have to visit the bank in Derby to finalize the details but I think we are wealthy," and in his joy he embraced her.

That week David and Annabel made excuses and after a three-hour journey down rutted lanes their coach entered Derby at the Old Friars Gate. The coachman, driving in the centre of the streets to avoid the rat-infested sides that were strewn with rushes, made his ponderous way into Iron Gate Lane. Finally the coach rumbled to a halt outside the Dolphin Inn. And the driver skilfully negotiated the coach and horses through an arch into the cobbled courtyard. He dismounted and made arrangements for the horses to be watered and fed whilst David and Annabel entered the inn to partake of refreshments. Safely ensconced in a comfortable seat, she glanced around, letting her gaze wander from the flagged floor toward the stairway that led up to a minstrel gallery and to bedrooms. Annabel had no comprehension that she was looking at the stairway that Henry Cavendish had climbed with Sylvia Leach, her great-great grandmother, one hundred and twenty years earlier; a stairway that led to a room where a seduction had started the out-road to the foundation of the House of Cavendish.

Annabel's attention returned to David as he ordered glasses of wine and plates of boiled meats. An hour later, fully refreshed, the couple left the inn to stroll the short distance to the bank of Crompton, Newton & Company located a few minutes' walk from the cathedral of All Saints.

Abraham Crompton had founded the bank thirty-five years previously and with such an important deposit being placed at his bank, Abraham was at hand to meet them personally and escort them to his office.

"Please be seated," Abraham said. "I must say that this bank is honoured to be trusted to handle such a large amount of money from your benefactor. The sum of money is one hundred and fifty-five thousand pounds and means you are extremely rich but to make everything informative to you, I will read to you the letter of transaction in which there are some stipulations to which you must agree.

Abraham gave a cough and in a clear voice began to read, "The letter begins with our address,

> *Abraham Crompton Banker*
> *Iron Gate*
> *Derby*
> *Dear Mr Compton,*
>
> *This is to inform you that a client of our bank has instructed us to make a transfer of money to your bank.*
>
> *The benefactor of the money wishes to remain anonymous and the recipients are a Mister David Halton and his wife Annabel Halton of Wingfield Hall in Oakerthorpe South Wingfield.*
>
> *Our client has placed certain stipulations; those being, that the recipients shall not know now nor in the future seek to know the name of their benefactor and if the recipients shall accidentally discover the name of their benefactor, they will never reveal it to any third parties.*
>
> *The recipients of the gift shall nominate lawyers to put in place two trust funds; the first trust to be in favour of David Halton to the sum of fifty thousand pounds and the second trust in favour of Annabel Halton to the sum of one hundred thousand pounds. The sum total of both trusts is equal to the benefactor's total gift of one hundred and fifty thousand pounds.*
>
> *The benefactor of the gift has also declared that the imbalance he has made in favour of Annabel Halton is a deliberate attempt*

ease his conscious for a misdeed he did some years ago and for which he offers no explanation.

I am honoured to be
Your trusted colleague

Nathanial Brassey
Goldsmith & Banker
Lombard Street
London

Signed on this 25th day of July in the year of Our Lord 1720"

David and Annabel sat in silence, overcome with the magnitude of their fortune as Abraham continued, "I have corresponded with Nathanial Brassey in London and apparently your benefactor made investments in the South Sea Company but earlier this year, he sold all his shares and donated the profits to you. I have arranged with Nathanial Brassey to transfer the money from those profits into this bank and I would suggest that you use your family lawyers to arrange trust funds and other legal arrangements."

David Halton now found his voice. "The Haltons have a lawyer named Mr Jones in Chesterfield and my wife's family at Ufton Manor use the same lawyers so it makes everything easier for the family."

"Excellent," said Abraham. "Now remember your benefactor wishes to remain anonymous and you must never try to establish his identity or to contact him or reveal his name even if you discover it. Is that clear?"

David and Annabel both nodded.

"I shall await the instruction from your lawyers as to the trust funds that you wish to set up for your family."

In a daze, David and Annabel left the bank premises and slowly walked back to the inn. The coach ride back to

Wingfield Hall began with the couple in ecstatic mood but eventually David began to rationalize his actions.

"Annabel my love, when we get back home we must be discrete; go to our room and carefully pen a letter to Mr Jones in Chesterfield, requesting an appointment but don't mention the subject that we wish to discuss; and not a word to Winfield nor the rest of the family; for the moment it is our secret."

Annabel was very economic with the words used in the drafting of the letter but after two attempts she was satisfied. She gave David the letter to read before she sealed it then finding a groom, David gave orders for him to ride into Chesterfield and to deliver it to Mr Jones at the office of Middleton and Jones. Mr Jones responded with a written message that he looked forward to their visit.

"Excellent," said David. "We will take the coach the day after tomorrow."

* * *

David and Annabel entered the premises of Jones and Middleton and were met by a middle-aged clerk who took their calling card and disappeared into a side office. David looked around the office of the law company and saw three clerks silently and diligently writing at desks whilst seated on high-backed chairs.

The door of the side office opened and the clerk returned followed by a young man who gave David a firm shake of the hand. "I am Mr Jones, please step into my office."

David noticed a portrait on the wall of an elderly gentleman; seeing David's glance, Mr Jones said, "That is a portrait of my late father, he founded the business; I believe as far back as sixteen-eighty he was engaged as lawyer to the Cavendish family. Was he not, Mrs Halton?"

Annabel confirmed the fact as they became seated.

"So what can I do for you?" said Mr Jones.

David explained that a secret benefactor had given them a large sum of money and they wished to set up trust funds and also to legalize payments from the bank in Derby. "The first trust shall be in favour of our daughter Amelia," said David, "and it shall be to the sum of thirty thousand pounds payable in increments of one thousand pound per annum from the age of eighteen. The balance of twenty thousand pounds shall be placed in an accessible account at the bank for our own income."

Annabel now spoke. "I know that you may find it unusual and strange for women to be in charge of their personal financial circumstances but that is my situation because the benefactor has also bequeathed me a large sum of money and stipulated that I must set up my own trust fund with the money. Because of my health I am unlikely to have any more children. Amelia my daughter is well provided for, so I wish you to set up a fund in favour of my niece Elizabeth Cavendish and it shall be to the sum of one hundred thousand pounds. The money shall be made available to her in the event of my premature death but in any event it shall be made available in eleven years time on her eighteenth birthday in the year seventeen thirty-one."

* * *

In the spring of seventeen hundred and twenty the price of South Sea shares had begun their climb from one hundred pounds to reach a peak in August of almost one thousand pounds a share. Every class of society from inn keepers, lawyers and nobility engaged in a feverish investment of their total wealth and savings to feed the frenzy. The South Sea Company issued more shares to honour debts incurred when the original investors attempted to sell their original bonds taken out seven years previously. Fortuitously, Sir Thomas Halton sold his shares in the July.

The bubble finally burst and the level of selling was such that the share price started to tumble. Within four weeks the stock had fallen to one hundred and fifty pounds as banks and goldsmiths who could not collect loans made on worthless stock went bankrupt and thousands of individuals where ruined.

At the Clarke residence, Samuel took Ann into his confidence and informed her that the family was almost penniless. The family gathered in the drawing room to discuss the situation and a solemn-faced Samuel said, "It is with sadness and despair that I have to inform you that I am ruined. I have lost all my investments and most of my savings in the collapse of the South Sea Company. Thomas, I know you invested in them, how badly has the collapse affected you?"

"I have lost almost everything and fear I shall have to sell my property," said Thomas.

Fiona silently wept whilst an ashen-faced Ann sat next to Samuel clasping her hands in despair and anguish.

Finally Samuel said, "I have been in touch with James and Charles at Ufton Manor and they inform me that they did not invest. In hindsight, Charles did warn me to be careful and I may be able to continue to look after their London business interests and that will give me a small income."

"James has been in touch with me," said Thomas. "I shall salvage what I can and we shall move up to Derbyshire. William seems happy in the Cavendish household. He is a young man now and James has promised the boy a job as a groom, I will probably get employment in Derby as a clerk and James says he will try and find us a small house."

Life however for David, Annabel and daughter Amelia remained almost unchanged; they continued to reside at Wingfield Hall. David purchased a few acres of land from Winfield Halton and began to farm the pasture while Annabel spent more of her time with her books and art.

They had their benefactor and his legacy to thank . . .

Chesterfield

Elizabeth had read Daniel Defoe's description of Chesterfield as '*handsome, populous well built and well inhabited*', which she often verified on her excursions into the town. Her journeys had become a weekly occurrence and as the coach rattled and swayed along the road that forged the thirteen-mile link between Ufton Manor and the town; Elizabeth reclined in the semi-comfort of the leather upholstery within her coach.

She had completed her shopping with a visit to the milliner and her thoughts drifted as she recalled James telling her of the days before the road was constructed, times, he said, when the lanes were so rutted and uneven that it was a common occurrence to use pack horses or horse-drawn sleds to convey produce from the town.

It was eight years since her grandfather had died of the flux in 'twenty-five. Vivien the long serving maid and widow of Ben also died of the flux in that cold harsh winter.

Her father had suffered severe melancholy at the loss of his father and friend, and that had been exacerbated three years later by the sudden death of his daughter Annabel. In his depressive moods Charles would often sit at the side of their graves and talk to the dead souls in the corner of the churchyard that was set aside for the Cavendish family.

It was an exceptionally mild autumn with the russet-leafed trees adding a warm glow and as the coach meandered along the lanes William was also deep in thought as he admired the beauty of the woodland. William slowed the coach and as the horses proceeded at walking pace, he bent down and glanced through the small window by his knee to ensure that Elizabeth was comfortable.

Elizabeth still in pensive mood, shuffled to a new position on the coach seat, her thoughts were of her childhood when, from the age of seven, she had grown up with William. They were like brother and sister, but her feelings of friendship had changed and she was confused; in his presence she had begun to feel an attraction. The change had been slow and begun three years earlier when William took responsibility to care for the mare that papa had purchased as a surprise present for her seventeenth birthday.

The vibrations of the coach wheels as they rumbled over a stretch of stony ground brought her back to reality, and Elizabeth grew tense with an inner fear. Her parents would surely soon discover her secret, and then her father would be plunged into an even deeper depression. She was in love with a suitor that her parents would consider outside her social station. Her thoughts wandered to William the groom, her coachman, the object of that love and affection; a man who was her mother's nephew. She thought of him having no mother to turn to as a child, for Sarah, his mother, had died in childbirth, leaving Thomas Clarke to bring him up; then when Thomas Clarke was bankrupted thirteen years ago, Charles had employed him as a stable boy and when Ben had passed away in 'twenty-three, two years prior to the death of her grandfather, William had adopted the mantle of coachman and groom for the Cavendish household.

* * *

On a similar return journey three months previously, her coach had just passed the crossroad leading to Wingfield Hall and taken the lane to Upton Manor when the incident occurred. As the coach negotiated a sharp bend a flock of starlings rose from the woodland disturbing a cock pheasant that strutted arrogantly into the path of the horses. Reining sharply, William was unable to halt the pair in time and the bird lay beneath the hoofs of one of the trembling horses.

William dismounted to calm the horses while Elizabeth nervously opened the coach door to question the reason for the abrupt stop.

"It's all right, ma'am, just a pheasant startled the horses," William said. "Would you be alighting for a moment?"

Elizabeth accepted the offer and he placed the footstool for her to descend to the ground. "Are the horses all right?" she enquired.

"Yes, ma'am, just a little startled, that's all." The horses had calmed under his gentle murmurings as he stooped to retrieve the dead bird and place it beneath his seat at the rear of the coach. *Cook'll no doubt make use of that*, he thought.

There was a long pause in the conversation as William noticed his mistress appraising him with her azure blue eyes from beneath the brim of her fashionable straw hat and being manly, his disposition didn't fail to notice the curvature of her waist and hips or the roundness of her shapely bosom that exuded the sexuality of a mature young woman.

The pause was broken as Elizabeth stepped off the lane to the edge of the woodland glade. "What a beautiful afternoon, just smell that lovely fresh odour from the trees and shrubs. It makes me think it's the last breath of nature before the long harsh winter that will be coming soon," she remarked as she recalled her grandfather speaking of the times before she was born when the winter snow isolated them for weeks. "What do you do on those long winter evenings, William?"

Taken aback at her cheerful familiarity, William murmured, "After a hard day's work attending to my duties, ma'am, it is about all I can manage but to take a glass of hot mulled wine around the table in the kitchen and talk for half an hour with the downstairs staff before climbing the stairs to my room."

They continued to talk freely for some time before Elizabeth said, "Let us proceed home, William."

"Yes, ma'am," and he held her arm to support her as she placed a shapely ankle onto the footstool and stepped into the coach. At that moment her fingers brushed against William's outstretched hand and her body tingled at the touch; she felt her heart race and quickly she averted her gaze and took her seat.

William had noticed the reaction to his touch and he too became flushed at the thought of her presence. But fearful of the obvious danger to his employment from a courtship with the daughter of his employer, he pushed the thoughts away. Although a distant family member, he knew that Charles Cavendish had aspirations of grandeur for his daughter.

Contrarily, Elizabeth sat alone and confused in the coach, nervous of the social implications her emotions would arouse. Her mind was in turmoil. It had happened so suddenly . . .

* * *

The crystal chandelier in the music room glistened from the flickering flames of countless candles. Elizabeth was at the harpsichord, playing an instrument that was becoming unfashionable and as Charity and Charles listened, he commented that he really should purchase a pianoforte, an instrument that he heard was growing in popularity in the music salons of London society.

As the evening wore on, Elizabeth grew weary and by ten o'clock she said, "I am so tired I think I must retire. Goodnight, Mama and Papa," and she kissed them both before closing the door of the music room and ascending the staircase to her bedroom.

The housemaid had turned back the bed linen. Elizabeth undressed, stretched her arms to her full height and admired herself in the mirror, then putting on her nightgown she climbed into bed. She lay for some time thinking of William, anticipating her next journey to town, and gradually she felt a warm glow course through her limbs. She tightened the muscles on her legs and experienced unusual feelings as she squeezed her thighs together; finally slumber overcame her as she drifted into a deep sleep . . .

* * *

During the next visits into town their familiarity increased and she was soon conversing freely with him. Meanwhile, William became enslaved with the charm and wit of his mistress. Within three months, they had become more open in their feelings for each other and one day, as Elizabeth sat deep in thought, William reined in the horses when the coach entered a secluded, wooded area of the journey. Dismounting from his driving seat, he led the pair onto the grass where they lowered their muzzles and chewed contentedly.

Opening the coach door he climbed in beside Elizabeth, gently took her in his arms and they embraced, her lips meeting his. They shared a long lingering kiss, but she pulled away when his hand reached beneath her petticoats. "No, William, we mustn't," she whispered. "Someday we will, my love, when we are together."

William drew back. "When will that be, and how? Your parents will never agree to a marriage and I will definitely lose my job without any chance of a reference."

"I know it looks hopeless but trust me, my sweet dear William, and I will think of a way."

With that reassurance the young lovers embraced once more and this time she allowed him to fondle her breast. He felt the nipple harden under his touch as her breathing deepened.

"That's enough," she said, disentangling herself from his embrace, "we must be circumspect."

Reluctantly William placed a hand on the coach door and as he stepped down she whispered, "I do love you and I promise I will think of some way for us." Then patting her hair in place and smoothing down her dress, she resumed her composed posture on the seat. It was as if nothing had passed between them. What could she do?

From that day when she declared her love to William, the problem vexed Elizabeth for most of her waking hours until an idea began to form in her mind. She found it difficult to conceal signs of her affection for William, but if they were to be together, then arrangements had to be made carefully. Elopement featured in her plans . . .

Drawing on Trust

Elizabeth gazed into the embers of a dying fire in the drawing room at the manor. The family were all gathered together but were in a quite mode; each engaged in reading or embroidery, the silence broken only with the occasional crackle as an ember gave a final crackle and a small flame leapt forth to illuminate the hearth for a brief moment of time.

"Papa, may I visit Cousin Amelia? I would so like to take the coach and spend a few days in her company." Charity who was engaged in embroidering, remained silent, waiting for her husband's response to the unexpected question posed by their daughter. Constance continued to sew as if the question was unheard.

Charles placed Daniel Defoe's book *A Tour through England & Wales* on the table at his side. He had been engrossed in the book, which had become popular since Defoe's death two years previously. Constance and Charity continued in occupational mood at their needlework while Elizabeth continued to gaze into the embers.

"I suppose a visit from Elizabeth will possibly be good for Amelia," said Charles. "David has informed me that she has been disconsolate since Annabel passed away."

At the mention of Annabel, Charity noticed a falter in his voice as he continued, "It would be good for both the girls, and the young ones have so little company."

Constance and Charity smiled and said nothing; the wiles of the women had won . . .

* * *

Elizabeth couldn't wait to inform William of the news and sought him out in the stables.

"Father has given permission for me to visit Cousin Amelia at Wingfield Hall, William," she said. I can stay for a few days and he has agreed for you to drive the coach. He says you can be housed in the servant's quarters at the Hall until the return journey so Amelia and I will have a coach if we wish to go out into town."

* * *

William had risen at six on the chilly October morning for the start for their journey; he had fed and watered the horses and given the coach a final polish, then driven it to the front portal of the manor in readiness for Elizabeth to embark. On the hour of ten, the front door opened and Elizabeth, accompanied by Constance and Charles, descended the steps of her home. George the butler followed carrying her baggage and with William's help secured it safely on the coach.

Constance embraced her granddaughter then Charles kissed Elizabeth on the cheek. "Drive, carefully and take care of her," he instructed William.

Oh, he will be taking care of me soon enough, thought Elizabeth as she warmly embraced her father and Charity. "Give our fond felicitations to Amelia," said Charles. "We know it is four years since her mother died and possibly her grieving may have lessened; we all miss Annabel, so do encourage her to visit us in the spring."

"I will, Papa."

Elizabeth stepped into the coach and took her seat. While William stowed the mounting stool she leaned forward to wave through the window. He climbed into the driving seat, flicked the whip and the horses took the strain. Elizabeth reclined, closed her eyes and thought of four blissful days away from the strict family regime at Ufton Manor. Slowly the coach gathered momentum.

* * *

Wingfield Hall, situated a few miles from Ufton Manor, had been built thirty years previously from the stonework of the old manor, a splendid fifteenth-century building built by Ralph Cromwell, the royal treasurer to Henry VI. A fact that was visually confirmed whenever Elizabeth and Amelia wandered up to the old manor and into the quadrangle, for over the stone gateway was carved money purses, symbols to the original owner's status as the royal treasurer. The ruins of the old manor house, stood as a shadow of its former self, due mainly to the fact that during the English Civil War a garrison of royalist cavalry had used the manor as barracks.

When Amelia had first told her the story Elizabeth had exclaimed, "How romantic!" but Amelia went on to tell her that Oliver Cromwell had '*slighted*' the castle for giving support to the royalists. "My papa David says they pulled down the walls so it could never again be used as a fortress and it was Great-grandpapa Halton who built Wingfield Hall, in which we live today. He had workers use stones from the old manor half a mile up the valley. I fear the remaining ruins of the manor will never be restored."

The young ladies were conversing in the drawing room; it was the first time they had spoken to each other for months and Amelia was in full verbal flow with very few signs of a grieving daughter. In her excitement she chattered incessantly, telling Elizabeth more tales of intrigue and treason about the old manor home. "Do you know there was an attempt to rescue Mary Queen of Scots from the manor? Father tells us when recounting the family history that it was all a trap to ensnare Queen Mary in a very secret rescue attempt plotted by Queen Elizabeth's secretary Frances Walsingham who was her 'spymaster'. Walsingham arranged for the Earl of Shrewsbury, who was married to Elizabeth Cavendish – or as we call her, 'Bess of Hardwick' –to move Mary Queen of Scots to the secluded home of the Earl of Essex at Chartley Castle in Staffordshire. Once at the castle, papa says Walsingham knew he had access to all of Mary's communication with the outside world."

Amelia stood up and stretched her legs. It wasn't often she had a captive audience, even if Elizabeth did look a little bored; then smoothing her dress and pacing before Elizabeth, Amelia continued, "Walsingham then persuaded Queen Elizabeth to discharge your ancestor's husband from his position as warden to Mary Queen of Scots. A post he had held for fifteen years and Walsingham personally selected Sir Amias Paulet as the replacement warden who apparently was so strict that he removed all the queen's liberties. She was not even given access into the gardens for walks and exercise. Father says Walsingham, had hundreds of spies in his pay and he wanted to trap Queen Mary into writing letters of a traitorous nature against Queen Elizabeth so he employed a local brewer of beer to join in the plot to smuggle letters in to the queen by placing them in a waterproof casing inside the beer bungs of the beer casks when they were delivered to the castle."

"How deceitful and devious," exclaimed Elizabeth. "My papa always says he thought Queen Mary was innocent of plotting and that Walsingham wanted her dead as she was a threat to restoring a Catholic monarchy."

"Oh, there is much more," answered Amelia. "Apparently, Walsingham intercepted all letters going in and out to the queen and one letter from a Catholic supporter of Queen Mary in Paris recommended that she should trust a young gentleman who was a loyal Catholic named Anthony Babington. Mary wrote to Babington asking for his assistance in her escape but Babington went too far and planned to rescue Queen Mary and have Queen Elizabeth killed. The escape failed and Anthony was arrested and tried as a traitor." Amelia's voice droned on as Elizabeth listened. "He was hanged till almost dead then they cut him down and cut off his manhood and put it in his mouth, then he was disembowelled."

Elizabeth gasped and her countenance turned pale as Amelia went on and on. "And then they chopped off his arms and legs and finally his head."

"Stop it, Amelia," Elizabeth cried in protest and exasperation. "Stop prattling on, your story upsets me and I have important things on my mind that I mean to convey to you."

"Oh, Elizabeth, I am so sorry." Amelia was now all contrite and sympathetic. "Tell me now, dearest cousin, what secrets are you hiding?" She put a hand to her mouth in horror. "Oh, you're not with child, are you?"

"Indeed I am not," Elizabeth said indignantly. "In fact, I have not lain with any man yet but that would probably solve my problem. I will tell my secret after dinner tonight in your bedroom, I have many things to tell you. But for now, how is your needlework? Are you still working on your lacemaking? It will be very useful for your wedding day when Uncle David finds you a suitable husband . . ." And so the girls chatted on . . .

* * *

With the supper finished Amelia and Elizabeth made excuses to retire for an early night and amidst girlish laughter they ran up the balustraded staircase to Amelia's bed chamber, where a welcoming coal fire glowed in the grate. The young girls giggled and sat on the floor in front of the embers.

"Now tell me – tell me your secret," Amelia implored. "I am bursting with curiosity to know."

For the next hour Elizabeth confided the problem of her secret love without disclosing that the source of that love was the groom, who at that moment was partaking of supper in the servants' quarters before being housed with other grooms and stable hands above the coach house. Amelia, always a romantic at heart, gave an excited clap of her hands and begged for more detail.

"Do you really love him, is he handsome, and is it true that your heart flutters when you are in love?" Her questions all poured out in an instant.

"Pray calm yourself, Amelia dear, I do declare that you are over-excited – and promise me you will keep our little secret."

"What ever will you do when Uncle Charles finds out?" was Amelia's response.

"That's my problem, what am I to do? I love him so much and yes, my heart does flutter. I am so frightened that I will not be able to withstand his advances much longer but I want him so much that I fear we may elope."

"If you run away with him, what will you do for money? How will you live, where will you live?" Amelia's questions seemed endless.

Elizabeth paused for thought "I am not exactly a pauper, dear cousin. You forget that when Annabel, your mother, who was my aunt and godmother, died four years ago, she bequeathed a trust fund to me, which is for a substantial sum of money in my own right. That inheritance is in the hands of your family lawyers in Chesterfield. The money in the bank is mine and not papa's," Elizabeth continued, "and I can and will make demands on it when the time is right."

And so they talked into the small hours; the wood embers in the grate were still glowing when Elizabeth retired to her own bed chamber. Sleep did not come easily; as her mind spun with thoughts until a plan began to form in her mind. At last she had made her decision.

The few days with Amelia fled past and as the girls embraced on the last afternoon and amidst whispered farewells, Elizabeth promised to let Amelia know of her plans.

On the way back to Ufton Manor, William halted the coach in a secluded glade and for a brief time the lovers caressed each other. Elizabeth allowed William to raise the hem of her petticoat skirts and for the first time he fondled and caressed her until she experienced the feelings that she had previously only experienced in the solitude of her bedroom.

Elizabeth was now at a crossroad in her life; she was home with the knowledge that her parents would never approve of what they considered an unsuitable marriage. She must begin to plan for an elopement with her William.

*　*　*

Autumn passed, and in her mind Elizabeth formulated a plan to elope in the spring. The plan necessitated her gaining access to her trust fund and to do that; when next she went into Chesterfield she must visit Middleton and Jones the family lawyers. But first she would pen a carefully worded letter requesting an appointment. She raised the sloping lid of her writing bureau and carefully grasping the back plate handles she slid open the single drawer and withdrew a sheet of her personal note paper. Elizabeth composed her thoughts then began to write in her best Italian lady's hand; a letter that had to convey to the reader some discretion. After two discarded drafts, she was satisfied as she read,

Dear Mr Jones

As you are aware, you hold in trust a legacy bequeathed from my dear Aunt and Godmother Annabel Halton to the sum of one hundred thousand pounds. This sum to which you have been entrusted shall be made available upon demand for my own personal

needs. Therefore bearing my request in mind, may I respectfully partake of your valuable time and request an appointment for us to discuss the matters more fully and in strictest confidence.

Believe me yours faithfully
Your client
Elizabeth Cavendish

Signed on this 23rd day of October in the year of Our Lord 1733

Folding the paper four times, Elizabeth carefully poured sealing wax onto the letter then taking her initialled signet ring, she pressed it into the hot wax. Picking up the quill again she carefully inscribed the sealed letter with the address "Mr Jones, Lawyer, St Mary's Gate, Chesterfield" and she waited for an opportunity to pass the letter to William.

"Take my mare, William, and ride into Chesterfield and deliver this letter; it is for our future. Await a reply," said Elizabeth.

As he rode off, she was well pleased with the correspondence that would now set events in motion, suddenly she felt a weight was taken from her shoulders and she eagerly awaited the reply.

William returned with a brief note from Mr Jones that informed her that he would see her next time she was in town. Over the next few days Charity noticed that Elizabeth seemed to have developed a carefree spring in her step.

* * *

The Cavendish coach drew to a halt in front a row of Tudor half-timbered buildings. Scanning for the sign outside the premises of Middleton and Jones; William drove the coach forward a few more yards and drew rein again at the front door. Placing a stool at the coach door, Elizabeth climbed down and ordered William to wait while she entered the premises. Once inside she was met by a clerk who took her card, knocked on the door of a side office and then entered. Silence pervaded the room as four clerks scribbled diligently at desks. Elizabeth waited.

The door of the side office opened and the clerk returned followed by a bewhiskered middle-aged man.

"Good afternoon, Miss Cavendish, I am Mr Jones, please step into my office and be seated," he said, and closed the door as she sat down, he continued, "My late father and I," Mr Jones paused as he pointed at a framed portrait behind his desk, "have represented the Cavendish family since sixteen-eighty. Now you are here to discuss your trust fund. It was a sad business the passing away of your Aunt, Mrs Annabel Halton; I had the pleasure to meet her when I was a young man. She and David Halton were left sums of money and it was her wish to put her legacy of that money in trust for you."

"I shall be taking a very long tour of England in the spring and I wish to have available five thousand pounds from the trust for my needs. As you are aware, since Aunt Annabel's death in 'twenty-eight, I can draw on the fund for my own needs. Am I correct, Mr Jones?"

"You are a very well versed young lady," said Mr Jones. "Yes, the total sum is held in the Derby Bank of Crompton, Newton & Company. I can arrange for my clerks to draw up notices of withdrawal to Crompton and Newton. If you sign each the letters we can witness them. I suggest five letters each to the sum of one thousand pounds; you can date and present them to a bank of your choice on your travels."

"That seems very satisfactory, Mr Jones, and I shall wait to hear from you that all is ready for my journey in the spring. I trust that this matter is totally confidential from all members of my family including the Haltons?"

"Of course, Miss Cavendish, in the legal fraternity, client confidentially is our byword, it is similar to the Hippocratic Oath taken by the medical fraternity."

Elizabeth smiled as she wished Mr Jones good bye, sceptical of his response . . .

Elopement

Elizabeth Cavendish had the promissory letters of credit from Mr Jones. Each letter was in her name to the sum of one thousand pounds and all were undated and unsigned to be drawn on the Derby bank of Abraham Crompton. She now planned the final stages of her elopement and on the pretext of visiting the better shops in the city, William drove the coach into Derby for her to present one of the letters for payment to the bank, where she collected nine hundred pounds in bank notes, ninety sovereigns and the remaining money in silver.

Abraham called for his clerk who brought in a small security box with iron clasps and a lock; Elizabeth placed her money inside the box watched by Mr Crompton and his clerk.

"Well, that concludes my business for today and thank you very much for your assistance," said Elizabeth. "However, I intend to go on a tour in the spring; I have letters of credit which I may present at other banks for you to honour."

"It will be a pleasure and we look forward to being of further service when needed. Good day, Miss Cavendish."

Mr Crompton and his clerk escorted Elizabeth and her chest of money off the premises and into the safety to her coach.

* * *

The festive season of seventeen thirty-three was to be the last for Elizabeth at Ufton Manor and she tried to suppress thoughts that in February she would be leaving her family to be with her true love. Tonight in the drawing room, the family had selected several bound editions of

Shakespearean plays from the library and they were taking turns to read extracts from their favourite scenes. Charles as always had read passages from *Henry V*, finishing with "*Cry God for Harry, England, and Saint George*", Charity followed that with a selection from *The Taming of the Shrew* which had everyone laughing. Elizabeth had already entertained at the harpsichord, and when cook brought in some pastries and hot mulled wine, she sat quietly thinking of her future, idly leafing through a copy of *Hamlet* that had been brought in from the library. Her eyes fell on some lines spoken by Ophelia:

> "*Pray you, let's have no words of this;*
> *but when they ask you what it means, say you this,*
>   *Tomorrow is Saint Valentine's day*
>   *All in the morning bedtime,*
>   *And I a maid at your window,*
>   *To be your Valentine.*
>   *Then up he rose and put on his clothes,*
>   *And opened the chamber door,*
>   *Let in the maid that rejected a maid and*
>   *Never left again.*
>   *By God and by Saint Charity,*
>   *Pity, and for shame, for shame!*
>   *Young men will do it if they come to it,*
>   *By God, they are to blame.*
>   *Said she, "before you slept with me,*
>   *You promised to marry me.*
>   *So I would have done, by yonder sun,*
>   *If you had not come to my bed."*

Elizabeth pondered on what she had read; her elopement plans culminated in her leaving on Valentine's day. Now in her mind was Ophelia's response to Othello; a response, she hoped desperately, was not an omen that William would let her down.

* * *

Towards the middle of January Elizabeth confided to Charity that she had not been feeling well lately. "Mama, it is every month you know, woman's problems, and I have been reading about a doctor who says that Harrogate has become a fashionable Spa with the discovery of several mineral springs renowned for the excellent quality of their waters. And Mama," she paused before continuing, "it says that there are several good hotels in the town. Would you ask Papa to allow me to partake of the waters for a few weeks? William could drive me and when I am ready to return home I will write and William can drive to collect me."

At first Charity was reluctant to speak to Charles about Elizabeth's intended journey but eventually agreed to do so.

Charles was in a receptive mood when Charity broached the subject and at first he gave no answer to Elizabeth's request but said, "I find it interesting that Elizabeth wants to visit Harrogate. I have just been reading the *Derbyshire Mercury* news sheet; and there is an article about a book written by Dr Thomas Short, titled *A History of Mineral Waters*. It mentions the waters at Harrogate and a strange natural characteristic of some stones that seems to be caused by the mineral properties of the local spring water. The article says that, following a rain shower, when the sun shines on recently ploughed ground up to two hundred yards from the spring, small crystals – beautiful as diamonds – are revealed, and although they are not actually diamonds, they are hard enough to cut glass. Heaven knows what that water will do to Elizabeth's stomach if she drinks it."

"But can she go?" Charity asked once more.

"Oh, I suppose so. So long as it is for medical reasons, I suppose she will be safe."

* * *

Elizabeth packed her bags and with a tear in her eye she kissed Charles farewell. She embraced Constance and Charity and climbed into the coach to leave Ufton Manor for the last time. It was Valentine's Day seventeen thirty-four.

William was driving her to a new life . . .

Epilogue

Elizabeth reminisced on the days of her youth, recalling the Valentine's Day thirty-four years earlier when William had driven her away to begin their new life together. He had taken her to Harrogate on that February day and made sure she was safe and accommodated in the new and fashionable Queens Hotel, then he had then driven the coach back to Ufton Manor so that he would not be accused of theft. A few days later William had intimated to Charles that he wished to leave his employment and seek work in Sheffield. Naturally Charles had tried to dissuade him but William said he was determined to make a life where he could earn more money and meet a young lady and possibly get married. Charles was reluctant for him leave but gave him a good reference. A week later, William joined Elizabeth in Harrogate and they had married.

Elizabeth Clarke thought of their first nine years together; they had been years of passion and heartbreak as they had tried to start a family. She had miscarried twice then at the age of thirty she finally managed to conceive and bear a son that they had named Robert. Today she was seeing that son getting married.

"Where have the years gone?" she asked William. "It is thirty-four years since we left Ufton Manor and I have never been home."

All she had to show to her son Robert of her previous life and the House of Cavendish were a few letters from her cousin Amelia. One letter in particular, dated seventeen thirty-six, informed her that Charles had died of a broken heart.

"We must visit Chesterfield soon, William," Elizabeth said. "I must set up a new trust fund to leave the ninety-five

241

thousand pounds still in the original fund to our son Robert and to his children when they are born. We don't want the money to die with us when we go, do we?"

Appendix

The House of Cavendish – Preston Chamade is set within the framework of historical events encompassing the Jacobite rebellion of 1715 and the events through until 1734. The Battle of Preston was a bloody battle with hand-to-hand street fighting that lasted for three days in November seventeen fifteen. Over the years many interesting artefacts have been uncovered but none as strange as those discovered by workmen excavating for sewerage works in the nineteenth century in the area of Back Ween and Patten Field, now the site of Trinity Church and near to the Sun Inn on Friargate. At the point where Back Ween merged with Friargate Brow, they uncovered five or six skeletons. Also buried nearby in a separate trench they uncovered the remains of a gigantic individual who measured six feet seven inches as he lay in this grave. In the skeleton's right hand was the remains of a basket-hilted sword and in his left hand was a massive iron key measuring nearly a foot in length. The key ring was large enough to admit the entire hand of the dead man. The nature of the key has never been determined but being a romantic I have forged a tale of love linked to the key and the tale is told in a brief episode in the battle scene.

The battle standard with the motto, '*Regis et patriae tantum valet amor*', translated to '*So much does love of King and country avail*' was retrieved from the river from the body of an escaping officer and are the colours of the Lancashire Tyldsley family.

The White Bull Inn was used as the hospital of the Jacobite Rebels. Today the inn is named The Old Bull.

Peter Kendall, the landlord of the Peacock Inn, eventually married and had a beautiful daughter named Ann, who in the fashion of the day wore wide-hooped dresses. On her Sunday visits to church the wide hoops necessitated that she had to enter the church doorway sideways. Ann Kendall was courted by a young local farmer who seduced Ann and she fell pregnant. The farmer then deserted Ann and left her to give birth to a daughter. The disgrace so weighed upon Miss Kendall's mind that she died on fourteenth of May seventeen forty-five of a broken heart. Shortly after Ann's funeral, the man who had betrayed her was riding past the church; suddenly the bell rang out, his horse reared and the farmer was thrown to the ground, breaking his neck. There was another funeral but gossip said that the judgment of God had fallen upon him. It is not known if the lovers lie together in peace nor if the bell ringer was in the church at the time of the accident. Maybe a supernatural hand was at work that day; or more rationally, the bell ringer was Peter Kendall.

Sir Thomas Halton, who resided at Gloucester House in Woodford Green, was the third Baronet Halton, of Samford Parva in the County of Essex. A title created for William Halton his grandfather on 10 September sixteen forty-two by Charles II for the first Baronet. The title became extinct on the death of the sixth Baronet in eighteen twenty-three.

Brigadier William "Old Borlum" MacIntosh (1662-1743) was a tall, sharp-faced man with fair complexion, beetle-browed grey eyes, he was an obstinate character that spoke in a broad Scotch accent. He was cultured and well educated for his time. MacIntosh led the Clan Chattan in the seventeen fifteen capture of Inverness and then led an independent column across the Firth of Forth to threaten Edinburgh and join up with the English Jacobite forces to march into England. Captured at Preston he escaped from Newgate Prison and with the price of one thousand pound on his head, he became a public hero in England as well as Scotland. Fighting with the Spanish at Glenshiel in seventeen nineteen he became so famous for his cunning and daring that he was a principle thorn in the side of the English forces. In seventeen twenty-seven he was eventually captured in Rossshire and imprisoned in Edinburgh Castle for the rest of his life.

James Radclyffe, 3rd Earl of Derwentwater (1689-1716). The bastard son of the daughter of James II, spent his adolescence in the Jacobite Court as a companion of James and returned to England in seventeen hunded and ten. Five years later at the age of twenty-six, extremely rich, and happily married with a new home and a second child in the offing, he chose to serve under General Forster. At Preston was vigorous in the defence, working alongside the men to erect barricades. He surrendered and was imprisoned, suffered impeachment and was the first to be executed, though he expected a pardon. On the scaffold he stated that if he had known his fate, he would have bought a new suit of clothes. His death turned public opinion in favour of the Jacobites.

Lord Widdrington and his two brothers were taken prisoner at the Battle of Preston. He was convicted of high treason and condemned to death, later he was reprieved but his title and estates were forfeited.

Colonel Henry Oxburgh the son of a man of considerable property in Lancashire was born in Ireland and educated in the most rigid principles of the Roman Catholic religion. He served for a short period as a captain in the army of James II. He emigrated to France in sixteen ninety-six, and acquired the reputation of a brave and gallant officer in the army of Louis XIV. Returning to England, he purchased an estate in Lancashire and in seventeen fifteen General Thomas Forster granted him a commission in the Jacobite army that marched south into England and Preston, where he became the principle negotiator for the capitulation of the town. After a brief trial in London on charges of treason, he was found guilty on 7 May seventeen sixteen and sentenced to be hanged, drawn, and quartered on Monday the 14 May seventeen sixteen at Tyburn. After every application for mercy was unsuccessful, Henry spoke on the scaffold with sincerity in which he said he considered the Pretender to be his lawful sovereign, and never thought of himself as the subject of any other prince. After his execution, the act of displaying his head upon one of the spikes on the top of Temple Bar provoked indignation in the populace and the Jacobite cause gained more sympathy which in seventeen forty-five turned to open rebellion with the Young pretender Bonnie Prince Charles laying a final claim to the throne of the Stuarts.

Reverend Robert Patten, chaplain to Thomas Forster. Patten took part in the rebellion but was released from Newgate Prison after turning king's evidence. He later wrote THE HISTORY OF THE LATE REBELLION published seventeen-seventeen which is an invaluable, first-hand account of events of the seventeen-fifteen Jacobite Rising and is the primary source of information on the subject.

Captain James Innes who defended the flat roofed house was sentenced to transportation to the American colonies to serve a seven year term as an indentured servant after being captured at Preston, Lancashire. He was transported on 15 July seventeen sixteen from Liverpool to Barbados on board the *Africa Galley*.

Rev William Paul Vicar of Orton, Leicestershire carried letters for the Jacobites. He was captured at Preston and executed for treason at Tyburn on the 18 July seventeen sixteen.

Captain Charles Wogan, served under Henry Oxburgh at the battle of Preston. After the defeat he was imprisoned in Newgate Prison, London for a year but on the eve of his trial he managed to escape to France were he became a Jacobite agent and was sent to rescue a Catholic Princess from Poland who was betrothed to marry James III, Wogan travelled to Urbino, Italy where he heard that the Princess had been taken prisoner in Innsbruck by Emperor Charles VI of Austria at the request of George I of England. Wogan, disguised as a French merchant, rescued the Princess and took her to Rome where the Pope awarded him a Roman Senatorship for his gallantry. He died in Barcelona in July seventeen fifty-four.

Lord Charles Murray, the fourth son the Duke of Athol, received a British army commission and served as a cornet in the 5th dragoons in Flanders from 1712 to 1713 but he abandoned his military posting to join the Jacobite rising. He was well liked as a commander, often dismounting to walk with his men at the head of the regiment wearing highland dress. At the battle of Preston he defended one of the barricades and was taken prisoner when the Jacobites surrendered. Court-martialled because he still held an army commission as a half-pay officer, he was found guilty of mutiny; his father influenced King George to grant an official pardon thus he escaped execution.

The following list is the British Regiment of Dragoons and their Officers under the command of Major-General Charles Wills's Regiment of Foot at the Battle of Preston seventeen fifteen

Commissions renewed by George I, on 25 March seventeen fifteen

CAPTAINS	CHAPLAIN Alexander Innes
Major General Charles Wills	ADJUTANT James Baker
Colonel Cotton	SURGEON David Hall"
Richard Cobham, Lieutenant-Colonel	
David Ward, Major	
John Saunders, Grendr. Cy.	
Charles Williams	
Walter Palliser	
Hugh Palliser	
Charles Davison	
Michael Midford	
William Scott	

1st LIEUTENANTS	2nd LIEUTENANTS
William Davison, Captain-Lieutenant	Henry Aylmer
Richard Lethat	Edmund Quarles
John Roper	John Hobart
Rothwell Stow	Charles Rainsford
John Thompson	Patrick Aylmer
Thomas Dawes	Ventris Scott
Thomas Newdigate	Edmund Martin
Thomas Burston	Tiddeman Roberts
William Cooke	William Pritchard
Henry Long	Benjamin Sladden

BRIGADIER HONEYWOOD'S REGIMENT OF DRAGOONS.

Brigadier Honeywood

Donald McBane sergeant guard of regimental colours

COLONEL PRESTON'S REGIMENT, THE CAMERONIANS

Colonel George Preston

Lieut. Colonel Lord George Forrester

Major Lawson

Captain Preston

REGIMENT OF DRAGOONS COMMANDED BY LIEUTENANT GENERAL CARPENTER

COLONEL George Carpenter   ADJUTANT Philip Carpenter

LT.-COLONEL Joshua Guest   SURGEON George Chapel

MAJOR Samuel Foley   CHAPLAIN Francis Gore,

CAPTAINS Alexander Mullen, Alexander Read, Thomas Browne

CAPT-LIEUT. George Carpenter

LIEUTENANTS William Ogle, William Smelt, John Hoare, Richard White, Abraham Dupuy

CORNETS Thomas Shore, John Hawksworth, William Carr, Churchill Lloyd, Thomas Haley, Nathaniel Carpenter

Lightning Source UK Ltd.
Milton Keynes UK
UKOW052111150812

197603UK00001B/30/P